STONEMASTER

ALSO BY CE MURPHY

THE GUILDMASTER SAGA
SEAMASTER * STONEMASTER * SKYMASTER (FORTHCOMING)

THE WALKER PAPERS
URBAN SHAMAN * WINTER MOON * THUNDERBIRD FALLS
COYOTE DREAMS * WALKING DEAD * DEMON HUNTS
SPIRIT DANCES * RAVEN CALLS * NO DOMINION
MOUNTAIN ECHOES * SHAMAN RISES

THE OLD RACES UNIVERSE
HEART OF STONE * HOUSE OF CARDS * HANDS OF FLAME
BABA YAGA'S DAUGHTER * YEAR OF MIRACLES * KISS OF ANGELS

THE WORLDWALKER DUOLOGY
TRUTHSEEKER * WAYFINDER

THE INHERITORS' CYCLE
THE QUEEN'S BASTARD * THE PRETENDER'S CROWN

THE STRONGBOX CHRONICLES
THE CARDINAL RULE * THE FIREBIRD DECEPTION

BEWITCHING BENEDICT
MAGIC & MANNERS
ATLANTIS FALLEN
ROSES IN AMBER
TAKE A CHANCE
STONE'S THROE
REDEEMER

STONEMASTER

Book Two of the Guildmaster Saga

C.E. MURPHY

A Miz Kit Production

MKP

STONEMASTER
ISBN-13: 978-1-61317-160-8

Editor: K.B. Spangler / kbspangler.com
Cover Design: Miz Kit Productions
Cover Art: Aleksandar Sotirovski

For Seirid

ONE

"Get up, Sunbaby. Sunsquirt. Sun..." Desimi al Ilialio's sneer appeared over Rasim's berth. "...burn! Sunburn, except you're never going to get a sunburn because everybody knows you can't learn to use more than one magic—"

Rasim groaned and pulled his pillow over his head. Desimi's insults had lacked an edge for weeks, ever since he'd helped saved the king's life. He'd been given the mark of the King's Guard in thanks, and wore the pearl-embedded silver necklace under his shirt all the time. No doubt his pride would eventually fade and his usual mean streak would return. Until then, Desimi's insults were so uninspired that even Rasim had been trying to come up with better ones, even though he'd get stuck with them.

"Sunstar," Desimi tried, but he sounded as though he knew it wasn't any good. "Get up, sunsquirt."

"Firestarter," Rasim suggested from the depths of

his pillow. "Scorchmaster." No one in the Seamasters' Guild had ever been really insulting about the other guilds. They each had their own separate domain—water, earth, air and fire—and their rivalries tended to be friendly. Rasim had never heard any genuinely cruel teasing from other guilds.

Then again, no one had ever crossed from one guild into another, either. Not until Rasim, anyway. Not until the king had informed Rasim that *he* didn't get a pearl necklace for his part in the king's rescue. No, Rasim had, to quote King Taishm, "slain a sea serpent, befriended pirates, discovered treachery, rescued a kidnapped girl, been imprisoned, and saved his home city of Ilyara."

And for some reason, King Taishm thought a boy who had become that entangled with politics ought to have some diplomatic training. He'd made Rasim the first journeyman to ever study with a second guild, and because nobody had ever *done* that before, they didn't *have* names for them. But by the goddess Siliaria, Desimi was determined to find one.

Maybe if Rasim just ignored him hard enough, Desimi would go away. It hadn't worked in the thirteen years they'd grown up together, but it couldn't hurt to keep trying. He said, "Scorchmark," beneath his breath, and tried to go back to sleep.

Desimi yanked the pillow off Rasim's head, holding it out of reach. "Didn't you hear me say it was time to get up, Sunburn?"

"Really? Sunburn? Is that the best you can do?" Rasim made a hopeless grab for his pillow, then sat up to rub his eyes. "What bell is it?"

"Half sixth." Desimi threw Rasim's pillow back into his face.

Rasim barely knocked it away in time, squinting at the bigger boy. "What are you even doing up, then? It's not bakery day until tomorrow." He reached for his shirt, dragging it on and feeling the two bars on its sleeveless shoulders bump over his cheek. The sea-blue marks were as important to Rasim as the pearl necklace was to Desimi. They symbolized everything he'd ever wanted: becoming a seafaring journeyman, able to sail and see the world. He was the weakest witch in the guild, though, and it had never seemed likely that he would earn those sea-colored bars.

Desimi waited until Rasim could see him before announcing, "Everybody's up early except you, Sunburn Stay-In-Bed. You've been so busy with the *Sunmasters*," he sneered the word, "that you're the only one who doesn't know."

"Doesn't know *what?*" Rasim scrambled for his trousers and tried to keep a wary eye on Desimi at the same time. For once, though, Desimi was so smug about knowing something Rasim didn't, that he stopped teasing.

"Asindo's being made Guildmaster."

Rasim fumbled his clothes through fingers suddenly gone cold. His heart began to beat wildly, making his face hot even when his hands were icy. He didn't even try to pick his trousers up again, just stared at Desimi. "Is Guildmaster Isidri...?"

"Nah." The necklace and the king's regard really had changed Desimi. Six weeks ago he'd have refused to answer right away. He'd have enjoyed letting Rasim think the venerable Guildmaster had died. She nearly *had*, after pouring out an incredible amount of magic to thaw their half-frozen harbor. For weeks, the Seamasters had been waiting in unspoken fear for word to come that Isidri was dead. Asindo, captain of the fleet's flagship, had been the acting Guildmaster during her illness. It would have been easy — it would have been *expected* — for Desimi to let Rasim assume the worst for as long as possible.

Relieved, Rasim sat hard into his berth, but misjudged and hit the hammock's edge. It rolled and dumped him on the floor. Desimi shouted with laughter, but Rasim didn't care. It was almost inconceivable that Isidri would step down as Guildmaster, but her death would have ripped a hole through everything Rasim had ever known. She'd guided the Seamasters for at least a generation. Anyone might deserve a quiet retirement after that. Rasim tried to make himself laugh at the idea, but it still took two tries to pick his trousers up again because his hands trembled so hard with relief he could hardly control them. His tongue felt too thick to make words. "What time is she stepping down?"

"Seventh bell. And we're all supposed to be washed and in our finest."

Which Desimi *was*, Rasim finally realized. He wore loose, undyed linen trousers and a tunic mostly like Rasim's. Desimi's, though, was vibrant blue, and Rasim's had been washed so many times it wasn't any particular color at all. Desimi's thick, tight curls were growing out, just as Rasim's black waves were, but Desimi's shone with water that toweling hadn't been able to absorb. It would be at least a year before either of them had hair long enough to start braiding into the tight que that marked an adult Seamaster. Still, even with his hair unkempt, Desimi looked mature, like the man he was growing into. And less angry than the man he'd *been* growing into: the king's notice really *had* made a difference.

Rasim, befuddled, said, "How are you bathed and dressed already? And—" It started to settle on him that the sleeping hall was empty save himself and Desimi. "Where *is* everyone?"

"The bells rang at five and half five to get us all up. Kisia rattled you until your teeth clattered but you wouldn't wake. I said I'd get you after we washed." Desimi gave Rasim a grin that was more like his old one: toothy and not especially nice. "You should just make it, if you hurry. Sunburn."

"Sunburn, *really?*" Rasim dropped the trousers he'd been trying to put on and dug into the small box beside his berth, searching for his own finer clothes. "How did I sleep through two bells?"

"Hm, well, let me think. Who's been working the docks and studying on the ships every morning, then running across the whole city to work on his sunburn into the evening? It hasn't been *me*, that's for sure."

Rasim tipped his head in weary acknowledgment. The hard physical labor of the mornings followed by the hot afternoons in the Sunmasters' ascetic stone halls, reading and hearing stories of diplomatic ingenuity, wore Rasim down until he barely remembered getting home every night. He was only *certain* that he was eating breakfast because Kisia always thrust a bread bowl of warm fish stew into his hands every day. He supposed he had to be eating at other times, too, but his memories of doing so were sketchy.

It didn't matter now. Rasim found his good tunic, the blue one that matched Desimi's, and his own unbleached linen trousers, and ran for the hall door with them clutched against his chest. Just before he left the hall, a thought occurred to him and he slid to a halt. "Desimi?"

The bigger boy, ambling along behind him, had a satisfied smirk. "What?"

"Thanks. For letting me sleep in and still waking me up in time to get bathed and dressed before the ceremony."

Desimi's smirk faltered and he looked across the room before meeting Rasim's eyes a little uncomfortably. "Sure. Whatever. Sunburn."

Rasim grinned hugely and ran for the baths.

Everyone, it seemed, was not only awake, dressed, and ready for the day, but also ready for Rasim to be running late. He skidded into the bath houses, and dropped his clothes in a lump beside the first bathing room. He jumped in, splashing water everywhere, and came up with a gasp. The baths were usually warm to hot, but this one was cold as sea water in winter.

Masira, the bathhouse mistress, appeared to bark a laugh as he stood up streaming with cold water. "That'll teach you to be late. This one's been drained and refilled, and I've not had time to warm it yet. Nor am I going to, young man. Get washed and get out before I turn it to ice on you."

Rasim gulped and splashed back under the water, scrubbing his fingers through his hair and catching a palmful of grit from the bath floor to rub briskly over his skin. He'd never *seen* Masira turn water to ice. That was a rare talent, and the only person Rasim knew for sure could do it was Guildmaster Isidri. But he didn't know anybody else who could heat the large baths as fast as Masira, either, and if she could heat water, he saw no reason she couldn't freeze it.

He clambered out, skin red from washing, and discovered Masira had left him a towel, a comb, and his clothes neatly folded on a bench where they wouldn't get wet.

"Thank you!" Rasim's shout echoed through the empty bath house, ringing off stone walls and making him feel unusually alone. No one was ever *alone* in the guilds. There were always people around the corner, underfoot, in the way, and there to help. He dried off as fast as he could, pulled the comb through his hair, and scrambled into his clothes before sliding wet-footed across the smooth stone floors back toward the entrance. Normally Masira would have his — or anyone's — ears for leaving the floor dangerously wet, but just this once, when he was clearly the last person in or out of the baths, he thought it was safe. And fun. A wild grin smeared across his face again as he ran from the bath house.

Kisia, holding a bowl and a chunk of bread, waited for him just outside the bath house doors. Rasim nearly crashed into her and she lashed a hand out, catching his upper arm and saving him from, but sending the bread to, a spill on the sandy earth. Once she was sure he was steady, she let go and thrust the bowl, full of fish stew, into his hands, then bent and collected the hunk of bread from the ground. She brushed it a few times, getting sand off its thick crust, then plunked it into the stew, where it steamed with its own warmth. "My mother says you're too skinny," Kisia announced. "She sent bread for you. If you spill on your tunic, I'll cut a pair of gills in your throat myself."

Instead of laughing, Rasim swirled the bread in the stew and lifted a huge sopping mouthful to his lips. "Oh, tides, that's good."

"Of course it is." Kisia's family were bakers, but Kisia had—for the first time anyone could remember in Ilyaran history—given up her family name and trade to join a guild. It hadn't taken her long to learn the threats and curses the Seamasters used, and she was learning the magic just as quickly.

Rasim, splitting his time between guilds, knew that not just the Seamasters were talking about that. Orphans brought to the guilds began studying magic practically as infants, and everyone believed that only children *could* learn magic. But Kisia was fourteen, nearly an adult, and was taking to it like—well, like a fish to water. Some people thought that changed everything, but if Kisia herself thought so, she was keeping it to herself. She herded Rasim back to the guildhall like he was the apprentice and she the master, and he didn't complain. Kisia leading meant he could concentrate on eating.

"Hurry up," she muttered to him. "Desimi's waiting at the door."

Rasim glanced up as he gobbled the last bites of bread and stew. Desimi, looking superior and impatient, leaned against doors leading into the courtyard where both daily work and important gatherings happened. "Took you long enough, Sunburn."

Kisia wrinkled her nose. "'Sunburn,' Desimi? Really?"

Desimi shrugged and Rasim grinned again, turning his attention back to Kisia. "That was really good, Kees. Thank you. And hey, you look nice."

She did, too, with her loosely curling black hair cropped apprentice-short. It made her brown eyes look large and her cheekbones more prominent. The Seamaster blue of her tunic—a journeyman's tunic like Rasim's, even though she was really just an apprentice—was exactly the right shade for her dark skin, and showed off arms made strong by baking and stronger by hauling ropes. She had callouses on her hands where she hadn't before, and her feet, exposed by the calf-length trousers like those they all wore, were starting to get the spread-toed look that so many of the sailors shared.

"Wait." Rasim's gaze jerked back up to her sea-colored tunic. "Wait, Kisia, you're wearing a journeyman's tunic!"

Kisia, who was never nervous, gave him a nervous smile. "Guildmaster Isidri told me to. I don't really know what's going on, Rasim. Isidri's stepping down, but there's something else too, something—"

As one, the three of them swung open the guildhall gates to reveal a courtyard packed with Seamasters young and old. The youngest were still babes in arms,

new orphans brought by the river, and the oldest—
well, Guildmaster Isidri was the oldest by far, more
than a hundred years old. She sat in an enormous
chair, almost a throne, reserved for the Guildmaster
alone. The chair, in turn, sat on a raised platform big
enough to hold a whole ship. It had a ship's worth of
people on it, too: Guildmaster Isidri, dwarfed by the
Guildmaster's seat, and Captain Asindo, and dozens
of other Seamasters as well.

But also, unexpectedly, there were masters from
the other guilds as well: red-coated Sunmasters
looking serene as white-robed Skymasters flitted
around the stage greeting people, and Stonemasters
whose pale yellow clothes blended with the city's
pale yellow stone walls. Although they couldn't have
all been waiting on Rasim, Kisia and Desimi, they all
turned as the doors opened, fixing their gazes on the
three late-comers. The whole gathering in the
courtyard turned too, curious to see what had drawn
the masters' attention.

Under the weight of hundreds of pairs of eyes, all
three of them slowed self-consciously. Rasim gulped
and finished Kisia's thought in a whisper: "Something
big."

TWO

Sick or not, Guildmaster Isidri's voice carried clear and sharp over the enormous gathering: "I see our young friends have decided to join us after all. Kisia, Desimi." Isidri paused long enough for everyone to notice before finally saying, "Rasim."

Rasim swallowed hard as the Guildmaster beckoned for the three of them to come forward. The crowd parted and Rasim glanced at Desimi, who looked as nervous as Rasim felt. Strangely, that made Rasim less nervous. He peeked at Kisia, too. She held her jaw thrust out with defiance, just like she did when she'd been caught stealing extra honey bread for her friends. That usually meant she was scared too, but was trying not to show it. Rasim wondered if it would make her feel better if he took her hand. He was sure it would make *him* feel better.

Instead of taking his hand, though, Kisia looked at him. So did Desimi, which made Rasim realize they expected him to take the lead. Some of the apprentices nearest them grinned, sensing their nervousness. If they waited much longer, everyone would start to laugh. That would be worse than facing whatever Isidri had planned. Rasim nodded like he, Kisia, and Desimi were sharing some kind of signal, and they fell into step together as they approached the stage.

The *Waifia*'s handsome first mate, Hassin, stepped out of the crowd on the platform, a reassuring sight. Hassin was well-liked, and Rasim had the implicit belief that nothing too awful would happen to them if Hassin was on hand. The first mate winked and tipped his head sideways, indicating a short block of stairs at the stage's far end. People moved out of the way as Rasim led the other two up the steps, and they crowded behind Hassin once they were on the stage. For once, Rasim was grateful to be small. He was almost hidden from the gathering as he whispered, "What's going on?" to Hassin.

"Masters, apprentices, and journeymen!" Isidri's voice cut through any answer Hassin might have given. Everybody, including Captain Asindo, came to attention. Isidri hadn't lost an ounce of her command, even if Rasim could see that she was slighter than she'd been, and that her color wasn't as good as it used to be.

She still looked fierce and uncompromising, though, with blue bands of rank woven into her wrist-thick white braid. It swung over her shoulder as she rose from the Guildmaster's seat, first glowering ferociously out at the gathered guild in the courtyard, then at the smaller crowd on the platform itself. "I've been Guild-master for forty-seven years," she said. "Most of you haven't been alive that long, never mind in charge of something, and frankly, most of you never *will* be in charge of anything but your own lives for that length of time. It's a blessing," she informed the gathering. "By and large, it's a blessing to not have to worry so much about others, but having to gives you a certain perspec-tive. Mostly that perspective is people are all the same, silly and smart, foolish and fearless. Mostly they're good. A few are mostly bad, and nobody is all of one or the other. And once in a while somebody who is mostly bad makes a terrible mess of things for every-body else, which is why we're here today."

A low chuckle ran through the gathering, though Rasim didn't think it was exactly funny. Roscord, the Islander prince who had bought the loyalties of five ships' worth of Northerners, had indeed been mostly bad, and Ilyara had nearly fallen to him. Isidri's unparalleled magic had saved the city—there was a *reason* she had been Guildmaster for nearly half a century—and so it *was*, Rasim supposed, because of one bad man that they were there. Without Roscord, Isidri might have stayed Guildmaster until she died of old age, instead of burning up so much magic that she nearly died, and now felt she had to step down. If that was funny, it was the dark humor of a man who'd nearly drowned.

"But like most messes, there's some good come of this. When I was a girl—"

Rasim and every other youth in the guild perked up, hoping Isidri would be as specific about that as she'd been about her number of years as Guild-master. Everyone said she was a hundred years old, maybe more. She looked, Rasim thought, like she was *three* hundred, especially now that she was frailer and the network of wrinkles on her brown face had collapsed inward more, deepening.

The ancient Guildmaster paused like she'd heard the collective in-drawn breath of hope, and gave the entire gathering one scathing look. "That's none of your business."

Another laugh burst through the crowd, this one much stronger. Pleased, Isidri continued. "This may surprise you, but when I was a girl the Stonemasters held sway at the palace. When *my* elders were young, it was the Skymasters. Then, the guilds worked together more closely, in and out of the palace all the time, teaching the royal children to their particular strengths, and the ascendant guild supporting the monarch's strongest magics. That changed with Queen Naisa."

Rasim's eyebrows lifted. Naisa had been the current king's great-grandmother. She'd ruled almost ninety years earlier. Isidri really *wasn't* far off a hundred years old, if she remembered the monarchs *before* Naisa.

"Naisa was a nice girl," Isidri said in the same tone she used to say Desimi was a simpleton or Rasim a trouble-finder. "But she was *only* a girl when she became queen, and not much more than that when she died. She was gifted in sunmastery, and had she lived longer, perhaps things might not have been what they are. But her son was born with sunwitchery ascendant, too, and he was only nine years old when Naisa died. By the time *his* children were born, it had become tradition: Sunmasters taught at the palace."

Glancing around, it was clear to Rasim that nobody younger than Captain Asindo had much knowledge of this. Even Asindo looked as though he knew it was true, but didn't quite believe it in his heart. To Rasim, it was like suggesting the sky had turned red and the earth as blue as the sea. The Sunmasters had *always* held sway in the palace. They had *always* been diplomats, guiding the royal family in delicate matters at home and overseas.

Another chuckle ran through the crowd. This time Isidri—and everybody else—looked at Rasim, who slowly realized he'd voiced the thought aloud. Heat rushed his cheeks, but Isidri's expression was unusually fond. "You're right, Rasim. The Sunmasters *have* always been Ilyara's diplomats. It's their magic," she said idly, as if no one had considered it before, and maybe they hadn't. "Sun witchery is so dangerous that those who master it have to be extremely steady of temper. It's a trait that stands diplomats well, too. And that made it all the easier for their magic and faith to gain ground in the palace."

"Who started it? Who *let* Queen Naisa be that short-sighted? What Sunmasters took advant—"

Isidri shook her head, cutting off the barrage of questions. "It doesn't matter, Rasim. The sky had gone dark and cold, and we needed the sun witchery. By the time that need faded, tradition had begun. There's almost no one left who remembers, and there's no one left to blame." Her ancient gaze softened. "There's a lesson for you to learn, lad. Blame almost never matters, in the end. Neither does credit, when you get down to it. You accomplish so much more if you don't care who gets the credit."

Desimi shifted uncomfortably next to Rasim. Rasim ducked his head, trying not to look at the other boy, and Kisia snorted loudly at both of them. Isidri's soft expression broadened into a smile as she turned away from the three of them to address the larger crowd again. "The point is that in the past few weeks things have changed again, and we have an opportunity. Rasim al Ilialio is studying with the Sunmasters—"

Rasim bit his tongue on saying he wasn't so sure he *wanted* to anymore, if the Sunmasters were—were—he didn't even have words for them. They weren't *traitors*, exactly, but it seemed like they'd taken everything to

their advantage, and not to the betterment of Ilyara or
its people. Of course, if he'd been raised a Sunmaster he
might have thought differently, but he hadn't, and
from where he was sitting—

—from there, his Guildmaster had just told him
not to waste time laying blame. Rasim gnawed his
lower lip and tried to pay attention again. "—which
means," Isidri was saying, "that for the first time in
generations, the guilds are making a move toward
working together as a whole unit instead of as four
individual groups. Working individually has been
fine," she acknowledged, "but the royal family is
weaker now than it has been for many years, and
smaller, too, which is saying something." A laugh
whispered through the gathering: Ilyara's royal
family was historically known to be a small one,
rarely having more than two children in a
generation. "If one guild's predominance within the
palace is part of that, we need to change it. Not for
the good of the Seamasters, or the Sunmasters, or
any single guild," she said firmly, "but for Ilyara
itself. For our home, and for our place in the world."

Approval roared up from the gathered
Seamasters' Guild, startling Rasim so badly he
flinched. The group on stage didn't roar, but they all
looked quietly satisfied. Isidri had clearly hand-
picked them to attend her last act as Guildmaster.
Rasim wondered how many others *didn't* know what
she was saying here, and how much resistance her

ideas would meet.

"*To that end,*" Isidri called over the fading cheers, quieting them further, "to that end, the journeymen on this stage with me will all be studying with other guilds. This is my final wish as the Seamasters' Guildmaster. We may not be able to practice each other's witchery, but we can still learn what goes on beyond guildhall doors, and build on friendships that have gone neglected for decades."

Another cheer rose up, though Rasim thought the sea witches would cheer if Isidri sneezed, just then. From her expression, so did she, but she put a hand over her heart anyway, appreciating their enthusiasm. Then she brought the noise down, patting the air with her palms to calm the cries. "A more blended guild system is my wish as Guildmaster. I also have one last thing personal thing I would like to do before stepping down. Kisia al Ilialio?"

Kisia stiffened like someone had thrown cold water on her, and jolted the few steps to Isidri's side. "Guildmaster?"

Isidri bestowed a positively benevolent smile on Kisia. Rasim hadn't even known the Guildmaster could *do* that. "Kisia al Ilialio is another remarkable case, one who casts clear water over old, muddied ideas. Kisia is the only witch I've ever known who has *chosen* to leave the life she was born to and join a guild, or been allowed to. She did this at age fourteen, and has proven beyond a doubt that witchery can be learned even by those who aren't brought into the guilds in young childhood. She has studied very hard in her time with the Seamasters, and it is my delight to entirely ignore tradition and raise her up to journeyman status now. Journeyman, you are assigned to the *Waifia*. Congratulations."

Kisia went as pale and then as red as her brown skin could, her mouth hanging open with surprise. Rasim shouted with pride and punched the air, then grabbed the person next to him for an exuberant hug before realizing it was Desimi. The bigger boy only grinned, though, and smacked Rasim's shoulder when the hug broke apart. "She deserves it, Sunburn. She's more of a witch than you'll ever be."

That was true, but Rasim's pleasure was greater than any sting of regret could be. He hit Desimi's shoulder in return, for the first time unafraid that it would lead to a fight, and spun to hug Hassin, too. The first mate pounded Rasim on the back, shouting cheerfully, and beyond the stage Rasim saw that any envy or ill will was swept away by the *Waifia*'s crew's response to the news. Kisia was holding Isidri's hands, both of them smiling through tears. Tears! Rasim never imagined Isidri could cry! The venerable Guildmaster turned Kisia to face the crowd, lifting their joined hands in triumph.

Through the arch of their lifted hands, Rasim caught glimpse of a green-clad Seamaster working his way through the crowd, a hood pulled up to conceal his features. Two larger men in dun-colored cloaks and a smaller woman in the uniform of the King's Guard followed in his wake, close enough to seem protective.

Despite his excitement, Rasim's stomach went to knots. Last time the city guard had come, it had been to disband the Seamasters. That had led directly to the events that had nearly killed both Isidri and the king. Rasim couldn't think of anyone in the guild who would have called the guards for a Guildmaster changeover, but many had clearly known of Isidri's other plans. Someone might have thought she was going too far, inciting revolution, and gone to the guards for help in stopping her. Rasim barely heard Isidri as she lowered Kisia's hand and sent the girl back into the group on stage. Kisia stumbled happily, and it was Desimi who caught her and hugged her first, rumbling congratulations in her ear. She beamed at him, then turned to Rasim with such joy that he put aside his worries just long enough to squeeze her tight.

"You deserve it, Kees. You're already a better witch than I am. Congratulations."

"I'm not," Kisia said with mild determination, but her smile stayed in place and she grunted as she returned Rasim's hug. "I didn't know she was going to do that!"

"I don't know if anybody besides Asindo knew it!"

"—my final act as Guildmaster to the Sea Guild.

All that's left," Isidri was saying as she began to unwind the blue ribbon of office from her hair, "is to announce Asindo as my official successor, and go get a cup of sakka."

"Ah, no, Guildmaster." Captain Asindo smiled, stopping Isidri from loosening the ribbon. "If you don't mind, I'll take the rank, and my first act as Guildmaster will be to insist that my predecessor retain her mark of office. Not even I remember you without that braid in your hair, Isi. Don't confuse me at this late stage."

Isidri, who was turning out to have quite the soft side after all, held still for a moment, then smiled and kissed Asindo's cheek. "Thank you, Asi. May Siliaria smile on your guild."

As she spoke, the hooded Seamaster broke through the crowd and regained Rasim's attention. All of the oldest, highest ranking Seamasters were already on the stage, and he couldn't think of anyone younger who might want to challenge Isidri or Asindo so openly, on such an important day. If Rasim only knew who the hooded master *was*, what he *wanted*, then maybe he could distract from his presence—

The man threw back his hood and revealed himself as King Taishm.

THREE

A shock of silence swept out as those nearest to him recognized the king. Then, as quickly as the silence rolled in, everyone knelt, like a wave rolling back through the gathering. It rolled forward, too, most people on the stage kneeling as swiftly as the crowd did. Rasim was too surprised to kneel, and Kisia, who was terrible at showing deference, didn't either. Since they didn't, neither did Desimi, so they made a trio of guards just like Taishm had, except they flanked Isidri, the only other person in the courtyard who hadn't knelt.

Taishm's gaze flashed to Rasim and his companions. Rasim thought he saw amusement in the king's eyes, but his voice was nothing but solemn. "Rasim. Kisia. Desimi. I see congratulations are in order, Journeyman Kisia, and I'm pleased that you wear the mark of the king's guard, Desimi."

Kisia flushed with pride again. Desimi clutched the necklace's heavy pendant in one hand and tried not to look overwhelmed. Taishm waited another moment, then, dryly, said, "Kneeling might be appropriate."

"Oh!" Rasim wasn't sure which of them had blurted the sound, but they all hastily knelt. That time Rasim was *sure* he saw humor in Taishm's expression, but he still kept it from his voice as he turned his attention to Isidri.

"Guildmaster."

"That would be Asindo." Isidri's tone was bright, as if masking something, and after a moment she bowed. "Your Majesty."

"Yes," Taishm agreed. "I'll want to speak to that Guildmaster as well. I suppose, Seamaster Isidri, that in deference to your age I won't ask you to kneel. Siliaria forbid you shouldn't be able to get up again."

A tittering gasp ran through the crowd. Isidri's mouth went sour. "You've arrived at my hall in the garb of my guild, Taishm. Here, I outrank you. You might have come at any time in the past weeks," she said much more softly, so the words might reach the king alone. "Why wait until today?"

"So I could gauge the response of those who knew nothing of your plans," Taishm said just as softly.

Rasim realized he was holding his breath so he could hear the conversation. Beside him, Kisia hiccuped a little gasp of air, too, obviously doing the same thing. They caught each other's eyes and for a sudden, desperate moment, they had to fight off body-wracking laughter. It lasted until Desimi caught Rasim in the ribs with a sharp elbow and glared, his own gaze darting to the sparring Guildmaster and king. He clearly didn't want to miss anything either. Tears of laughter burned Rasim's eyes and he bit the insides of his cheeks, trying to calm down. He didn't even know what was going on, but it was definitely important, and they were going to ruin it all by giggling.

Neither Taishm nor Isidri paid any attention to them, though Rasim was sure they were both aware of the hysterical journeymen. Isidri, still almost inaudible, said, "And?"

"And I think a monarch less lenient than I would accuse you of instigating rebellion in Ilyara."

All of Rasim's humor vanished in an instant. Of *all* the people to accuse of treason, Guildmaster Isidri, who had nearly *died* for Ilyara and for Taishm —he didn't know his head had snapped up or that he was glaring outrage at the king until Taishm's attention slid from Isidri to the three journeymen again. "I said a monarch less lenient than I. Call off your sharks, Rasim al Ilialio, lest we have words."

Bristling, not understanding, Rasim looked around. On his left, Desimi's jaw was set and his breath held, making his big shoulders and chest look even broader. On his right, Kisia's lip was curled and her fingers were braced against the stage, like she would use it to launch herself at the king. Rasim wasn't the only one prepared to fight for Isidri.

Not the only one by *far*. Tension filled every line of
Hassin's body, too. In fact, of the sea witches on stage,
only Captain Asindo—Guildmaster Asindo—was *not*
prepared to fight. Everyone else who had heard any
of the conversation was tense, angry, and ready to de-
fend Isidri. The weight of gathering sea witchery was
massive, almost as heavy as Rasim had ever felt it.
Taishm was king, and gifted in all manners of magic,
but Rasim doubted he could stand against the full onslaught of the Seamasters' Guild.

Rasim, very carefully, exhaled his anger away and
lifted a hand to spread his fingers wide, signaling to
the gathered masters that they should calm
themselves. The weight of magic in the air didn't
change. Concern twisted Rasim's belly and made
sweat stand out on his skin. They *had* to listen, even
if his command was silent. *Call off your sharks*,
Taishm had said, and call them off Rasim would. He
stood, drawing everyone's attention, and met every
belligerent gaze with his own determined calm.

One by one, face by face and magic by magic, the
Seamasters let their power go. The aura of threat
lessened, then faded, and finally, as Rasim knelt
again, disappeared entirely. Kisia and Desimi were
the very last to relinquish their witchery, like they
were protecting Rasim as much as Isidri.

Taishm al Ilyara, king of the city-state, pursed his
lips and studied Rasim. Rasim shivered, unable to
read anything in the king's expression, but feeling

like he was being judged, or maybe more than judged. Like he was something new and potentially dangerous, and that the king was deciding whether he should be allowed to live.

For the moment, it appeared he passed muster. Taishm's attention snapped away from him as if it had never been there, returning to Isidri. "You certainly have the hearts of your people," he said, soft once more, and then so quietly Rasim thought it wasn't meant to be heard at all, "Would that I had such loyalty." More clearly—much more clearly, permitting the assembly at large to hear him—he said, "The Great Fire made hundreds of orphans, swelling the guild ranks to greater numbers than have ever been known in Ilyara's history. I have watched Guildmaster Isidri these past weeks as she has worked to begin building a legacy unlike any other, and I see now that she has the support of her guild and," he nodded to the array of masters represented on the stage, "at least some backing within the other guilds."

A rumble of agreement went up, no one quite willing to break into cheers and interrupt the king's speech. Taishm smiled faintly and climbed the steps to the stage so he could face the larger audience. "I would take Guildmaster Isidri's vision one step farther. It is no secret that the royal family is smaller and weaker in magic than it once was—"

That got a response whether Taishm intended it to

or not. It was one thing for the city to gossip about its weakening monarchs. It was something else to have the king himself admit it. The whispers and murmurs reached a peak and faded quickly as Taishm continued to speak over them, not dwelling on the topic and therefore not allowing the crowd to. "—nor that my cousin's decision to marry a Northerner was unpopular. But he was not wrong in that the al Ilyara needs new blood.

"It's commonly believed that only those of al Ilyara blood can master all four forms of witchery. But then, it was common knowledge that only young children could learn witchery at all, and Kisia al Ilialio has proven that wrong. Perhaps we all have the talent for more than one kind of magic. I would like to find out. I propose a new guild, called the King's Guild, which will take apprentices and young journeymen from each of the others, and ask them to study all forms of witchery."

Excitement burst in Rasim's chest. Kisia bumped her shoulder against his, her expression bright and enthusiastic. The youngest apprentices in the crowd looked equally thrilled, their high young voices suddenly rising in squeals. Several journeymen looked sour, perhaps fearing themselves too old to take part in Taishm's new guild, and many masters were clearly uncomfortable. Taishm's proposal went too much against the way things had always been. Rasim shook his head impatiently. If they'd been willing to support Isidri, it was silly for them to not embrace Taishm's interpretation of the same idea.

Taishm, though, seemed pleased at the response, as if understanding that it was the youngest guildmembers whose support he most needed. "It may not work," he admitted, "but even if it doesn't, I believe it will accomplish what Seamaster Isidri wishes: a greater understanding between each of our guilds, and perhaps with the palace as well. This, I hope, will be *my* legacy as well as Isidri's, but I have a final question to ask before it can go forward."

He turned to Isidri. "Will you, Seamaster Isidri, agree to become Guildmaster to the new guild, and select teachers from each of the guilds to train our new students?"

Isidri gave him a good hard look. "That's not much like retirement, young man."

Taishm laughed. "I was thinking of it more as keeping your meddling fingers out of Asindo's new Guildmastery, if you must know. It's a rare Guild-master who retires rather than dies in office, and I think that's to save their successors from all the scolding glances and clucking tongues."

Isidri looked affronted. "I would never!"

Anything else she might have said was lost beneath a howl of disbelieving laughter shared by apprentices and masters alike. Isidri chuckled, then did as she'd refused to before: knelt before King Taishm. "I'd be honored, lad."

"I'm thirty-eight," Taishm said dryly. "I'm nobody's lad, Isidri."

"At my age, everybody's a child. Do you want me to do the job or not?"

Taishm laughed too. "Yes. Yes, I do. Rise up, Kingmaster Isidri, and come with me to discuss your new guild." He took her hands and drew her up to a wall-shaking bellow of approval. Isidri's brown cheeks actually darkened a little with a blush, leaving her looking rather young and very pleased. Asindo caught her in a hug when Taishm finally released her hands. That was enough for all the other guild members on the stage, and they converged on her, hugging and offering congratulations. Rasim hung back, watching with a smile, until the shifting crowd brought him up beside Taishm.

The king arched a curious eyebrow. "Not in the thick of it?"

"I'll get my chance. I like to see everyone happy. Seamaster blue looks good on you, sire."

Taishm grinned down at himself. "It does. Better than Sunmaster red, to be sure. I've always thought it was too harsh for me. I'm surprised you're not wearing it."

Rasim shook his head. "I'm a Seamaster, whether you've got me studying with the Sunmasters or not."

"Perhaps I'll put you in coats of many colors," the king offered. "All of you, in the Kingmasters' Guild."

Rasim stumbled over his own feet, for all that he

STONEMASTER   37

wasn't even moving. "What? *Me*? In the Kingmasters' guild?"

"You began all this. Shouldn't you reap the benefit of that?"

"I—I..." Rasim's breath wheezed out of him, hope crushed by reason. "I...really? But I'm a terrible witch, your majesty. Everybody knows that. You should be asking, well, Desimi. Maybe Kisia. But me? I want to," he said wistfully. "I really want to. But...me?"

Taishm's manner went dry. "I *am* the king. I could insist."

"Insist on what?" Captain Asindo appeared beside the two of them, clapping Rasim on the shoulder. He was already wearing the arm-bar decorations that marked the Guildmaster, and Rasim, looking at the length of Asindo's greying hair, thought maybe he should adopt the colorful braid as well. It had made Isidri stand out, and it would be a nice nod to the witch who had been Guildmaster longer than any other.

"Insist that Rasim be part of the Kingmasters' Guild. He seems to feel he lacks the talent."

Asindo shrugged his big shoulders. He wasn't a tall man, but he was wide and burly, not the sort to trouble with. He ran the *Waifia* with thoughtful silence, making his crew think twice about their duties, and Rasim expected him to run the guild the same way. "I'd think a small talent in many magics would be as worthy as a great skill in one."

"It's done me well enough," Taishm said dryly.

Asindo beetled his thick eyebrows, then chuckled. "I meant no offense, majesty. I was thinking in terms of the ordinary populace, not the royal family. But at the moment you can't have Rasim."

"What?" Taishm and Rasim both said the word, though Rasim snapped his mouth shut so a wail of protest wouldn't break free. The king, however, suddenly made the most of his height and his rank, staring incredulously at Asindo, who wasn't bothered at all.

"I said you can't have him. Nor Desimi nor Kisia, for that matter. The *Waifia* sails on the afternoon tide, and my journeymen will be aboard."

Rasim said, "What?" again in a much smaller voice. Ships' schedules were set weeks ahead of time, but he'd heard nothing about the *Waifia* setting sail. Of course, with as busy as he'd been, running between guilds, maybe that wasn't a surprise. He wondered if Kisia and Desimi would have bodily hauled him onto the ship the same way they'd gotten him out of bed that morning.

Taishm rolled his jaw and scowled at Asindo. The Guildmaster lifted his eyebrows and waited patiently, a tactic Rasim had seen him use ship-board dozens of times. Just like the freshest apprentice, Taishm slowly lost his edge, irritation sliding into exasperation. "Well, Siliaria's—*hair,*" he said with a little too much emphasis, obviously substituting a milder curse for whatever he'd had in mind. Rasim eyed him in amusement. If the king thought he hadn't heard—and said—worse in his time, then Taishm was much more sheltered than any Guild orphan could hope to be.

Asindo smiled in a self-satisfied way that reminded Rasim of Isidri. It wasn't a smile he was used to seeing from Asindo, and he wondered if it came with being Guildmaster. "That's what I thought," Asindo said, then said, "Well?" to Rasim.

"Nothing. I just didn't know we were sailing this afternoon. And how can you take the *Waifia* when you've just been made Guildmaster? Isidri never had time to sail her ship."

"First, it's a poor sea witch who doesn't know when his ship's due to sail, Rasim. I don't care if you're studying with the Sunmasters. I expect you to keep up on your duties here." Asindo flicked a finger up as he spoke, then a second one as he continued. "Two, Isidri officially retired the *Waifia* into my hands when she turned seventy-five, so for twice your lifespan and more she's had no ship of her own to sail."

Rasim's eyes popped, though he kept his lips pressed shut as he did the quick calculation. He was thirteen, so twice his lifetime was twenty-six, which meant Isidri was at *least* a hundred and one years old. And she'd just taken on a new position as King's Guildmaster. It seemed likely she intended to live forever. Rasim couldn't quite imagine anyone stopping her.

"You're not paying attention," Asindo said drolly.

"I am! The *Waifia*—I didn't know she'd been Guildmaster Isidri's. I thought Guildmasters gave up their ships."

"They do, but there's no sense in having a good ship put to shore for years on end, which brings us to three." Asindo lifted a third finger. "I'm sorry to say it, but I won't be the *Waifia*'s captain for this journey. And that's why you and the rest of the crew are going, no questions asked. I'll not have a new captain on board with a crew who doesn't know the ship."

No journeyman would argue with a captain on that, much less the Guildmaster. The king, though, drew breath to protest and was silenced by a look from Asindo. "My guild, my crew, my laws, your majesty. You can have Rasim when they return."

Taishm's eyes glittered. "It's your guild, but even the guildmasters are mine to command. If the *Waifia* must sail today, then sail she shall, but to the destination I desire. I didn't come here today only to hear Isidri's plans made public. I have also come to send Rasim to the Northlands."

FOUR

"You have?" Rasim heard his own voice a little distantly. He had just come from the Northlands six weeks ago, and had only faintly imagined returning there someday. "But winter has come on. Their harbors will be frozen..." He glanced toward Ilyara's own harbor, not actually visible through the thick guild walls. Weeks ago, Northerners had frozen that warm water with a magic no one had known they'd had. Their own harbors might well be ice-free after all.

"Queen Jaana was able to send a ship," Taishm said without inflection. "She asked for you in specific, Rasim. I thought you hadn't met the queen."

"I didn't. I met Inga and Lorens. Lorens is..." Rasim looked around, as if the tall Northern prince might be nearby. One of Taishm's guardsmen threw his hood back, exposing pale yellow hair and a quick grin. Rasim's ears went hot with surprise. He hadn't expected Lorens to actually *be* there, certainly not masquerading as a guard. It wasn't how royalty *worked*, at least not in Rasim's mind. "Lorens is right there," he said feebly.

Taishm suddenly looked as though he was trying hard not to laugh. "Yes. He'll be returning home with you."

"Why—" The question popped out before Taishm had finished speaking. Rasim's ears got even hotter. "Not why is he coming home with me, but why—"

"Why has my mother asked for you in particular?" Lorens planted a hand on the stage and vaulted up, showing his strength and vigor to good advantage. Showing Taishm up, Rasim thought, frowning. Taishm, as king, had to be formal in approaching and addressing the guilds. Lorens, although royalty himself, wasn't a prince of Ilyara, and didn't *have* to be as formal, even if royalty usually was. But his casual manner made Rasim feel like Lorens was trying too hard. Perhaps, like Rasim, he hadn't forgotten the ugly moment in the palace weeks earlier, when it had seemed as though he had been part of the plot against Taishm. The moment had passed, but it left a lingering caution at the back of Rasim's mind.

Still, it was hard to be wary of the Northern prince as he clapped Rasim on the shoulder, then dragged him into a friendly hug. "That may be my fault, Journeyman. I wrote to her about your efforts in saving Taishm, and she already knew of your heroic venture into our salt-poisoned lake. She wants to meet you, and," he said, pausing for emphasis, "she hopes you can help us to restore fresh water to that lake."

"Me? Lorens, I told you, maybe a whole ship full of sea witches—"

"—which we'll have," Lorens caroled cheerfully.

Rasim stuttered over the truth of that, then surged on. "Well, even with a ship full of them to purify the water, you'd need Stonemasters to go to the bottom and stop that, that *fountain*—" He ran out of words again, remembering the eerie light and the endless spout of salt that he had discovered at the bottom of Hongrunn's lake. "It's not that I don't want to go, your highness," he said to Taishm. "I just don't know what help I could be."

"Have you not been studying diplomacy with the Sunmasters for weeks? Think of this as your journeyman test," Taishm suggested. His voice turned a bit sour. "After all, you *have* already negotiated one treaty. Surely a lad who can pocket an army of his own can hold his ground when he speaks with another foreign queen on his king's behalf."

Rasim's ears went hot a third time, the blush burning its way down to his cheeks this time. "It's not an army in *my* pocket. I meant that treaty to be for the good of Ilyara, not *me*. And mostly I was just trying to bargain because something for nothing is never a good idea. I don't know that she'd really give me—us!—an army."

"And yet just in case," Taishm said drolly. "You'll continue your studies on board the *Waifia* with Master

Endat, who is perhaps the most diplomatic of my Sunmasters. His journeymen will join you. Between them and the Skymasters who will come to help you fight the winter winds, you'll have nearly an entire King's Guild aboard the ship, Captain Asindo."

"*I* won't," Asindo said.

Taishm looked almost startled, then smiled, a brief and bright expression. "Of course not, Guildmaster. Who will be captaining the *Waifia* in your place?"

"Captain Nasira." Asindo transferred a stern gaze to Rasim. "She's less lenient than I am, lad, so watch yourself. No diving off ship to slay sea serpents, you hear?"

Rasim, very dryly, said, "I'll try to avoid it."

Asindo grinned at his tone, then slapped Rasim on the shoulder, nodded to the king, and slipped off into the crowd to begin his Guildmaster duties. Taishm watched him go, then turned a thoughtful expression back on Rasim. "You'll need Stonemasters, will you?"

Rasim slumped. "To fix the lake, yes, but..."

Taishm's eyebrows elevated. He waited, and finally Rasim mumbled, "But nobody likes sailing with them. They weigh the ships down."

Amusement creased Taishm's forehead. "Do they now. How is that? Does a Stonemaster weigh five times that of another man? Perhaps seven times that of a Skymaster, who work with wind and therefore must be lighter?"

If Taishm's guards weren't just an arm's reach away, Rasim thought he might kick the king's shin. "It's the magic. You must know how it has different weights. Stone witches weigh the ships down."

A curious half-smile wrinkled Taishm's face. "Different weights. Tell me about that, Rasim."

Exasperation flooded Rasim. "Any big magic has a lot of weight. But if it's just one Sunmaster, their power usually feels light and crackling, like fire. Seawitchery is slower than that, heavier, until it gets up to full force and then it can be terribly fast and dangerous, like floods or riptides. And sky magic is lighter than even sunwitchery, even in a storm. I haven't worked with Stonemasters, not really, so I don't know it as well, but I know there's not a captain in the fleet who wants to sail with them because they slow the ships down. Their magic weighs too much."

Taishm's smile kept getting bigger, though it looked more astonished than pleased. "That's utterly fascinating, Rasim. Excuse me," he said as if Rasim was the king and he an ordinary citizen. "I have some matters to attend to." He strode away, Lorens in his wake, with no more ceremony than Asindo had taken. Rasim blinked after them, then shrugged and went to pack for the afternoon's sail.

#

There were Stonemasters on board.

Rasim knew it before he'd even made ship. It was something in how the *Waifia* listed toward the docks, and something in the heaviness of the hot afternoon air, but mostly it was Captain Nasira's tight jaw and clenched fists, and the look of loathing she sent toward Rasim as he approached the ship. Rasim faltered in dismay. Desimi, two steps behind him, crashed against Rasim, swore, and shoved him forward. Rasim stumbled forward reluctantly, moving far more slowly than before, and Desimi snarled, "What is *wrong* with you, Sunburn?"

"*Really?*" Kisia breathed the question as she slipped around the two boys and glanced at the ship. "Captain looks like she's in a mood, that's all. Come on, Rasim, she's not going to hold you under until you drown." She leaped lightly onto the gangway, digging bare toes against the damp wood, then got a better look at those on deck and faltered, too. "Oh. Maybe she *will* drown you. How long can you keep air under water, Rasim?"

Rasim squared his shoulders. "Long enough to slay a serpent." He stepped onto the gangway and past Kisia, his own brash answer giving him a little confidence. "Journeymen Rasim, Kisia and Desimi requesting permission to come aboard, Captain."

For a moment it looked like Nasira al Ilialio might refuse them. She was tall and rangy and whipcord quick, with her black hair tied in a narrow que down her back. Not very many Ilyarans had straight enough hair to make a braid that thin, and to Rasim's eyes it looked like a weapon in itself, something Nasira could use to strangle someone with. She snapped, "*You*," at Rasim. "*You're* responsible for this," and jabbed a finger toward the gold-clad Stonemaster and her two uncomfortable-looking journeymen.

Rasim took a breath, ready to argue, then held it in his chest. Technically the king was responsible, but Nasira was unlikely to appreciate the distinction. Rasim let his breath out on a sigh. "I'm sorry, Captain."

"I don't want you to be sorry. I want you and them off my ship."

That was the kind of argument Desimi often used, demanding things he knew he wouldn't get. Rasim kept his mouth shut, knowing better than to point that out to a captain of the guild. When he remained silent, Nasira stabbed a finger toward him. "They're *your* responsibility. I want them out of my sight and out of my way. And if I catch you neglecting any of your other duties —!"

"That," Kisia breathed at Rasim's elbow, "isn't fair."

"Doesn't matter." Rasim tried not to move his lips so Nasira wouldn't know they were talking. Aloud, he said, "Yes, Captain," and waited until Nasira growled, "Permission to come aboard granted," before leaping ship-side.

For a few seconds, with the gentle rock of the
Waifia beneath his feet, the first hints of his sea legs
coming back, nothing else mattered. Not the bustle
on deck, not Nasira's frustration, not even the weight
of the Stonemasters on board. His whole life, Rasim
had wanted nothing but to sail on this ship, to learn
the stars at sea and to work with the water. It had
never seemed likely, given his wretched lack of magical talent, but it seemed Siliaria, the goddess of the
river and sea, had smiled on him. Nothing could be
completely unbearable as long as he got to sail, and
maybe someday he would captain his own ship.
Maybe even *this* ship, the Guild's fastest and most-
beloved. A broad smile split Rasim's face, pure happiness at being in the place he loved best in the
world.

"Something *funny*, journeyman?"

He would not, by Siliaria, let Nasira dilute his
love of the sea. He said, "No, Captain. I'm just glad to
be back on the *Waifia*," and refused to let his smile
fade while she glared at him.

"We haven't got room for your cursed stone
witches," she snapped. "Find somewhere for them,
and if it means you sleep on deck, you'd best find a
place I can't see you. Kisia, Desimi, get your things
below and get to work."

All three of them echoed, "Yes, Captain," and even
Desimi shot Rasim a slightly sympathetic glance as
he and Kisia scurried to do Nasira's bidding. Rasim

groaned. If *Desimi* was sympathetic, there were unknown depths to the trouble Rasim was in. He puffed his cheeks, then turned to examine the Stonemasters the king had thrust on them.

They were *not* the ones Isidri had selected to participate in her cross-guild studies. All three of them looked faintly bewildered, even the gold-robed master, though she tried to mask it. She was of ordinary height but had good shoulders and arms that any sailor would admire, muscle built up from a lifetime of working with stone.

Both of the journeymen were boys several years older than Rasim. One looked like the most typical Stonemaster imaginable: he was a broad chunk of youth, barrel-chested and thick-waisted, though Rasim bet four weeks at sea would take some of the thickness from his waist. Of the three, he looked the steadiest by far, his discomfort fading into fascination with the goings-on around him.

The other boy was one of the tallest, thinnest people Rasim had ever seen. He was all knees and elbows, and as pale as any native Ilyaran could be, his skin a light golden-brown. He didn't, Rasim judged, spend much time outside, and hadn't for years. Besides being pale, though, he was pallid. Sweat beaded on his upper lip. Every time the ship rocked—and it did constantly, of course—he spread his hands widely, or grasped uselessly at the air. His feet were spread wide too, knees bent as he tried to steady himself on the shifting deck.

"I'm afraid Journeyman Milu doesn't feel well," the Stonemaster said. "It may be a sickness of the sea."

"He can't be seasick," Rasim said in astonishment. "We're still *docked.*"

As if the very word was too much to be borne, Milu wrenched his feet up and raced for the ship's railing, knocking aside working sailors as he ran. A moment later he doubled over the rail and the sounds of his retching silenced all activity on deck.

Rasim closed his eyes. It was going to be a *very* long journey.

FIVE

Hassin generously offered his cabin to Stonemaster Lusa, who made space in the small room for Milu and the broad journeyman, Telun. Not that it mattered to Milu: being below deck made his sickness even worse, and no one wanted to clean up the messes he left. After an incident that left Hassin's cabin smelling vinegary and vile, Milu returned to the deck and huddled miserably at the *Waifia*'s stern, where he said the sea's pitch was ever so slightly less noticeable. The *Waifia*'s healer, Usia, had tended to Milu half a dozen times already, and came away sourly bemused. "It's as if the water in the lad's ears refuses to be stabilized," he told Nasira within Rasim's hearing. "Coluth's power is too strong in him. A stone god's disciple isn't meant to sail."

Captain Nasira looked as disgusted as any human being could, and shot Rasim a positively filthy glance that sent him scurrying away. A little while later, between tending to Milu and his own shipside duties, he found Hassin and said, "The sea is barely rippled," to the first mate. "What's he going to do if it storms?"

"Wish he was dead," Hassin said cheerfully. "It *will* storm, too. It's winter weather in the north. If he pleads enough, maybe we'll blast the whistle until a serpent comes, and we'll feed him to it."

Rasim shuddered. "No."

Hassin's teasing expression fell into apology and he put his hand on Rasim's shoulder. "No, you're right. I shouldn't joke. We lost too many people to that beast, and we'd have all been lost if it wasn't for you."

"I thought you all *had* been." Rasim didn't like to remember that part of the weeks after he'd been separated from the fleet. Captured by pirates was bad enough, but captured and believing himself to be the last survivor of the Seamasters' fleet had been numbing. He never wanted to encounter another serpent, or see his friends' lives risked that way. "I'll stay on deck with him. You take my berth, instead of your smelly cabin."

"In the prow, where it pitches like crazy, and with Desimi snoring above me?"

"Below," Rasim corrected with a brief smile. "Kisia got to the top berth first, then gave it to me when I finally made it down there. I thought Desimi's head would spin."

"How is it with you two?" Hassin had broken up more fights—one-sided fights, with Desimi fighting and Rasim running—between the two of them than

Rasim could count.

"Better," Rasim admitted. "The king's regard helped."

"Good. Ah, Siliaria's child, there's Nasira. If she catches us chatting—" Hassin slipped away and swarmed up the mast. Rasim went back to his own duties, stopping often to insist poor Milu try a sip of water.

"It just comes back up," Milu protested miserably.

"I know, but if you dry up it'll be worse. Just a sip." And then Rasim was off again, doing the tasks assigned to him, and sometimes more than that. By sundown he was grateful to simply collapse on deck not too far from Milu, whose misery kept them both awake most of the night. Exhaustion won over in the small hours of the morning, and Rasim slept through whatever sickness Milu spat up.

He woke to Sunmaster Endat squatting right beside him and examining him in the pre-dawn light. Rasim gave a strangled squeak of alarm, knowing anything louder would wake his sleeping crewmates and probably get him thrown off the ship. "What are you *doing*!"

"Having a look at you," the Sunmaster said. "I'm supposed to take over your instruction during the journey, but I've barely laid eyes on you, lad. I had no idea a ship was so busy when it sailed."

Rasim, only half awake, gave the Sunmaster a doubtful stare. "I thought you were one of the king's best diplomats. Haven't you been on a ship before?"

"Certainly, but I've never needed to find time to teach a sailor while he was working before. It changes one's perspective. Have you been taught to feel the fire yet?"

It was such a peculiar conversation that Rasim considered the possibility he wasn't yet awake. Rubbing his eyes, however, suggested he was, and after a tired moment of contemplation he sat up to squint at the Sunmaster.

He didn't, in Rasim's estimation, look like much, and since that was a term often used to describe Rasim himself, he felt he knew what he was talking about. The Sunmaster was of no particular height, and large around the belly. He shifted from his squat into a sit, cross-legged on the deck. It made him look as big around as he was tall. His short curling grey hair had receded, and now revealing a shining and very round brown pate. Everything about him was round, in fact, including his face, which would be moon-shaped even if he wasn't fat. He'd abandoned Sunmaster-style robes and wore the calf-length pants and tunic of a sea witch, though his were whiter and of finer cloth than the usual stuff worn by the sailors. His expression was pleasantly curious, and Rasim couldn't help thinking that perhaps he wasn't too clever.

"No," Rasim finally said. "No, no one has taught me to feel the fire yet. What does that even mean?"

"Ah. Well, we'll have to begin with that. I suppose they've got you reading histories. That's all very well, but it's nothing like teaching you sun witchery. I'm Master Endat, by the way, and I'm pleased to meet you, Journeyman. The whole city has been gossiping about your adventures. Now, do you have a torch?"

Master Endat *definitely* wasn't too bright. Rasim, carefully said, "Yes, Master. I know who you are. And no, Master. Only a few people on shipboard tend to fires. They're very dangerous at sea, you know."

"With a ship full of sea witches who can douse one with a sneeze? Don't be absurd. And with three Sunmasters on board right now, if you burn this ship to the waterline you've more talent in you than anyone could have ever dreamed. Now go get a coal from your galley, boy, we've work to do."

Rasim put his face in his hands. He was on second shift, from the second afternoon bell until the tenth at night, and it wasn't yet sixth in the morning. He had no excuse beyond not wanting to do as Endat instructed, and knew it. "All right," he said into his palms, "but if Milu starts throwing up again I have to keep him out of the Captain's way."

"A bargain is struck," Endat said with satisfaction. Rasim staggered off to get coals and, if Siliaria had pity on him, to learn to feel the fire.

Siliaria, he reflected later, wasn't known for her pity, and what of it she had to spare had already been given to Rasim and the other Seamaster orphans. She had chosen not to drown them when they'd been cast into her waters during the Great Fire. That was as much as any sea witch could ask for. They certainly shouldn't dare hope for her pity in regards to learning sunwitchery, a magic that was anathema to her. Especially, perhaps, since Riorda, the sun goddess, had usurped Siliaria's place as the most beloved and highly esteemed Ilyaran deity. Whatever the reason, Rasim had clearly asked too much. He couldn't feel the fire except when it burned him, and after the third blister, Usia refused to tend to him any longer. It was one thing, Rasim was informed, to accidentally burn himself. It was something else to hold coals in his hand and expect to come out unscathed. If he hadn't the sense Siliaria gave a goldfish, then it wasn't Usia's duty to treat him.

Endat looked encouraging every time Rasim failed, assuring him he would succeed next time. That was almost worse than jeers and mockery. Escaping to support poor sick Milu became a relief, at least until one morning when Rasim returned from that duty to find Kisia sitting cross-legged and thoughtful before Endat's pyre of coals. Desimi leaned on a huge coil of rope just a few feet away, his toes dug into it for support and his arms folded over his chest as he glowered at the coals. Rasim's mouth got dry, like he'd bitten into one of those coals, and a taste nearly as bad as charcoal rose from the back of his throat.

Kisia looked up with a smile that faded at Rasim's

expression. "What? There's no point in only one of us trying, right? Isn't Isidri and Taishm's whole idea—"

"His Majesty," Endat said severely.

Kisia paused, then said, "Isn't Isidri and the king's whole idea to see if anyone, everyone, else can learn more than one magic?" through her teeth. Endat looked no more happy than she did with the compromise, but he didn't correct her again. Desimi smirked, though, catching Rasim's eye for a heartbeat. Neither of them said out loud that they thought Kisia had more than earned the right to refer to Taishm casually if she wanted. It didn't seem like an argument they could win.

Rasim couldn't even make himself admit that she was right, that they *were* supposed to be finding out if the journeymen could learn more than one magic. Of *course* Kisia—and Desimi, and everyone else, even miserable Milu—should be studying with Endat too. So it didn't make any sense for him to feel betrayed, like he'd been hit right in the stomach with a ball of frustration and jealousy. It didn't make sense, and he knew it.

It still took him a long time to even be able to nod an admission that she was right. Her eyes were large and stricken with worry, but he didn't care. He left her to study, and for the first time on the week-long journey, clambered the mast to the distant crow's nest.

Sesin, a slightly older journeyman, was there, keeping watch. Rasim jerked a thumb, indicating she could leave. She hesitated, surprised. "You're not on shift until second bell."

"I know, but I need some fresh air. I guess it's your lucky day."

Sesin's gaze fell to Kisia and Endat, hunched together near the prow, and Desimi watching them like a sea hawk, before she met Rasim's eyes. "I guess it is. Thanks, Rasi."

Nobody had called him by that nickname in years, not even Kisia. Rasim smiled and Sesin's face lit up. "I could stay if you wanted company."

"No, it's..." Suddenly Rasim did want company. He slumped down into the bowl of the crow's nest, sitting on a coil of ropes and putting his head on his knees. "Yeah, that'd be good."

Sesin balanced her backside on the edge of the nest, wrapped a rope around her ribs to keep herself steady, and put her feet on the opposite edge of the nest, above Rasim's head. "I can see what it is plain enough. You're afraid she'll succeed."

"No!" Rasim buried his head further against his knees. "Yes. I mean, it's not that I want her to fail, it's just..."

"That you want to be good at something, and you want to be good at it *first*. Come on, Rasi." Sesin crooked a sympathetic smile when he looked up, surprised at her understanding. "We grew up together. Don't you think I noticed how hard you worked at being..."

"Barely good enough? Well, no. Why would you? There are hundreds of us fire orphans, and you're older and..." *Very pretty,* was what he'd been going to say, but all of a sudden it sounded ridiculous. His face heated and he glared at his bare toes instead of continuing. Sesin *was* pretty, with a kind of softness in her manner and her brown eyes, and in her quiet smile. He'd expect a young journeyman like himself to know who she was, but not for her, several years older, to have ever noticed anything about him at all.

"Well, I did," Sesin said. "Maybe because you worked so hard when Desimi was playing around. And you still weren't very good."

"Is this supposed to be making me feel better?"

Sesin laughed and leaned back, trusting the rope around her waist to keep her from falling. "No. I just meant I understand why you want to succeed with sun witchery before Kisia or anyone else does. It probably means more to you than almost anyone else."

Rasim mumbled, "I don't know," into his knees. "Kisia's got a lot to prove too."

"*Keesha,*" Sesin said, emphasizing Kisia's original merchant name, "has already proved she can be *Kisia.* She's turned the whole idea of who can learn magic, and when, upside-down, and that's really as much as she'll ever need to do. You, on the other hand...well, you're clever, Rasi. But that's not the same as being powerful, is it?"

"I don't care about powerful. I just want to be good at something." It was true. At least, Rasim thought it was true, but the knot of frustration and uncertainty in his belly twisted even harder. It wasn't *power* he wanted. He didn't care if he could trounce Desimi magically, or at all. He just wanted to be good at something magical, not just telling other people what to do. Anybody could do that, if they thought fast enough, but magic needed a talent. He could keep water in a bucket and keep it out of an air bubble, but that was about it. Even if he only learned to light a candle, being able to master two magics would be something new, something unique, something special to him. *That* was all he wanted. A small special magic, like everyone around him seemed to have. If that meant being able to feel the stupid fire, whatever Endat meant by that, then that was what Rasim wanted. He wanted to feel its quick flickering life, its constant fear of dying, so completely unlike water's patient and persistent wearing away of everything that attempted to thwart it.

"But I don't know *how!*" Rasim thrust his hands down, palms slamming against the ropes he sat on. At the same time, down below, Kisia and Desimi both shouted, and every rope on the ship disintegrated into flame.

SIX

Sesin fell backward, her feet over her head and surprise greater than fear in the instant Rasim could see her expression. He surged forward, clawing at her ankle, and felt the fabric of her trousers brush his fingers, but he couldn't clench them in time. He was still bent double over the crow's nest railing, reaching for her, as salvation unfolded.

The massive sails, no longer bound to the mast, fell with Sesin. One billowed open beneath her, heavy canvas slowing her fall. She twisted, quick as a fish in the water, seizing the sail in clenched fists. Her weight slammed it back against the main mast, and one of the crosspieces caught her in the belly. She doubled over it, making a retching sound. Fabric settled over and around her, but Rasim could see from the shape wriggling in the sails that she had thrown a leg over the crosspiece and was clinging to it, safe from falling.

His knees turned to water and he would have collapsed if he hadn't already been bent over the railing. Relieved exhaustion trembled every muscle in his body, and he squeezed his eyes shut for a moment, whispering a prayer of thanks to Siliaria. Then, still shaking, he pushed himself upright and forced his eyes open to stare at the disaster below.

It had happened so quickly the crew was mostly still gaping upward, wondering what was going on. Great swaths of the ship were covered by sails, making Rasim appreciate their size in a way he'd never done before. It wasn't that he hadn't handled them hundreds of times, on and off ship, or seen them being completed and inspected before bringing them inboard. But they weren't normally spread open across the deck and draping over the sides of a ship. They dwarfed the *Waifia*, making her vulnerability without them very clear.

As he watched, one of the upper-most sails finally settled to the deck, but the bulk of its weight was over the ship's rail. The *Waifia*'s forward momentum, as yet unchecked, allowed the large piece of cloth to be dragged overboard. Rasim swung around, realizing there were other huge chunks of sail already in the water. He spread his hands toward them in a desperate attempt to call enough magic to save them.

Sailcloth was heavy, though, and soaked sailcloth *much* heavier than that. Even trying to lift them was enough to drag Rasim to his knees. A sob of frustration broke in his throat. He had dived with a sea serpent. He had scuttled across the bottom of an icy Northern harbor. He *had* to save the sails, or the *Waifia* would be becalmed and lost at sea for good. His heart pounded, sweat rolling into his eyes as he strained to keep the sails from sinking. For a desperate moment he imagined blowing the ship's whistle until sea serpents came, imagining that they would rise up directly below the sails and save them.

Then suddenly the weight of magic was in the air and Rasim's strain lessened. Hassin, Captain Nasira, Desimi—the whole crew working together as they struggled out from under fallen sails and came to understand the problem. They didn't just lift the sails from the water, but lifted the water around the sails, separating them from the depths. It was much easier, then, to skim the enormous pieces of cloth back to the ship, excess water streaming away like tiny rainstorms. As the nearest sail approached the ship, it swung around to offer a narrow end, and half a dozen sailors scrambled to lay hands on it. The crew twisted the very water, making the sail twist too. As it became damp instead of drenched, the sailors pulled it in, folding it with quick efficient moves. They would force the rest of the water from it through witchery once the other sails were saved.

But they still had no way to bind the sails to the masts. Rasim's gaze swept the deck, searching for rope that had gone unscathed. There was none, and as he got a better look at the sails he was astounded they hadn't all gone up in a flash of fire as well. They were singed around the copper rings that had held the ropes, and there were black streaks against the cloth where ropes had been touching it when they burst into flame.

Shouts were coming from below decks, and that water was leaping from the sea to enter the *Waifia*'s portholes. There had been ropes below, too, huge coils of spare rope, rope to hold cargo in place, rope that bound barrels of water and food against the walls. Every hammock on the ship would be lying in a puddle on the floor, or worse, alight: they were lighter material than the sails, and if they fell burning to the lower decks, then the *Waifia* was in real danger. The tar that helped keep her waterproof would go up all at once if any of it caught fire.

The anchor. Rasim turned toward the *Waifia*'s aft, dread making him nauseous. But no: the anchor had settled hard in its moorings rather than slipping free to sink deep into the ocean. Not that it would do them any good with its thick rope eaten by flame, but at least they hadn't lost it. They *had* lost the rowboats, all of them. They drifted in the sea in the *Waifia*'s wake, and even if someone went to fetch them, Rasim didn't know how they could be bound back onto the sides of the ship.

Sesin finally struggled free of the sail that had saved her, gasping for fresh air. She lay on her belly with her arms and legs wrapped gratefully around the spar. Her tunic was burned in two, a band of it

looped around her hips and the rest where it belonged. Rasim could see her trouser's waistband and
the leather belt that kept them up through the gap in
her tunic, suggesting the fire had gone out so quickly
that the leather had saved her from a terrible burn.
Rasim turned again to climb down the ladder and
help her, only to discover that the ladder, too, had
been burned away, its rope sides disintegrated like
everything else. He could still climb and slide down—
a ladder rung was nailed into the mast every few feet
—but the discovery took him aback and he stayed
where he was a moment, swaying with surprise.

Rasim finally met Kisia's eyes across the distance,
and saw fear and horror in her face. Only then did it
actually strike him how foolish, how *dangerous*, it
was to try mastering sunwitchery aboard a ship. He
had made the argument to Endat already, but he'd
let the Sunmaster talk him into it, and now Kisia had
tried as well, and—

—and she had succeeded, to the detriment of
them all.

Captain Nasira, Rasim realized with sick clarity,
was going to confine Kisia to the brig if she was *lucky.*
The worst had already passed: water was no longer
pouring into the portholes, suggesting the fires below
had been put out. The sails were back on board, only
one or two witches attending to each of them now and
getting the last of the water out. Now that the moment of crisis was over, everyone was beginning to

stare and ask questions. Within seconds, they would turn on Kisia and the Sunmasters.

Hands shaking and heart throbbing, Rasim began to climb down. He didn't know what he could do, but he wasn't going to let Kisia stand alone. Halfway down he stopped to reach a hand toward Sesin, whose gaze was fixed blindly on the mast he clung to. "Come on," he said. "I'll help you."

Sesin shook her head, a tiny, pained movement. "I'm stuck." Her light voice was strained. "My ribs. I think I cracked them when I hit the spar. I know I have to move but I can't make myself. It hurts too much."

"All right. I'll come out to you."

"And do what?"

"Probably make you hate me forever." The spar was easily wide enough to scoot out on. Once he reached Sesin, Rasim wrapped his legs around the mast and extended a hand. "All you have to do is not fight me. I'll get you to sitting and put your arms around me and get you back to the mast and carry you down. It'll hurt, but if you relax I can do it."

Sesin whimpered, "I don't want to," but she nodded anyway, then scrunched her eyes shut and bit her lower lip as she tried to relax her grip on the yardarm. Rasim touched her arm gently, then startled badly as Hassin called, "Rasim!"

The first mate sounded unnaturally loud, using a voice meant to carry over the sounds of snapping sails and rushing wind. Rasim looked down at him.

The sail that had saved Sesin dangled nearly to the ship's deck, stopping a few feet above it. Hassin caught an edge, then snapped his fingers for others to do the same. Together they stepped back, drawing the sail taut. "You can slide down, Sesin. We'll catch you."

Sesin gave first Hassin, then Rasim, a wild-eyed stare. "I can't. It'll hurt too much."

"Your other choice is to stay up here until your ribs heal. Want me to push you?" Rasim offered a crooked smile.

Sesin's lip curled, but she nodded. "I can make myself let go," she whispered. "I don't think I can make myself roll. But I'll fall if you nudge me."

"All right. Are you ready?" Rasim asked the question of both Hassin and Sesin. Hassin glanced around at the witches who had gathered to hold the sail, then nodded. Rasim nodded too, then said to Sesin, "Relax. On three, all right?"

"Yeah." She exhaled, putting as much looseness into her body as she could. "Ready. On three."

Rasim stretched to put his hands on her shoulder and hip, said, "One," and pushed her down the sail before she had time to tense up again.

She screamed, which she hadn't done when she'd fallen, and slid down the sail in a whipping rush. It sagged with her weight and she rolled off the bottom edge. Hassin caught her under the arms and knees. Sesin screamed again, turning white, then buried her face against Hassin's shoulder. From his expression,

Rasim thought maybe she'd bitten him to keep from screaming a third time, but he didn't say anything and he certainly didn't drop her. They looked like an image from an old romantic story, the handsome first mate bearing the lovely journeyman across troubled waters. "I'll get her to the healer," Hassin said to no one in particular, and strode below decks.

"*You* can climb," somebody else said to Rasim. He grinned, a little disappointed—sliding on the sail looked fun, since *he* didn't have broken ribs—and scooted back to the mast to climb down.

Captain Nasira was out of sight, checking her ship. Rasim hurried to Kisia, whispering, "Kees, what happened? How did you—?"

"Rasim, I *didn't do that.*" Kisia grabbed his hand and squeezed until it hurt, her face pale with fear.

"What do you mean, you didn't? I heard you shout."

"She's right, Journeyman." Master Endat studied Rasim thoughtfully. "She didn't call the flame. I felt no power in her. What happened up there? You looked angry."

"I was—" Embarrassment swept Rasim and he looked at his feet. "I was frustrated and jealous because I was afraid Kisia would learn sun witchery before I could. She's already better at seamastery than I am."

"Rasim," Kisia said unhappily.

"It doesn't matter," Rasim said just as miserably. "If it wasn't you, who was it? Who would *do* that? It's only Master Endat and his journeymen who *can*, if it wasn't you, and it wasn't Master Endat—"

Rasim searched the deck with his gaze, looking for the Sunmaster journeymen. They, like everyone else, were on deck now. Maybe they had been all along. Desimi, helping drain water from the sails, stood near Pynda, a big, often mean-faced girl who reminded him of the old Desimi. She looked appalled, though, not guilty. The other sun witch, Daka, who was slight and delicate, had an expression of reverent joy as she looked around the ship. "*Daka*?" Rasim asked in quiet astonishment. "Why would she do that?"

"I do not believe it was Daka al Riorda, Rasim," Master Endat said gently. "I believe it was you."

SEVEN

Rasim barked a bitter laugh. "Because I was angry when it happened? Master Endat, if things caught on fire when I was angry, I'd have burned Desimi to a crisp when we were ten."

Unexpectedly, Desimi looked up from his work and said, "Nah." Rasim stared at him incredulously, but the bigger boy shrugged. "You always kept your temper when I gave you a hard time."

"No, I just didn't let it get the better of me. You were always going to become a master, no matter how mean you were. I was never going to unless I proved myself some other way, and fighting you wasn't going to do it."

Master Endat's eyebrows rose with interest. "I had no idea you were so disciplined, Rasim. That may be why—"

"Not. One. Rope." Captain Nasira came up from below decks, her jaw so tight muscles bulged and words could barely be forced through her teeth. "There is not one rope left on this ship, not even the one that was holding up the third mate's trousers. Who did this?"

The small gathering of sun and sea witches exchanged glances. Rage contorted Nasira's jaw even further. "If you think you'll *hide* it—"

"Me." Rasim stepped forward, feeling small and miserable. "Nobody was trying to hide anything, Captain. We're just not sure what happened. But Master Endat thinks it was me."

"You're a sea witch," Nasira spat. "A poor one, but a sea witch. You really expect me to believe this nonsense of studying sunmastery has given you some kind of special talent for a second magic? I might believe it of Kisia, just because she's already a freak."

Kisia stiffened like an angry cat, her brown eyes darkening to black, though she managed to hold her tongue. Rasim wanted to cast Endat an *I-told-you-so* look, but figured it would make things worse.

"I could even believe it of Desimi. *He's* got talent to spare. But not you, Journeyman. You're too pathetic. Don't imagine all of us believe that story about the sea serpent, either."

Desimi caught his breath, then stayed silent too, clearly wanting to protest that he hadn't even been *studying* sunmastery, only watching, but also obviously flattered that Nasira imagined him to have enough power to master two magics. "But you're the clever one," Nasira snarled to Rasim. "So clever us out of *this*, Journeyman. Maybe a guild's worth of Skymasters could bring up wind enough to shove a sailless ship to land, but we've only three, and a trio of Stonemasters to anchor us down. As for *you*." She thrust a finger at Endat and his journeymen. "You'll be confined to quarters until we make land, and the first landfall I make I'm putting you off-ship. I'd drown you all if I could."

Someone said, "You can't do that," and to Rasim's horror he realized it was himself.

Nasira's hot rage went cold so fast Rasim thought he could feel a chill waft off her. She pulled herself up tall and looked down at him with terrifyingly little expression. Dizziness ran through Rasim and he made fists, his blunt fingernails digging into his palms. "Excuse me, Journeyman," Nasira said in a low, deadly voice. "What did you say?"

Rasim whispered, "I said you can't do that. We're on a diplomatic mission from the king, and Endat is his chosen envoy. You can't just put him off the ship. I think it would be treason."

"And you should know about treason." Nasira's voice remained soft and dangerous. "You're the one who went North and brought back a ship captained by the man who tried to kill King Taishm. The whole *guild* was disbanded and marked as traitors for that journey north."

Rasim's jaw fell open. "Guildmaster Isidri sent the

fleet north and you know it. All the captains agreed with it, even you, Captain Nasira. You could have refused to sail to the Northlands if you'd thought it was a mistake. You could have — "

"Put him in the brig," Nasira said. "Him and any of those who support him."

Kisia instantly stepped forward. Rasim stomped on her foot, making her swallow a yelp and hop back again. He shook his head once, hard and fast. There was no point in more than one of them being thrown in the brig. Nasira was so angry that she was already remembering things the way she wanted instead of what had really happened. Showing support for Rasim would only make it worse. And Nasira was right about something: it *had* been the ships lent to him by the Northern royal family which had carried the traitorous Northern captain to Ilyara's shores. It had nothing to do with the current situation, but Nasira had it on her line and wasn't going to let go.

Hassin, stoic-faced and silent, put a hand on Rasim's shoulder. It seemed the whole crew had gathered to watch Nasira take Rasim down, and now as first mate it was Hassin's duty to do as she ordered. He put his other hand on Endat's shoulder, even more lightly. The Sunmaster nodded to his journeymen, and both the girls fell into step with the little processional being brought below. Daka's gaze was still high and reverent, looking at where the ropes had burned with so little other damage, but Pynda's rage was close to Nasira's in magnitude. If she didn't calm herself, they might be in far worse trouble than just having lost the ropes.

Endat touched Pynda's shoulder, as if reminding her to let her anger go. Her jaw rolled, and though none of the rage left her, the sense of danger somehow did. Endat nodded again, and Hassin brought them all below. The Sunmasters were allowed to go freely into their quarters, but Hassin escorted Rasim all the way to the tiny, cramped brig built into the *Waifia*'s prow.

Rasim had cleaned and tarred the little room many times, but he couldn't remember anyone actually being sent there. Asindo ran a smoother ship than that, no power struggles and no one foolish enough to confront the captain so openly. Of course, no one had ever incinerated all the *Waifia*'s ropes when Asindo had been captain, either.

"I'm sorry, lad," Hassin said unhappily as he opened the brig door.

Rasim shook his head. "Just don't let Kisia do anything stupid, all right? Captain Nasira's..." He trailed off, unable to even put it into words, and Hassin smiled faintly.

"Yes. She is. She's a good captain, Rasim. Never doubt that. You wouldn't know it, but she lost her son and husband to the Great Fire, so she hates fire with everything that she is. She came back to the guild, after, because she had nowhere else to go and nothing else left. Then she lost her ship and a dozen crew when the serpent attacked, and now the guilds themselves are changing. It's hard for her."

"You don't need to explain." Rasim took a deep breath before stepping into the brig, as if the free air outside its walls was somehow different from the air within. "This fire is a disaster, and if it really is my fault, then the captain is right to put me here. I didn't know," he added. "About her family. I didn't know. I'm sorry."

"So were we all." Hassin closed the door gently, as if that made Rasim any less a prisoner, and left him alone in the brig.

It was large enough to stand in because he was short, but its floor sloped up and the keel split the room in half. A small bed took up half the remaining space. Rasim sat on it and looked at the tiny space. There were no portholes, not this far forward, and the only light came from the window in the door. Even in full daylight, the brig was hardly more than shadows. At night it would be completely dark.

Within about ten minutes, Rasim thought he would probably go mad with boredom long before sunset left him in the dark. Then it struck him that Nasira had given him a task, whether she'd meant to or not: she'd told him to be clever and find a solution to their becalming. Right now the *Waifia* rocked very gently, barely disturbing the water it lay in. Poor Milu might appreciate that, though quiet waters hadn't yet settled his stomach. Rasim lay back on the bed, studying the ceiling in the dimness. Braiding clothes might make rope strong enough to tie the masts in place, but even if every pair of trousers and every tunic on the ship was used, it wouldn't be enough. The Skymasters might be able to call up enough wind to shove the *Waifia* along for a while, but it would exhaust them. There had to be another answer.

Whatever it was, it escaped him for the moment. The quiet still air and the small close room worked together, warming Rasim until he drifted into uneasy sleep. Memories flashed through his dreams, the cold terror of diving with the sea serpent mixed with playing games of sailing ships in the guildhall's water barrels. Sticks were ships, powered by sea-witchery moving the water below them, and then serpents rose up and crushed the stick-ships in their coils, bringing sailors to their doom. Huge paintings appeared in the air, like the murals in the Northern palace that showed great heroes fighting terrible monsters. Rasim's own face was among them, brown in a sea of pale-skinned warriors. The sea serpent twisted him in its coils, then released him into the cold grey heart of Northern mountains, where another monster lurked.

Rasim flinched awake, sitting up so fast he cracked his head against the low brig ceiling. Spots danced behind his eyes like sunlight on the water. He sank down again, holding his head and wincing. The Northlands had already sent monsters—

assassins, at least—to Ilyara. He didn't want to imagine there was another monster of any kind waiting for them, assuming they were ever able to reach the North.

"Oh." Rasim sat up again, more carefully this time, and stared at the door as if thinking hard enough about him would summon Hassin.

It didn't. Rasim drifted into sleep at least twice more before the first mate finally came to the brig carrying a leather water flask and a bowl of cold fish stew. "Captain didn't say *not* to feed you," he said dryly as he opened the door. "Let's just keep this between you and me."

Rasim hopped off the bed and seized the food and drink, putting them onto the bed. "I figured it out, Hassin. I know what to do. Oh! How is Sesin?"

"She's all right. Won't be doing much work for a few weeks, but the healer's bound her ribs and strengthened the bones somewhat. I'll tell her you asked. You figured what out?" Hassin was a dark shadow against the dim light that spilled through from the lower decks, but Rasim could see the curiosity in his eyes.

"That we don't have to move the ship!"

Hassin arched an eyebrow and Rasim flapped his hands impatiently. "We just have to move the water around it. Not all of it, just enough of it. Like playing ships in water barrels." He brushed his fingers in a long line, mimicking the movement they'd used when they played that game. "We make a corridor of moving water around the *Waifia*, deep enough that the current can't snatch it back, but not much wider than the ship. It'll work, Hassin."

The first mate pursed his lips. "A current of our own under the ship. That might work. It'll be difficult with this much displacement and the ocean's pull to fight against, but it might just work."

Triumph splashed through Rasim and was instantly quashed. "Maybe you shouldn't tell the captain it was my idea."

Even in the dim light, Hassin's surprise was obvious. "It might turn the tide in your favor."

"Or it might make her even angrier. She told me to figure it out. I don't think she really meant it. Besides, Isidri just told us it doesn't matter who gets the credit, right? What matters is that we make it to land."

A long silence met that argument, before Hassin sighed. "You're a far-sighted lad, Rasim. All right. I'll suggest it and let her think it was my idea, but if we get home safe, I'll be telling Guildmaster Asindo the truth."

"Fair enough." Rasim settled back onto his hard bunk and picked up the water flask gratefully. "Thanks for this, Hassin."

"You're welcome. And if you feel the ship surge in a few minutes, know that I'm thanking you as well."

That was higher praise than anything Rasim could ask for from Nasira. He beamed and ducked his head, not even minding when he was again left alone in the dark. Several minutes later the ship *did* surge. Rasim bit back a cheer, afraid Nasira would hear it and deduce the truth. Hours passed, long enough for night to fall, and Hassin returned with more food and a wink of approval. Happy despite the circumstances, Rasim ate and fell asleep, barely even hearing the whistle blasts that marked shift changes.

From the light pouring into the hold and the relative brightness of the brig, it had to be twelfth bell, the hottest and brightest time of day, when he had his next visitor. To his surprise, it was Nasira, who flung the door open with an angry smile of satisfaction creasing her features.

"We're making landfall," the captain announced. "I'm putting you off the ship."

EIGHT

They were *nowhere*; that much was obvious from the position of the sun and the cold air. Rasim stumbled coming up from below, his eyes not fully adjusted to daylight's brightness. They hadn't been at sea long enough to reach the Island nations, never mind to sail far enough north to reach Lorens's homeland. The Northern prince had stayed out of shipboard politics, but he was among the gathered crew now, as Rasim followed in Nasira's wake.

A shadow blurred the horizon in a distant announcement of land. Rasim's gaze latched onto it, his thoughts racing. It couldn't be *much* land, or it would be on the Ilyaran charts. Come nightfall he might be able to determine where he was by the position of the stars, but he already knew it was too far to swim to a larger island, much less civilization. And winters in the Islands might not be as harsh as they were in the North, but storms coming off the sea could kill as easily as cold or snow. Surviving on an island too remote for the Ilyaran fleet to bother mapping would be—

Rasim clenched his fists like he could stop his speeding thoughts with the action. There was no use in borrowing the trouble. Maybe the tiny island would prove more hospitable than he was imagining. Either way, he'd find out soon enough. He set his jaw and drew himself up to his full, unremarkable height. Nasira could put him off the ship, but she wouldn't, by Siliaria's teeth, see him sniveling when she did it.

"We'll use the currents to put in to shore," Nasira snapped. "We'll scavenge what we can to make rope for our sails, and when we leave, we'll leave this troublemaker behind."

A collective gasp ran through the crew, but Nasira glared them down. "I'll not risk my ship or my crew to mad sun witches."

Someone—Rasim couldn't see who, and the voice was low enough that quietness disguised it—muttered, "So he's a sun witch now after all, is he?"

If Nasira could have commanded sun witchery, Rasim thought she'd have done it in that moment. Rage blasted off her with a heat of its own. "I don't believe it for a minute, but he's the fulcrum of this nonsense. I'll put off anyone else who's been mixing magic studies too, to keep us safe."

Kisia made a small triumphant sound and stepped forward defiantly. Rasim winced, wishing she wasn't quite so eager to tar herself with his brush, but grateful for her steadfast friendship, too.

"All of you, then," Nasira snarled at Kisia. "You and all of his friends. Desimi. Sesin." Her gaze even flickered to Hassin, but she held *that* threat behind her teeth. Hassin's expression never changed, but Rasim felt a spike of black humor. Journeymen were low enough ranking that the crew might not be brave enough to stand up and support them, but Hassin was second in command and well-liked. Nasira would be a fool to try throwing him off the ship too. "The Sunmaster journeymen will go too," Nasira snapped. "I won't have them on my ship."

A murmur ran through the crew, disbelief and uncertainty. Rasim closed his eyes momentarily, no longer thinking about his island fate. Nasira's anger would see her in a serpent's maw, if she wasn't careful. A captain's word was law shipboard, but the king himself had sent them on this journey, and this crew was used to Asindo's lighter touch. Nasira could push them too far, and bring mutiny on herself. Someone would speak soon, and this would go from bad to worse. Rasim tried to catch Hassin's eye, hoping to signal to the first mate that *he* not challenge Nasira. They would be in far worse trouble if Hassin mutinied and lost.

Lorens, softly, unexpectedly, said, "No."

Silence swallowed the crew's voices. Rasim's heart leaped, then fell again in a nervous pattern twice as fast as normal. Nasira turned by slow degrees to look for the one who had dared to speak. Lorens's lips twitched in faint amusement. Nasira's face went black with anger. "You are in no position to forbid anything. This is my ship."

"And Rasim is the invited guest of my royal mother," Lorens said mildly. "I can hardly imagine she'll be very welcoming to any treaties if the boy she specifically requested is not among the Ilyaran envoy. Of course, if you wish to risk the anger of two monarchs, by all means." He flicked his fingers at Rasim dismissively. "Put him off the ship. Let him fend for himself on a barren island. I might remind you, though, that this particular lad seems to thrive in impossible situations. Gods know how he'll come out on top if you do leave him here, but *I* wouldn't want to explain myself to King Taishm when Rasim washes up on his shores again."

Rasim could see fear first take the strength from Nasira's anger, then turn to anger itself. He understood that: it felt better to be angry than afraid, a lot of the time. In this case, though, he wished Nasira would choose fear over anger, since it was his own fate being decided.

"I'm sorry." Lorens sounded bland and not in the least apologetic. "I'm afraid I'm putting you in an awkward position, aren't I, Captain? Please, let me put this to you as a request from a foreign dignitary. Leave the children aboard ship until we reach the

North. My own fleet will take them home, when our business is concluded. You'll be obliged to deal with them for as little time as is possible. I swear this on my honor as my mother's son." By the time he finished, his voice and eyes were absolutely sincere, though Rasim was certain the Northern prince was only putting on a performance.

Still, it was what Nasira needed to back down grace-fully. Or as gracefully as she could, at least. She spoke stiffly, anger glittering in her eyes. "In the name of peace between our nations, it is of course my pleasure to accede to your request, Highness. But there will be no more practice of sunwitchery on my ship."

Lorens smiled brilliantly. "Of course not. I think we can all agree that was a terrible mistake, and that it's only through Seamaster Hassin's cleverness that we're not all to be stranded at sea after such an accident. I will commend you to my mother, Hassin."

A pained smile shaped Hassin's mouth and he carefully didn't look at Rasim. "Thank you, High-ness. If I may, Captain, Desimi would be of use in getting us close to shore—"

Nasira nodded once, sharply. As if they'd been re-leased from chains, the crew suddenly burst into action, dozens of them returning to the work of shap-ing the currents that carried them across the water. Others ran to the stern, where Rasim saw the ship's rowboats had been rescued after all, and stacked pre-cariously. He wondered where poor Milu had been sleeping, but thought it was better not to draw attention to himself by asking. Instead, he slipped away from Nasira and the crew's bustle, knowing that his own witchery was too weak to help with the heavy but delicate work of moving the *Waifia* closer to shore. The best he could do was take the prow and send his senses deep, searching for sandbars and reefs that might catch the *Waifia* as it made landfall.

Lorens joined him at the prow, yellow hair stirring wildly in the wind. He brushed a few strands back, tucking them behind his ear. The wind seized them again and he chuckled. "I see why you Seamasters wear your hair long and braided. Are you all right, Rasim?"

"Thanks to you."

"You'd have come out on top. What's the captain's problem?"

"Same as Desimi's used to be, I guess. Hassin said she lost her family to the Great Fire, so she probably hates all Northerners."

The Northern prince glanced down at him. "Do you think of yourself as a Northerner?"

"Nah." The water in front of them changed colors subtly. Rasim extended his hands, trying to feel danger beneath the water's surface, and called, "Two degrees to port, Hassin, there's shallow water ahead." He waited until the ship's direction altered, then spoke to Lorens again. "I might not be much of a witch, but if I was Northern-raised I wouldn't be able to do that at all. And I look Ilyaran."

"All but the eyes," Lorens agreed.

Rasim crossed his eyes like he could see their color. "I forget they're green. I don't see them very often, and there are other Ilyarans with my skin tones, so sometimes it surprises me when people guess I've got Northern blood just by looking at me. Anyway, a lot of Ilyarans hate the Northerners, and you'll have just made it worse for Nasira by making her back down. But I'm glad you did." The island came into focus as they drew closer and Rasim shivered. "I'm really glad you did."

It was not hospitable territory. Black and sharp, it looked like it had just been coughed up by the ocean. Rasim couldn't see any glow that said hot rock was still being spat forth, but neither did he see any hint of vegetation or bird life. Resourceful or not, he saw very little chance that he could have survived on such a bleak land. They would be lucky to find anything to use as ropes, and if they couldn't, it would be a wrecked and weary crew that finally made port in the North.

"As am I." Lorens frowned at the upcoming island. "Rasim, *was* it you?"

"Was wh—the rope fire? No. I mean, I don't see how it could have been, and...did you see Daka's expression after it happened?"

"Daka." Lorens made a motion, suggesting the smaller Sunmaster journeyman's height. Rasim nodded, and Lorens shook his head. "No. What was it?"

"She looked enraptured. She looked..." Rasim fumbled for words, gesturing uselessly as he did. "Witchery comes from within. When it works right it's wonderful. Like you're connected to your ele-ment. There's nothing like it. It's like...like flying," he said helplessly. "It feels like you're everything. Like you're free. And that's how she looked when the ropes burned. Like the magic had taken her. But she would have to be crazy to do that on a ship at sea."

"Like it had taken her," Lorens said thoughtfully. "Does that ever happen? Does anyone ever give themselves up entirely to their witchery? Kill them-selves with it?"

With a shudder, Rasim recalled Isidri's weakness after she'd saved the city. "I've never heard of it, but I don't guess it's something they'd tell us about. I don't even think most witches would be able to. I think you'd have to be awfully powerful in the first place. Like Guildmaster Isidri." Or Desimi, he thought, but kept it to himself.

"Is Daka?"

Rasim shook his head. "I don't know. But..." He lowered his chin to his chest with a sigh. "No. Sun-master Endat would have said, if it had been her. Wouldn't he?"

"I'm not sure." Lorens leaned on the railing, frowning at the water below. "From what I came to understand while in Ilyara, the Sunmasters look out for themselves first."

The *Waifia* dipped as an undercurrent caught the witchery being worked. Rasim's stomach dipped too, even deeper than the ship's pitch accounted for. For a few seconds the air filled with voices, warnings flying about strong waves and bringing the ship safely in to shore, and for those same few seconds, his own mind rang with different warnings.

The Northern prince had just challenged the *Waifia*'s captain to keep Rasim safe. That was not the act of a man trying to hide his own involvement in the attempted assassination of a king. That memory came back to Rasim in a rush, though. Lorens had looked so cold, so calculating, and so obviously guilty to Rasim's eyes, with the Island lord Roscord dead at his feet. Rasim had thought — *believed* — in that moment, that Lorens had killed Roscord to hide his own involvement in the attempt on King Taishm's life. But it would have been easy for Lorens to support Nasira and be rid of Rasim just now, if the Northern prince had anything to hide. A knot loosened beneath Rasim's heart. Maybe he'd been unreasonably suspicious, after all.

Captain Nasira barked orders, dragging Rasim's attention away from his own thoughts. "We can't go closer without beaching her! Drop the rowboats! Hassin, take a crew of eight to shore. The rest of us will hold the *Waifia* in the surf, since we've no anchor rope." The furious look she shot at Rasim made his cheeks heat. "Take the troublemaker," she snarled at Hassin. "I don't want him on my ship any more than he has to be."

Hassin nodded and beckoned Rasim without changing expression, then called half a dozen others, including Kisia. Desimi stepped forward, but Hassin shook his head. "I'd like to have you, lad, but holding the *Waifia* steady in these waves will take witchery such as yours."

Conflict swept Desimi's face. He was obviously flattered to be considered necessary on the *Waifia*, but equally dismayed not to be one of the explorers. But he didn't argue, and Hassin looked pleased. Desimi's shoulders straightened at this sign of the first mate's approval, and Hassin clapped his shoulder as he passed by on the way to the rowboats. A dozen crew heaved the topmost boat onto their shoulders as Hassin reached them. He inspected it briefly, then lifted one hand, palm upward.

Whitecap waves surged up, caught in his witchery. Sea water flowed over the ship's rail and grasped the bottom of the rowboat, taking its weight from the crew. Hassin grunted, but others came to help, their witchery blending with his until the rowboat floated gently over the rails and hung in a fountain of water by the *Waifia*'s side. Hassin stepped across the rails into the rowboat and flashed a grin at his small crew as they too came aboard. "This is much more elegant than sliding down ropes into the rowboats. We should do this all the time."

"This is a lot more trouble than sliding down ropes," someone else muttered. Hassin laughed in agreement, and cast the captain a sharp open-palm salute as the witches lowered the rowboat into the sea.

Nasira glowered at them all, and at Rasim in particular. "Listen for our whistle. If danger approaches, you'll know by its blast."

NINE

"There's nothing going to be here," one of the crew said as soon as they were out of Nasira's earshot.

Hassin glanced at the woman and she subsided, though her sentiment was clearly shared by the others. Rasim muttered, "There has to be," at his hands, and the same woman gave him a look as cold as any Nasira had bestowed on him.

"Captain's right. We should put you off here, no matter what that Northern prince says. He's got no business ordering a Seamaster around, especially after his own people near killed Guildmaster Isidri. First they burned Ilyara, then they half froze it, and now Taishm wants to make treaties? The royal line's more than weak. It's gone soft in the head."

"Shut up, Missio!" Kisia's thighs bunched like she would launch herself at the crewman, but Hassin spoke quietly instead.

"Kisia. Missio." Warning filled both names, though there was far more emphasis on the second. Rasim gave Kisia a faint, appreciative smile, but Missio scowled darkly and left Rasim to shift uncomfortably. He had spent years dealing with Desimi's dislike, but the older guildmembers disdaining him so openly was much worse. A lot of accidents could happen ship-board, if too many of the sailors felt like Missio and Nasira did.

"There's a bit of a harbor yon," said another of the rowboat's crew, and for a little while they were occupied with bringing the boat in safely to shore.

Even Hassin looked dismayed when they leaped to the barren rock, though. Craggy fresh stone rose from the water, with tide pools lying here and there, but the barnacles and crabs in those pools were the only immediately visible life on the island. Hassin looked around grimly, then broke the crew into two groups with a few points of his fingers. "It's not a big island. You four head around it to the right, we'll go to the left. Break into pairs when you reach higher ground that needs exploring, but don't go off alone. Siliaria alone knows what's hidden in this rock."

He hesitated, looking at Missio and Rasim, who were in the same group, but Rasim shook his head. If Missio—or anyone—thought he needed Hassin's protection, then he would become that much more of a target. Hassin nodded, then glanced at the sun. "Move as quickly as you can. Best to be back on the *Waifia* by nightfall, I think. Be cautious, but be thorough. We need *something*, or this journey will be a long, tiring one."

Kisia sent Rasim an unhappy look as she left with Hassin. Rasim tried to smile reassuringly, but from the worry furrowing Kisia's eyebrows, he'd failed. He was pretty sure she would be mad at him for that, even if it wasn't his fault. Sighing, he followed the others of his group.

Within half an hour it was clear Missio was right: there was nothing to the island but tidal pools and slick rock. Rasim, smaller and more lithe than the other three on his crew, darted up to higher ground as often as he could, searching shoal-ridden slopes for anything that might pass as rope. The shoal made for uncertain footing, even when he paid attention. Rock skittered from beneath his feet and proved that the actual ground lay as much as a palm's depth below the shifting stone. He watched the others from the corner of his eye, when he could see them, and caught glimpses of them slipping and digging their toes in as well, Once in a while someone called up to him to say they hadn't found anything, and he shouted that he hadn't, either, back to them.

Then a passage opened up behind a jut of sharp rock, hardly more than a cut in the stone face. Rasim yelled, and Missio, the next smallest of their team, clambered up the sharply slanted hills behind him, squeezing through the passage to find more of the same beyond it. They explored in silence, Rasim keeping an eye on the sun's position in the sky. Hardly more than an hour took them across half the territory they needed to explore, with no luck.

"You're right," he said over his shoulder to Missio. "There's nothing here."

She curled her lip, accepting his acknowledgment gracelessly. Rasim tried to smile as he turned away again, not paying enough attention to where he stepped. Shoal scattered beneath his feet and he slipped, landing hard enough to knock the wind out of him.

In an instant, the slippery stone beneath him surged in a little landslide and threw him into a crevasse as easily as a waterfall might throw him down a cliff face. Too breathless to cry out, Rasim twisted, scrabbling at the crevasse's lip with his fingertips. He caught, but slipped again as his weight broke more pieces away from the sharp edge. A few inches deeper he caught again, this time on a stronger section of stone. It held, leaving him dangling. Shoal bounced and clattered against the crevasse walls, the sounds seeming endless, as if they were falling forever. Rasim glanced down once, trying to judge how wide, how deep, the chasm below him was.

Even with noon sun pouring from above, he could see no bottom and more than enough width for him to fall much, much farther before becoming stuck in its maw. His fingers went cold, terror suddenly setting in. He hadn't had time to be afraid when he'd fallen, but with the terrible depth beneath him, Rasim's heart beat so hard he thought it would shake him loose from the crevasse wall. He could find no purchase with his toes. His fingers began to sweat, weakening his grip. The first time he tried to shout for help, all that came out was a cough. The second time his voice was thin, but it carried. Within a few seconds, he heard cautious footsteps.

Missio appeared above him. Nervous relief soured Rasim's belly. He tried for a smile, but it fell apart. "Help."

Missio crouched, hands falling between her knees as she studied Rasim's precarious position. Then she smiled. "No problem. Hold on a minute and let me go get some rope. Oh, *wait.*"

"You don't need rope. Just lie down and grab my wrist!"

"And risk you pulling me in?"

"I wouldn't—!" But she would, Rasim realized from the glint in Missio's eyes. If *she* had slipped, if *Rasim* was above her, offering help, she would pull him in, throw him into the abyss and risk her own life to do it, rather than simply save him. That was how deep her fear and anger ran. "Missio—!"

Missio picked up a large piece of rock and slammed it across Rasim's right hand.

Pain splintered through his fingers. They spasmed open, leaving his weight dangling from just his left hand. Rasim howled and scrabbled his toes against the crevasse wall, desperate to find any kind of purchase. Missio reached down and pried up his pinky finger, then the finger beside it. Rasim lurched, his weight hanging precariously from two fingers. "Missio, please, no, don't—!"

She flipped his index finger away from the stone, and the weak middle finger straightened, dropping Rasim into the fissure.

He bashed against one wall, then the other. His right arm smashed against an outcropping and instantly something felt *wrong*. Pain took his breath and he tucked his arm against his chest as he bounced from one wall to the other. It seemed like he'd already fallen forever when he finally managed to tuck himself into a ball. Every hit felt worse than the last, bruises upon bruises on his back and shoulders and shins, but at least his limbs weren't flailing and breaking.

Abruptly there was emptiness, no more walls to crash against. Rasim drew a shocked breath and hit water with an icy slap that flattened him against the surface before he sank. The crack echoed in his ears, blood rushing to his skin so fast that despite the cold, he felt a blast of warmth beneath the water. His witchery came to life, throwing him to the surface, where he gasped and lay on the cold lapping water, staring blankly into darkness. His right arm and fingers ached too badly to use. Rasim curled them against his chest, holding them with his left arm, and was almost grateful that he couldn't *see* how badly he was injured.

Not even the crevasse he'd fallen through was visible. He gazed upward, trying to make sense of that, and finally concluded that the crack in the earth angled so the sky couldn't be seen. Shivers came over him. If the crevasse was the only way out, he would die down here in the darkness, alone and very afraid.

But the water was moving. That meant the tide reached in here, and that meant there was a chance of getting free. Rasim rolled upright, half treading water and half letting his magic support him. The witchery could have done it alone, but he wanted to save what meager power he had, in case he needed it to break out.

Shadows started to break free of the dark, once he was upright. The sound of surf was louder in one direction, the same direction the faint shadows stretched from. Rasim kicked that way, then cursed as pain made him so dizzy he started to sink. He clutched his right arm again, ground his teeth together, and used witchery to push himself through the water. His hurt arm simply wouldn't let him swim. Better to risk draining his small magic than to simply drown in the darkness. Bits of light glimmered ahead, though, disappearing and reappearing with the shift of waves. Rasim took a deep, shaking breath, and ducked beneath the water's surface.

The light was easier to see from below water: larger,

more diffuse, inviting. A cave mouth of some sort, all but hidden by rising tides. Rasim exhaled noisily, a stream of bubbles bursting upward. He frowned at them a moment, barely understanding what they meant before dark humor washed through him.

No sea witch went under the water's surface without bringing a bubble of air with him. Even Rasim could do that, but for the first time in his life he hadn't thought to. His arm hurt an awful lot, but he thought he must have taken a hard knock on the head to forget such a basic lesson. If he could find a ledge to drag himself onto, he could dry off. Then he could slip back into the water warmer than he was now, and search for the way out to the *Waifia.*

Desimi, Rasim thought tiredly, wouldn't even need to get out of the water to do that, but drying off while still in the water sounded too exhausting. And he *needed* to dry off: now that he was paying attention, he realized he was shivering so hard his teeth were clattering. No wonder he couldn't tell if his head hurt. Still shivering, Rasim broke the surface again, eyes adjusting enough to pick out shapes in the dim light. There were ledges above the water's surface, and other half-familiar forms making monsters of the shadows. Rasim propelled himself to one of the ledges and forced water to fountain upward, bringing him to ledge's flat surface. Then he collapsed, gasping and trembling, as exhausted from the use of witchery as the cold.

It helped enormously to strain water from his clothes. He was still too cold, but cold and dry was much better than cold and wet. Rasim pulled his arms inside his tunic, folding his useless right one against his belly and rubbing his chest vigorously with his left. He was bruised *everywhere*, each rub causing a lance of pain, but at least he began to warm up. When the worst of the tremors had passed he tucked himself into a ball, squinting at the darkness and trying to make sense of the half-familiar shapes. Enormous curves, stretched high and wide like ribs, posts thrust high toward the ceiling—

Rasim laughed. It echoed around the cave, brightening it. He *had* been knocked on the head, if he couldn't recognize those shapes at a glance.

There was a *ship* down here. Wrecked, thrown against rocks, but a ship. It had to have been broken even before it found its way into the cave's mouth, because the entrance was too small a whole ship to pass through. But a wreck *had* passed through it, and he could see that its ruined pieces still carried the ropes that had once held sails and cargo in place. It was the *Waifia*'s salvation.

For an instant he imagined bringing the ropes back all by himself, being the glorious hero of the hour, and immediately burst the fantasy with a derisive snort. Even if his right arm wasn't banged into uselessness, he lacked the magical strength to haul that much rope through the water without it dragging him down. It would take others to untangle the ropes and more still to pull them out of the cave. And even if he *could* do it himself, most of the crew thought the rope fire was his fault anyway. At the very most, finding new ropes would redeem him, not make a hero of him.

Besides, he'd had enough of being a hero with the sea serpent. Others could take the credit here. All he wanted was to be safe on board the *Waifia* again...

...and to hear what story Missio had told the others.

TEN

It wasn't often that Rasim submerged himself without getting wet first. Desimi—even Kisia—had the trick of casually pushing water away as they leaped in, so that air surrounded them and closed over their heads as they splashed down, dry as a desert road. But Rasim's witchery rarely responded quickly enough, so he was typically soaked after such a venture. This time, though, he'd dragged himself out of the chilly, choppy water so he could dry off, and by Siliaria's fins, he would *not* get wet again. So he let himself into the water bit by bit, pushing water away slowly, and after a few careful minutes, was triumphantly dry and encased by a relatively warm air bubble beneath the water's surface.

The passageway out of the cave was larger than he'd thought at first, and more exposed by the falling tide than he'd expected. He popped his head out of the water to examine it quickly, then dove deep again to swim against the currents. The witchery worked by the *Waifia*'s crew to keep it in place was a weight in his mind, giving him direction without needing to surface. Swimming, especially with witchery helping him along, was faster than hiking over the island's rough terrain. Rasim thought he might even get back to the *Waifia* before Hassin's crew did, and shock Missio. Of course, Captain Nasira might have preferred it if Missio had succeeded, but that was another problem.

He came up on the *Waifia*'s far side, deliberately keeping the ship between himself and shore. Then he let loose a shout, waving as he struggled to keep from being drawn under by the magic holding the ship in place. Two of the sailors caught sight of him and lifted him from the water on a spout. He blurted, "I found rope," the moment his feet touched deck.

Jubilation lit the faces of those who heard him, and one sprinted off to tell the captain. She appeared a minute later, mouth held tight. "*You* found rope?"

The way she said it sounded like she imagined Rasim had orchestrated the whole thing, from setting the *Waifia*'s ropes alight to finding new ropes and making himself heroic. "I found a shipwreck in a half-submerged cavern, Captain."

"And you left the others behind to salvage it," Nasira said sarcastically, but her perpetual frown deepened as she looked him over more carefully. "You're injured, Journeyman."

"I fell into a crevasse. It was a long way down, but

I found a wreck at the bottom of it, and its ropes look like they're still sound. I couldn't check to be sure." Rasim lifted his damaged right arm in embarrassment. Most of the crew would have been able to lift themselves up to the wreck in a water spigot, even if they'd had broken limbs. "It's about a third of the way around the island to the port side, Captain. If you blast the whistle and call the others back, I think we can salvage the rope by sundown. At least enough to drop anchor so the crew can rest tonight without us drifting."

Nasira snapped, "Do it," and one of the other journeymen swarmed the mast to sound the sharp whistle that warned of danger and woke sailors for the next shift inboard. He'd heard it hundreds of times, but in the middle of the ocean it now made Rasim flinch, as if it might yet again call sea serpents from the depths. Nasira saw his blanch and sneered, though she said nothing. Maybe, Rasim thought, even she hadn't fully recovered from the terror of the serpent's attack. Then she cast a glance at the sky, judging the hour, and eyed Rasim. "How far around the island did you get?"

"We split into two groups, each taking half. My crew was more than a quarter of the way around when I fell." Rasim flexed his hand inside his tunic, feeling again the sharp pain of Missio's rock smashing against his fingers. "It took us a span and a half to get that far, so they won't be back for at least that long."

"All right. Go see Usia." It was as much compassion as Rasim had heard from the captain since he'd come on board. He ducked his head in a nod, and limped below decks to see the ship's healer.

Usia examined his injuries, listening to Rasim's account of his fall while giving the swollen hand a cursory look and tending to everything else first. Rasim had bruises everywhere, and more scrapes than he could count. "Not broken," Usia proclaimed of the right arm, "but bruised so deep it won't color for days. You'll take the herbs I give you, or that bruise will last you two years. Now." He straightened Rasim's puffy fingers, making Rasim gasp and sway. "Who did this?"

Too dizzy with pain to lie, Rasim said, "Missio," then inhaled sharply with surprise. "How did you know somebody did it?"

"You were hanging by your hands. If a stone big enough to do this so evenly had smashed onto your fingers, you'd either be stuck there under it or you'd have a bruise across your face where it bounced off your hand and hit you again. Only way it wouldn't is if somebody was holding it. You told the captain?"

"No."

Usia, who had probably been young once himself, smirked without surprise and wrapped Rasim's fingers. "I'll heal them properly later, but the captain's going to need to see this first."

"I don't want—"

"It'll come out, boy, whether you tell it or not, but don't try to fool me by saying you held your tongue for Missio's sake. You're just waiting to see what story she tells. Smart," the old healer opined. "She'll drown herself that way, and your hands are..." He glanced at Rasim's fingers and shrugged. "Clean. Go topside, lad, but stay out of the way. You're in no condition to work."

Grateful for the respite, Rasim returned to the deck and tucked himself out of the way among the rowboats. He could see from there, but couldn't *be* seen, and for the moment that was all he wanted.

Within another span of the sun, Hassin's rowboat rose beside the *Waifia* in the same manner it had been lowered, through witchery. This time, though, the first mate had no smiles or delight about him. Kisia was a huddled lump on one of the boat's seats, her face buried in her hands and her body shaking. Rasim's heart twisted. He hadn't wanted to cause her any pain, although it was hardly *he* who had done it.

"Hassin!" Relief sounded in the captain's voice. "Come along, we've found rope, but your witchery would be of use in fetching it—"

"Captain." Hassin spoke across her orders, his own voice raw and deep with sorrow. Nasira fell silent in astonishment at his tone, and the first mate climbed aboard to make a second, more solemn salute than the one he'd left the ship with. "Captain, Rasim al Ilialio has been lost. Missio saw him go into a crevasse, but she didn't get there quickly enough to save him."

In all his life, Rasim thought he might never see a more befuddled expression than the one on Captain Nasira's face. She took in the distraught gazes on the crew that had gone ashore as they, too, came aboard, and for long moments said nothing at all, just stared at them. Other crew seized the rowboat, hauling it back to the stern where Rasim sat hidden among the others.

Nasira finally spoke, saying, "*Rasim?*" incredulously. Rasim startled: she had not said his name one single other time on the voyage.

"I know you didn't care for him, Captain, but—"

Nasira's voice changed dramatically, becoming a command. "Rasim!"

Rasim slithered free of the rowboats, ducking under the still-wet one that had carried Hassin and the others to the *Waifia*. "Here, Captain."

Kisia made a broken sound of relief and threw herself at him. Rasim caught her, wincing at his bruises, but it wasn't Kisia whose eyes he sought. Missio went ashy, then grim, then struggled for an expression of joy. Hassin, bewildered, said, "Rasim? *Missio?*"

Missio blurted, "I saw him fall, I swear it—" as Usia lumbered onto the main deck and growled, "From *where*, crewman?"

For the space of a blink, Missio looked genuinely confused. "From the crevasse—"

Kisia hissed, "*Missio!*" and released Rasim so she could claw her hands and surge toward the older crew member. Missio flushed guiltily, but Rasim, feeling strangely calm, caught Kisia's shoulder and shook his head once.

Nasira, watching the interplay, became deadly serious. It was worse, somehow, than even the anger she'd shown to Rasim earlier. That had at least been passionate. Now Nasira looked to be locking down all her emotions, becoming remote and judgmental, as the captain of a sailing ship sometimes had to be. "Missio?"

"I saw him fall into the crevasse," Missio said again, desperately. "I told you, Hassin, I couldn't get there in time—"

"Rasim," Usia rumbled, "unwrap your hand. Show the captain."

Rasim did silently, surprised to see his hands trembling. He hadn't had time to be angry, before. His thoughts had been too taken up with first surviving the fall, and then the excitement of discovering the shipwreck. Even now it was more anticipation than anger that made him shake. It was one thing to fight a sea serpent, or even save a king. Those were done in the flood of the moment, with everything moving so fast the details couldn't be considered. But this had suddenly become a trial, and he was alive to stand witness against the crewman who had tried to kill him.

Tried to kill him. He hadn't really let himself realize that was what had happened, not until that very moment. Anger and fear flushed through him, making his bruises ache. His hands steadied, though, as he held them out to the captain.

Nasira looked at the bashed fingers expression-lessly, then looked at Usia. He came forward, his gait rolling even though the ship barely rocked, and told the captain what the injuries looked like from a healer's eyes: deliberate, caused by someone else.

Missio's eyes were so wide that Rasim thought she'd forgotten how to blink. Her cheeks were drawn and she looked around like she hoped an avenue of escape might open. Instead, more and more sailors closed ranks around her, until she was a prisoner in all but name. Hassin and the second mate took her arms, and she didn't resist. Nasira, thunderously cold, turned to Rasim again. "What happened in that crevasse?"

"I slipped, but I caught a ledge." Rasim's voice shook. "Missio saw me fall. I thought she was com-ing to help me, but she..." He had to wet his lips and swallow before he could continue. "She smashed my hand, and pried up the other hand's fingers so I would fall. And I did."

"And why didn't you tell me this the moment you came back on board the *Waifia*?"

Rasim couldn't very well say he thought the cap-tain might have applauded Missio's efforts. For a few seconds he struggled for an answer. Long enough that

Nasira — and most of the crew, he wagered — realized what he wasn't saying. Before Nasira's face turned ugly again, he forced a different explanation out: "I thought keeping quiet would be the best way to have the truth come out. It worked with Prince Roscord, in Ilyara. And—" His shoulders slumped. "Captain, you've not commanded the *Waifia* long enough to have favorites among the crew, but I thought telling tales on anyone might set you against me."

"Even more."

For a horrible moment Rasim thought he'd said those words aloud. He'd certainly thought them. But the whispers of surprise that darted through the gathered crew made it clear that *he* hadn't said them.

Nasira had.

"You mean set me against you even more," she repeated, clearly enough that no one could mistake it. Rasim, sick to his stomach with confusion and fear, nodded and looked at his feet. "I don't like you, Journeyman," Nasira said flatly. "I don't like the trouble you brought to the Seamasters Guild. I don't like that a guild orphan is involved with royal politics. I don't like that you dragged Stonemasters onto my ship. And I don't like anybody with Northern blood. But I am the captain of this vessel and I have done badly by you. Make no mistake. I recognize that this is my fault. Journeyman Missio would never have dared act on her own fears and anger if I hadn't been so ready to lash out with mine."

"Captain—" Rasim almost swallowed his tongue, uncertain what to say next.

"Do not." Nasira barely kept it from being a snarl. "Do not speak to me, Journeyman. Much of this is my fault, but Missio still chose to try to murder a member of my crew. There is no other penalty than death, for that transgression. Bind her hands." Nasira's voice shook with fury, and Rasim no longer knew if it was at him or at herself. "Lay out the plank."

There was no point in binding an Ilyaran sailor that way, or making them walk a plank, except that it was tradition at sea, even for the sea witches. Witchery worked whether they were tied up or not, and it was nearly impossible to drown a seamaster.

It wasn't impossible to starve one, though, or for one to die of exposure. Missio might be able to catch fish off the island's reefs, and would be able to purify water, but unless she found shelter, that would only prolong her death sentence. Either way, she would die cold and alone.

"Please." Rasim barely heard himself above the wind and the lapping waves. He cleared his throat and stepped forward, forcing his voice to a louder register. "Captain, please, wait."

Warning sparked in Nasira's eyes, but she lifted her hand, stopping the sudden rush of activity as the crew fell silently to doing Nasira's orders. "Why?"

"Because, Captain." Rasim took a deep breath. "I want her to live."

ELEVEN

Missio turned a gaze gone black with hope and disbelief toward Rasim. Nasira resumed her own dangerously neutral expression, hushing the startled whispers that ran through the crew. "Why?"

Rasim swallowed and met Missio, not Nasira's, eyes. "Because nobody deserves to be abandoned someplace like this, but more because..." He looked at Nasira after all. "Captain, killing people doesn't solve anything, does it? It might scare the ones who are left, but being scared just makes people lash out and do stupid things." He made a small motion toward Missio, using her actions as an example, then spoke even more softly. "Besides, it's one thing to kill somebody when you're fighting for your life. It's something else entirely to do this. To think about it ahead of time, and kill someone. That's not right."

"It's what she tried to do to you, Journeyman."

"Yeah." Rasim gave the captain a watery smile. "But it didn't work. And I'm—" He bit back the words *better than that*, because they wouldn't help even if they were true. He wanted them to be true, though. "I'm never going to sleep well again, knowing we left her here. Please, Captain."

Wind, water, the creak of masts; those sounds became loud compared to the silence of the *Waifia*'s crew. Rasim's right hand began throbbing, making him realize he was holding every muscle in his body tense as he waited for the captain's verdict. Missio's eyes were huge, her gaze locked on Nasira, and her lips parted like she was trying to gulp air and couldn't.

Everyone, including Rasim, watched the captain, but Nasira's attention was entirely on Rasim. He felt like he should say something else, but he couldn't think what. A plea to the sea goddess Siliaria's mercy, maybe, but neither Siliaria nor the oceans she commanded were known for their mercy.

Nasira finally shook her head once, sending Rasim's stomach into a plummet. But she lifted her eyebrows, shook her head again, and addressed Hassin. "Put her in the brig, then."

Missio's knees cut out from under her. Hassin's grip saved her from falling, but he had to brace himself to do it. Rasim caught the startled glance he shared with the second mate, as if Missio weighed more than they expected. Well, Rasim would too, he bet, if he'd just been spared a death sentence and all his muscles stopped working. Hassin hauled Missio to her feet, but she still stumbled as they walked her away.

Just before they brought her below, Missio shot one enraged look back at Rasim. Rasim gaped back, confused. He hadn't exactly expected gratitude, but Missio's anger didn't make sense to him.

"Get below yourself," Nasira said.

Rasim turned a dismayed gaze on the captain. Surely finding the shipwreck with ropes mitigated some of the trouble he'd caused. "To the brig?"

For the first time since he'd come on board in Il-yara, a hint of humor curled Nasira's lips. "To Usia's quarters, journeyman. You need that hand looked at."

"Oh." His hand began to ache as soon as she reminded him of it. Rasim cradled it and headed for the stairs. "Yes, Captain."

"Rasim."

His stomach clenched and he stopped, looking back. Nasira, more gently than she'd ever spoken before, said, "Stay out of my sight."

Rasim whispered, "Aye, Captain," and went below decks in weary confusion.

Usia was still on deck. Rasim sank down beside the healer's quarters, trying to work his way through everything that had just happened. Nasira had sounded almost teasing there at the end, but he thought she'd meant it as well: he should stay out of her sight as much as possible. Hers and everybody else's, too, probably, because he had just defied the captain and made her admit fault in front of the whole crew, even if that hadn't been his intention.

Anybody who didn't like Nasira might see him as someone to rally around, and everyone who did like her would probably be angry on her behalf.

And all he'd wanted, a few hours ago, was to not be stuck on a deserted island himself. Rasim shivered, then glanced up at the sound of footsteps, hoping it was the healer.

Instead, Desimi stopped a few feet down the hall and scowled at Rasim. "What is *wrong* with you?"

Rasim stared up at his rival, feeling dull. "I got stomped on and thrown in a hole?"

"No," Desimi said, annoyed. "I mean, you won't fight with me, you won't let the captain put Missio off the ship, you...what is *wrong* with you?"

"Nothing! I just don't want anyone to die because of me!" Rasim folded his fingers behind his neck, pulling his head down to his knees. His right hand hurt immensely, but somehow it felt better than the churning in his stomach. "I don't know why that made her angry. I thought she'd be happy to be alive."

Desimi didn't say anything, but his feet remained just within Rasim's line of vision long enough that Rasim finally looked up. "What?"

"There really is something wrong with you. You just...you just keep believing in the best of people. Nobody is that stubborn, or that dumb, or—or whatever it is you are. That *good*."

Rasim bellowed, "I'm not *good* at anything!" so loudly that Desimi stepped back. Rasim tightened the knots of his fingers until the deck he sat on went blurry with tears. "I'm not *good*, Desimi, I'm little and I'm terrible at magic and the only thing I *can* do is try to think ahead and see what's going to happen. What if the captain did make Missio walk the plank? What if she did survive somehow? What if then she got off that nasty little island and then she really, really hated me, and really had a personal reason to try to kill me? I think of all these questions and I try to think of the best answers and even that doesn't work because instead of maybe making a friend, or at least not an enemy, by trying to save her life, now she's even angrier than before!"

Desimi's gaze was a weight on Rasim's shoulders, but the bigger boy didn't say anything until Rasim's panting had faded and the tears had stopped dripping from his eyes. "It's like you don't know anything about how people work at all." Desimi's voice wavered between admiration and disgust. "You just keep thinking if you believe in them hard enough, they'll turn out nicer."

"What else am I supposed to do?" Rasim demanded. "I can't beat everybody up and I can't impress them with magic and I can't—I can't—all I can do is try to be smart and nice and hope people will be nice to me too! And Guildmaster Isidri says..." All his energy drained away and he slumped miserably against the wall. "She says people are mostly good, so what else can I do but treat them like they are?"

Desimi was quiet again for another long minute, and when he spoke, he sounded frustrated. "You better watch yourself, Sunburn, or that's going to get you killed." He stomped back toward the stairs, leaving Rasim staring after him in exhaustion. That would have been a more useful warning five hours ago, but he didn't think Desimi would have *made* it five hours ago. Weary to the bone and completely baffled, Rasim lowered his head and nestled down again, waiting for Usia.

The healer was longer in coming than he expected, though the pitch and roll of the *Waifia* told him why: the crew were bringing their witchery to the fore again, creating the currents around the ship's belly that would take it around the island to the cavern Rasim had found. It was late enough now that he thought they wouldn't get more than the rope to drop anchor with, but at least everyone would sleep well tonight and be able to face tomorrow's challenges refreshed. Usia would be up there making certain no one overstretched themselves. The crew's overall welfare was more important than Rasim's damaged hand.

And the crew, whether they all liked it or not, was intact, which hadn't been certain when this day had dawned. Rasim finally began to relax, bruised bones and muscles protesting as some of the tension left them. It had been a wretched, exhausting day, but it was turning out all right. He was warm and safe, Missio was alive, and Usia would come to him when he could. Satisfied, he tipped over to rest a little while, content to lie on the deck and let the *Waifia* rock him to sleep.

He had no idea how much time had passed when Kisia's voice rang down the hall: "Rasim? Rasim, you need to come up on deck."

"Whuh?" Rasim flinched out of his drowse, only half understanding her. He got his feet under himself before he was fully awake, putting his hand out for balance. It knocked against the wall, making him inhale sharply, but at least the pain woke him up. "What's going on?"

"The ship you found." Kisia's face was drawn, cheeks pinched and making her look older than her fourteen years. "It's one of ours, Rasim. It's one we lost when the serpent attacked. It's the *Sinaz*. It's Nasira's old command."

Rain lashed Rasim as he followed Kisia to the deck. He called witchery, repelling the fat drops of water in the same way he had pressed water aside when he swam through the ocean, creating a barrier of air between himself and the downfall. Everyone on deck did the same.

Almost everyone. Captain Nasira, standing at the *Waifia*'s side, was *wet*. Rasim had never seen a wet Seamaster captain before, or at least not outside of the bath houses. Water collected and rolled off Nasira's sleeves, and a steady stream drained down her narrow braid to make an ever-increasing puddle around her feet. Rain poured down her cheeks, off her chin, dripped from her ears and her nose.

Rain, Rasim thought, or tears. Maybe allowing the rain to soak her also let the captain cry in full sight of her crew, but without raising any commentary. The sailors were busy, and she could by no means be considered alone, but they still left a space around her, allowing her to be almost alone among many. She had lost her ship and at least a dozen crew to the serpent, and it was clear the wounds were still raw. Rasim took a step forward, then vividly recalled her order to stay away, and thought better of approaching her.

Kisia had left him the moment they came on deck. Rasim followed her now, though between his injuries and his weak witchery there wasn't much he could do to help. He took up a place at the ship's stern, perching on the stacked rowboats and watching the activity through the increasing deluge.

Half the crew was set to keeping the *Waifia* steady in ever-choppier waves. Hassin led the salvage attempt, his head popping in and out of the water like a slender seal's. Others, also in the water, dove deep. Rasim sensed their power at work, pushing back against the currents as they tried to navigate the cave mouth as grey skies grew darker with oncoming night.

Desimi burst out of the water only a few yards away from Rasim, his expression both triumphant and tired. Vast amounts of water followed him on deck, carrying the weight of the huge, thick rope he dragged with him. It piled onto the deck in broad loops, taking up most of the *Waifia's* stern. "It's the *Sinaz's* own anchor rope," he reported as he pulled one end of the giant rope free. "It's frayed, but it should get us to the Northlands."

Rasim scrambled down from the boats to help Desimi shoulder the rope's weight. "How is it in there?"

The bigger boy's face went bleak. "Bad. Tide's as low as it's going to get, but the sea is rough enough that it's throwing even the strongest of us against the walls through that narrow passage. Usia's going to be busy for a week, healing us up. I don't know how the ship got in there in the first place." He curled his lip. "No, I do. It's broken up pretty bad. But Siliaria herself must have wanted it in there herself, for it to fit. How's the captain?"

"Bad." Rasim could just about use his hand if he didn't think too hard about it, so together the boys lugged the sodden rope to the anchor before Rasim looked over the ship's rail, then eyed Desimi.

Desimi eyed him back. "You're going to use that hand as an excuse not to climb over and thread the eye yourself, aren't you?"

"No, I'm going to use being a weak witch as my excuse. If one of those waves catches me—"

"Hnf." Desimi put the entire weight of the anchor rope on Rasim, who nearly collapsed under it, and climbed over the rail. "Once we get it threaded we have to move the rowboats so we can get to the anchor spool—" His voice was lost to the wind and rain. Rasim lurched forward to give Desimi the slack he needed to thread the anchor's eye, and caught a glimpse of the bigger boy clinging to the *Waifia*'s stern, windblown and surprisingly rain-soaked. Not even Desimi could split his attention well enough to keep himself dry while doing this kind of work. Somehow that made Rasim feel better.

They were going to need rope to re-tie the row-boats to the *Waifia*'s sides, though, because there was no room at mid-deck to stack them, and the anchor spool needed to be clear for all this work to be of any use. Rasim fed Desimi more rope, but let his attention return to the diving sea witches, now nearly invisible in the raging storm. It might be nearly impossible to drown a sea witch, but the storm was trying its best.

A different, lighter touch of witchery swept by him. Rasim glanced toward the *Waifia*'s prow. All three of her Skymasters were there, embracing one another and standing with their faces to the sky. Rasim was used to seeing them fill the sails, not stand against a storm, but the worst of the wind suddenly failed, sweeping a greater distance from the ship. It howled over the sea, kicking up more

distant waves. A shout of relief rose up from the
sailors who were still trying to hold the *Waifia* steady
in the storm. Now that he knew they could ease the
storm, Rasim didn't know why the Skymasters didn't
just chase it away entirely. He would ask later, since
they were all supposed to be learning about each
other's witchery anyway.

A thought brushed him as lightly as the skywitchery had done, and he turned a slow blink
toward the storm-lashed Seamasters in the water.

"No," he said, mostly to himself. "No, you're doing
this wrong, you're doing it—Hassin!"

The call was entirely swallowed by the sound of
the storm. Rasim straightened, wishing he could
command the lightness of the skywitchery's touch. It
would be easy to get Hassin's attention if he could
only convince the air itself to reverberate with his
shout. He sent a desperate glance toward the
Skymasters, and thought for an instant that he
caught the youngest journeyman's eye. Rash and
hopeful, Rasim filled his lungs and bellowed again:
"*Hassin!*"

To his astonishment, his voice lifted and carried,
booming across the water.

TWELVE

Even with Seamasters and Skymasters working
the storm, it wasn't possible for the tempest to just
stop. But it seemed like it did, under the weight and
size of Rasim's voice. Raindrops hesitated in the air,
waves caught and held a moment before crashing
back into the sea. The wind itself was silenced with
surprise, and every head whipped around, a whole
ship's worth of witches gaping at Rasim.

"You need Stonemaster Lusa's help!" Rasim shouted
into the quiet.

Hassin's expression cleared as the storm roared
back to life. It *couldn't* have really gone quiet, Rasim
thought, but his Skymaster-assisted voice had been
so enormous that it certainly seemed like it had, and
now the storm was all the louder. Hassin signaled to
the swimming sailors, and they began returning to
the *Waifia* as Captain Nasira turned a resigned gaze
toward Rasim.

He hunched his shoulders and came forward. "The

seas are too bad, Captain. Somebody will get killed, going through that narrow cave mouth. But the Stonemasters could widen it, couldn't they? Make it safer?"

Nasira muttered, "Why do you have to be clever," but nodded to a nearby sailor, who ran to fetch the stone witches. Rasim studied his toes, caught between guilt and pleasure at the captain's grumpy compliment. Nasira, still between her teeth, said, "How did you do that?"

Rasim blinked up. "I felt the Skymasters start to do their witchery, and it made me think of the Stonemasters, that's all. I thought since they're here, we should use them—"

"No. How did you make your voice carry?"

"Oh." Rasim shook his head. "I didn't. One of the journeymen saw me trying to shout."

Something indecipherable washed across Nasira's rain-lashed face. Relief, maybe, but also surprise or maybe disappointment. Rasim frowned. "Captain?"

"You need me, Captain Nasira?" Stonemaster Lusa came on deck with her eyebrows tied in knots, they were so tight. She took each step carefully, attention fixed on the deck, and threw off the offers of help.

Nasira waited until the Stonemaster had joined her at the rail, then nodded to the raging sea and the barely-visible cavern mouth. "We need that cave mouth widened. Can you do it?"

"From here? No."

Nasira flicked an eyebrow upward and made a

small gesture toward the sailors in the water. "We can get you to the stone, if you can shape it."

Lusa, very evenly, said, "You want me to get in that."

Rasim bit his lip to hold in a laugh. The Stonemaster hadn't complained once during the journey, but it was suddenly clear she didn't like sea travel any more than poor sick Milu did. And the seas *were* awful right now. Rasim couldn't blame her for not wanting to risk them.

"In a rowboat," Nasira offered, but Lusa gave her a flat look that made the captain's lips twitch with amusement, too. Her humor disappeared quickly too, though. "We can survive the night without your assistance, Stonemaster, but it would be far easier for all of us if you can help."

"If it will get us out of this storm more quickly, I will do it. Journeyman, will you fetch Telun? His assistance would be appreciated." Lusa returned her regard to the pitching seas as Nasira signaled for a rowboat to be taken down and Rasim ran to summon the big Stonemaster lad.

The Stonemasters' cabin door swung just before Rasim rapped on it. His knuckles brushed air, and he remembered too late that knocking would exacerbate his injuries. "Thanks." He curled his fingers against his chest again, then blinked at Telun, whose oilcloth-wrapped shoulders filled the door. "You're ready to go?"

"It wasn't hard to figure out what the captain needed a stonemaster for, once she was summoned. And Milu's no use right now, so it has to be me." Telun tilted a few inches to the side, allowing Rasim to see into the room. Milu's gangly form stretched across the floor, with his fingers dug into the wood like he might be able to hold himself still despite the ship's motions. Rasim grinned a little and Telun gave Milu a fond, sympathetic look before leaving the cabin. "I've never seen anyone so miserable in my life. Do sea witches ever get ship-sick?"

Rasim shook his head. "Master Usia says it happens because there's water in our ears that gets sloshed around and makes us dizzy, but even I can keep that from happening. I know Master Usia has tried to do it for Milu, but it doesn't take. He thinks the stone god's power is too strong in him. But it's like breathing, for a Seamaster. You don't even think about it."

"Lucky." Telun stomped up to deck. Rasim followed, knowing that once again, having had the clever idea, he wouldn't be of much use to anybody until it had been implemented. Still, he hadn't often seen Stonemasters at work, and Usia was still above deck, tending to sailors injured in the pounding storm.

Master Lusa already stood in one of the rowboats when Rasim and Telun returned to deck. She might have been stone herself, her spine rigid and her chin lifted high. Hassin, though bedraggled and weary-looking himself, was with her. Rasim had no doubt it was the first mate's magic that would steady the boat and drive them toward the bleak island. Desimi, finished with the anchor rope, jumped into the skiff as well. Hassin didn't even try to put up an argument. Desimi's talent for witchery would be of great help in the waves.

"Rasim!" His name was barely audible above the storm, but Hassin waved him down. Startled, Rasim skittered across the deck and stopped by crashing his ribs into the railing.

His ribs shrieked protest. He'd done it thousands of times before, but never just after bouncing down a stony crevasse. Cross-eyed and wheezing with pain, he doubled over, keeping his hands on the rail so he wouldn't fall. He glanced up and saw Desimi's familiar smirk, which gave him the strength to stand and grit, "Yes, Hassin?" to the first mate.

"You're the only one who's been in there while it was at all light. Come on."

Rasim looked over his shoulder at the storm-whipped ship. "Should we get a Sunmaster for light? Master Endat is already keeping the torches alight so we can see what we're doing, but I can get one of the others."

"Sunmasters in a storm." Lusa sounded as though she found the idea appealing. "Do. At least I won't be the only one out of my element, then. Telun, come aboard."

The stone witch journeyman did as he was told while Rasim ran below a second time. None of the Sunmasters were prepared to go out in the storm, but to Rasim's surprise, Daka, the tiny Sunmaster journeyman, threw an oilcloth cloak on and followed Rasim eagerly. "I thought Sunmasters didn't like rain," he said as they scrambled into Hassin's skiff.

"I like everything." Indeed, Daka's face was alight, just as it had been when the ropes had burned. Desimi lifted a hand to guide rain away from her, but Daka shook him off and extended her arms upward, then laughed in glee as Hassin carried the boat away from the *Waifia*'s side.

The sea was much darker, away from the *Waifia*'s shuddering torchlight. Rasim took Telun and Master Lusa's hands, closing his eyes to concentrate on extending his own rain barrier around them. It would do no good for the stone witches to be so sodden and shivering they couldn't work. Nearby, Daka muttered a protest. Rasim squinted one eye open to see that Desimi was keeping the rain off her, as well. They said Sunmasters were hot-blooded, and got sick easily when cold came on, so it was smart of Desimi, no matter what Daka wanted. Besides, Usia and Captain Nasira would never forgive them if they returned with a boat full of sniveling, sick witches.

"What's the tunnel's shape, Rasim?"

"Almost straight. Downward slope." It was easier to remember when his eyes were closed, though he'd swum it with them open. "The cave isn't big. Desimi had to have seen it, to get that rope...?" Rasim opened his eyes again, but Desimi shook his head.

"Too dark. I was using echoes and witchery to tell stone from wood and wood from rope. It sounded big."

"Big compared to us, but not to a ship."

"And you need room to salvage the ship, or just to move freely through the passageway?" Master Lusa sounded dreamy, though Rasim didn't yet feel the heavy weight of stonewitchery at work.

"We don't have the tools to salvage," Hassin replied. "We just need to get the ropes without tangling up so much we drown ourselves. Even if the cursed walls were just *smooth*—!"

Lusa nodded. She had never sat down; now she lifted her hands as the little rowboat approached the half-drowned cave's mouth. Telun, moving unsteadily, joined her. "Can you hold the boat close enough for us to touch the rock?"

Hassin and Desimi glanced at one another, then nodded. "Rasim, you'll be our scout. Dive and keep an eye on the walls. Surface when it's clear enough for us to pass through. It doesn't have to be perfect," he emphasized. "Just good enough."

Rasim's jaw dropped before he collected it into a brilliant smile. "Aye, Hassin!" He stood, not caring that the water was cold or that he'd likely be drenched by the time his adventure was over. He hadn't expected to be of any use at all, and even a small task was an exciting balm.

"Wait, Rasim. Daka, are you bold enough to go beneath the surface with him? He'll need light."

If the girl was a sky witch, she might have flown straight into the sky at the offer. "I can burn bright enough that the *Waifia* will be able to see what we're doing!"

Rasim's excitement fell away. "That much fire will use up all my air in no time. Maybe..." He cast a miserable glance at the other Seamaster journeyman in the boat. "Maybe Desimi should go instead of me."

"No, I need Desimi's strength to hold this wretched tub at the island's side. Daka..."

"I don't *have* to burn that bright." Her eyes glittered and she shook her hands. Gentle flame licked to life around them, dancing and hissing in the downfall of rain.

Even the Stonemasters, reaching for the oncoming island, were distracted by her show of power. Telun, still wobbling and gaining his balance, breathed, "I thought you needed fuel for the flames. A spark to start it and something for it to burn besides naked air."

"Most of us do." The corner of Daka's mouth curled up. "You didn't think Master Endat brought just anybody along on this mission, did you? Pynda and I are two of his most promising students, but even Pynda needs the spark. Come on, sea witch," she said to Rasim. "Can you get us in the water without dousing my flame?"

Stung, Rasim pushed raindrops further away, creating a wider barrier of air between himself and the downpour. Daka stepped closer to him. Rasim, uncertain, put his arm around her waist to draw her closer still, and felt his face go hot when her smile grew even brighter. She put her arms around his neck, careful to keep her blazing hands well away from his hair, and put her lips by his ear. "Into the water went Sunchild and Sea, bringing to life Ilyara's new queen."

Rasim's vision turned red with embarrassment. It was a children's rhyme, a way of recounting Ilyara's history. The Sunchild and Seachild were lovers whose children became the queens of Ilyara, graced by Siliaria the sea goddess and Riorda the sun goddess. He made Daka laugh by stuttering, instead of sing-songing, the next lines. "Across the earth came Stonechild and Sky, fathers to all of the kings, by and by."

"Siliaria save us all." Desimi, rolling his eyes, pushed them into the water.

Daka shrieked, but they sank beneath the surface without getting drenched. Rasim shot a triumphant glance upward, but Desimi had already forgotten them. The rowboat moved closer to the cave mouth, and Rasim kicked deeper, avoiding the water-working magics that Hassin and Desimi held in place.

The tunnel looked far more dangerous by Daka's

light than it had seemed swimming out earlier that day. Rasim breathed dismay and Daka huddled closer to him, some of her bravado gone now that she was under water. "We won't drown?"

"No. If we run low on air we'll surface in the cave, where it's sure to be calmer. Oh." Rasim gazed upward again as stonewitchery's weight began pressing against the walls. He pushed back against the current with his own magic, holding Daka and himself in place as Lusa and Telun did their work from above.

The walls rippled heavily, like water somehow lived just beneath the black rock. With each ripple, they smoothed a little. "Like shaking a blanket out," Daka whispered, wide-eyed. "I've hardly ever seen stone witches at work."

"Me either. Just repair work around the city, fixing crumbling corners and things." That, though done by stone witches, was rarely a job done with magic. Only the palace was grown up from the sand and stone itself. Otherwise Ilyaran homes, streets and even the enormous sea walls that defined the boundaries of Rasim's world, were brick and mortar, chiseled into shape and laid into place. "It's like it's alive. It's beautiful."

"It is." Daka put her hand out, trying to touch the shifting stone, then squeaked in dismay as she broke the air barrier surrounding them. Her fire guttered and she yanked her hand back.

Rasim inhaled sharply, sealing the damage up. "Don't *do* that!"

"I didn't know it would break!"

"I didn't either! Nobody ever pokes it! There's a whole *ocean* out there! If you let it, it'll drown you!"

Daka swallowed, her thrill visibly fading. "The walls are creaking. Can you hear them?"

"They sound like they don't like being changed. Come on." Rasim pushed them forward with his witchery, going deeper inside the cave. "We'll see how far the changes have gone, and go report."

"Should we get some rope, so they don't have to make as many trips?"

And so Rasim could personally fix some of the damage Master Endat thought he'd done. He peered at Daka, who was so close he could hardly see her. "Daka, was it—who set the ropes on fire?"

Rapture flooded her face again. "I don't know. It came out of nowhere. I don't think it was Pynda, because she needs the spark. It could have been me or Master Endat, but it wasn't. You're sure it wasn't you? Kisia is sure it wasn't *her*."

"Kisia thinks a lot of strange things," Rasim mumbled. "I don't think it was me. Does that ever just...happen? Things catching on fire for no reason?"

"There's usually a reason we can't easily see. Maybe a bright light shining through glass, or an ember buried in a haystack."

"Well, neither of those happened on the *Waifia*."

Rasim brought them to the surface near the *Sinaz* and let out a slow breath as Daka's fire lit and warmed the cave. There were dry ledges nearby. He lifted Daka onto one, then climbed up after her, staring in dismay at the ruin of Nasira's old command.

The ship was nearly broken in half, its ribs and deck showing the marks of battle against the sea serpent. A hole punched through the prow caught Rasim's attention. It looked nothing like the other war wounds the fleet ships had taken from the serpent, and he found footing to crawl up and investigate.

A chunk of metal had fallen through to the ship's wrecked hull. Arrow-headed and clawed at its base so it would catch rather than fall backward into the sea, it was stamped with a pair of interlocked rings. Rasim felt his face drain of blood. "Daka, this ship was lost during the sea serpent attack. We thought the crew were all dead."

"What? Is there somebody alive in here?" Daka scrambled after him, only stopping when Rasim held up the claw.

"No. No one is alive here," he whispered. "But this is a slaver's mark, Daka. Someone has taken Sea-masters as slaves."

THIRTEEN

"We can't go in search of them." Hollows marked Captain Nasira's eyes, but her raw voice harbored no doubts.

It had not been a restful night. The discovery of the slavers' mark had fired urgency in the whole crew, as if their old friends and shipmates had been lost for mere hours, not months. They had worked the night through, alternating between holding the *Waifia* in place and scavenging ropes until the rowboats could at last be bound against the hull and the anchor itself dropped.

Even then they hadn't stopped, despite the storm, despite their exhaustion. There was little else on the *Sinaz* that could be salvaged, but what could be, was: figures of Siliaria that no sea witch sailed without, scraps of metal caught between broken boards, and a sea-tarnished silver necklace that everyone recognized as belonging to a broad-shouldered witch named Sirion. And then they had mourned, all hands on deck to sing the *Sinaz* into Siliaria's grace, and to speak of the friends who had sailed beneath Nasira's command that day.

Now dawn broke red and dangerous on the horizon, but the worst of the storm had passed. Captain Nasira stood on the captain's deck, Sirion's necklace clenched in her left fist. Someone had polished it during the dark hours of the night; now it gleamed crimson in the rising sun's light. It looked like a call to arms, a banner to be held up against impossible odds.

"We can't go in search of them," Nasira repeated. "I want to as much as you do. But they are months gone, and we have a mission from our king." Her eyes glittered but didn't linger on the Sunmasters, the Stonemasters, or Rasim. Others did look at them with accusation, but Nasira continued to speak, drawing their attention again. "I promise you this, though. When our duty is done in the North, I will scour the seas in search of our guildmates. I will pull down stone and sky and shine Riorda's own light into the dark cracks of the world. I will find those who have survived, and I will *bring them home.*"

A cheer cracked the morning sky. Rasim added to it as he looked at the captain with new, astonished eyes. She'd been so antagonistic toward him that he'd never imagined she could speak with such passion and conviction, but she suddenly seemed to be everything a Seamaster and ship's captain should be.

Pride filled him until his chest hurt, and he let go another cheer to help release the ache. Kisia squirmed up beside him and hugged his ribs hard, obviously as moved by Nasira's speech as he was.

His bruises protested the rough treatment, the eye-watering pain enough to knock the admiration and awe out of Rasim. He whimpered and Kisia laughed guiltily. "I forgot. I'm sorry. Usia hasn't healed you yet?"

Rasim wheezed, "He's been busy," then shushed himself as Nasira began to speak again.

"The guilds pride themselves on how few people they lose. They must: Ilyara's witchery is its strength among nations. If witches came and went idly from the guilds, our power might be taught the world over, and Ilyara's place weakened. We are *meant* to forswear our magic when we leave, whether we leave for love, as I did, or whether we are taken, as our friends were. I should know. I was one who left, only to return when the Great Fire took my family. I should also know—as does at least one other on this ship—that it's not as easy as that." Now her attention *did* settle on Rasim, and dozens of other gazes turned his way too.

"I was safe within Ilyara when I left the Seamasters Guild, and even I made use of small witchery to ease my day. Rasim al Ilialio was captured not by slavers, but by pirates, and to save his own life he taught an Island girl seawitchery. We must assume that our guildmates are doing the same. We can learn nothing at sea, but when we make land we can begin to search out rumors of Ilyaran witchery in foreign lands."

She turned to Hassin, who stood a few paces behind her, his hands clasped behind his back as he listened intently. "Take us north, First Mate. Take us north, so we can do our duty and then find our friends."

"Aye, Captain! Sky witches, ho!"

Wind sprang up, billowing newly-hoisted sails. Everyone who wasn't holding on—most of the crew —staggered a step or two. Raucous, surprised laughter broke the tension on board, and sailors fell to their jobs. Rasim, though, stayed where he was, staring at the horizon and lost in thought.

The guilds *did* pride themselves on losing very few guildmembers, whether to accidents, disasters, or even marriage and families. That was an unspoken acknowledgment in the guilds: there were enough orphans year in and year out that the ranks could be replenished that way, rather than the through older guildmembers becoming parents. Some did, of course: there were those for whom children were more important than witchery, but they left the guilds like Nasira had done. But some *were* lost from time to time: shipwrecks and sandstorms and slavers could strike at any time, and *someone* had been teaching Northerners magic lately.

"What's wrong?" Kisia plucked at Rasim's arm,

pulling him toward the rail where they were out of the way.

"Nothing's wrong. Why?" Rasim flexed his right hand, testing it for usability. It creaked and ached, his knuckles nearly too swollen to move. Well, the ship was under sail again. Usia would soon have a chance to heal him.

"You've got that thinking look again. What are you thinking about?"

"What they haven't told us." Rasim bit his tongue, even though he was talking to Kisia and not a master sea witch. His Sunmaster teacher back in Ilyara would be disappointed that hear the lessons about considering his words before he spoke hadn't had any real effect on Rasim so far.

Kisia, though, wasn't bothered at all. She folded her arms around herself and pursed her lips, examining Rasim like a close study would allow her to see inside his head and understand him. Maybe it worked, because after a few seconds she said, "You mean about the ones who leave. Like Nasira."

Rasim shook his head. "No, exactly *not* like the captain. We know where she went, what she did. But there must be some who just really don't want to be part of the guilds, right? People who find ways to leave without marrying. People who…disappear."

"I've never heard of any."

"Well, me either, but if you were the Guildmasters wouldn't you try to keep it quiet? Especially from the

younger journeymen and the apprentices? The
guilds have dozens or hundreds of members, and
did even before the Great Fire. The adults might
notice when another adult goes missing, but not
necessarily even right away, and the younger ones
like us?" Rasim shrugged. "We'd never know."

"So, what?" Kisia frowned at him even harder. "You
think there's a — a rogue guild out there somewhere?"

Rasim's jaw fell open in horror. Kisia laughed, then
clapped her hand over her mouth. "I guess you don't."

"I hadn't thought that far. Kees, that would be
awful. At least for Ilyara. I think." Rasim rubbed his
temple with his left hand. "Did you know other
countries used to have witchery? A long time ago,
when Guildmaster Isidri was a girl, maybe, or maybe
even before. But it died out, like it's doing in our royal
family now. They must hate us," he said more quietly,
as that realization came on. "I never thought about
why Ilyara never gets invaded, because the answer is
so obvious. We have witchery. But if there are rogues
out there — and there *have* to be, don't there? I never
want to leave the guild, but even Desimi chafed at the
idea that his future was set out for him."

"Desimi used to be angry about everything. The
truth is he'd never leave the guild either, because he's
strong. He's going to be a full Master someday. He'll
have a ship of his own, and a place at the Masters'
table. He might even be Guildmaster someday, if
that's what he wants."

"But what if he had all that power and somebody offered him something he wanted more than a ship of his own and a place at the Masters' table? What if they offered him..." Rasim's imagination failed and he waved his hand. "I don't know. Whatever Desimi wants? He could...*escape,* if he wanted to, don't you think? With his witchery, he could be halfway across the Ilyaran Sea before he even had to come up for air. There have to be people who have done that, don't there?"

"You're going to have to ask—" Kisia hesitated. "Well, not Captain Nasira. Maybe Sunmaster Endat. He'd know, and he's nice."

"The captain will hang me up by my ears if she catches me near Master Endat."

Kisia huffed laughter. "That's true. Maybe Stonemaster Lusa or the Skymasters."

"I'm not sure Lusa ever wants to see me again, after last night." Rasim wrinkled his nose, but nodded. "I'll ask Skymaster Arret. I need to thank them for making my voice carry last night anyway."

"That was them?" Kisia looked disappointed. "I thought it was you."

"You think the rope fire was me, too, but I promise, Kees, if I could make fire I'd have been a lot warmer when I got off that island yesterday." Rasim turned to frown at the receding lump of rock, hardly believing it had only been the day before that they'd first seen it. "Is Missio all right, after riding out the storm in the brig?"

Kisia gave Rasim another long, studious look. "She's probably banged up and uncomfortable, but that's the least she deserves. But I'll go check on her, if you want. You go see Arret, and for Siliaria's sake, have Master Usia look at you. You're purple with bruises, Rasim."

Rasim glanced at his arms in the bloody morning light. Kisia was right: every inch of visible skin was discolored and unhealthy. He didn't want to think what his wrapped-up hand looked like. "Aye, Cap—"

Kisia mashed her fingers over his mouth, stopping the teasing words, then waggled one finger under his nose. "Don't you dare jinx me, Rasim al Ilialio."

Rasim's eyebrows shot skyward, but he pressed his lips together and lifted his hand in apology. Seamaster apprentices might tease each other with the captain's title, but journeymen, especially those who had ambitions to become captains themselves, never made light of the honorific. Rasim hadn't had any idea that Kisia, so new to the guild, harbored such ambitions. As she removed her fingers from his lips, his mouth spread in a startled, delighted smile. "Really, Kees?"

"Shh," she said fiercely. "I don't even want to talk about it."

Rasim's smiled turned to a grin and he nodded, though the impulse to throw a salute was powerful. Kisia al Ilialio would make captain, if that was what she wanted. Kisia had a determined streak the width of the Ilyaran Sea, and he couldn't imagine anybody stopping her from what she wanted to do. He wanted to tease her with a different title: Seamaster, or even Guildmaster, but instead his grin just got wider and wider, until Kisia became self-conscious and muttered, "Be quiet and go see Usia, Rasim."

Still grinning—in fact, grinning so brightly now that his vision swam, though it seemed silly to be misty-eyed with pride over someone's ambition—Rasim waved and turned to go below decks.

He nearly crashed into Prince Lorens, who stood unexpectedly near, with his arms crossed over his chest and thoughtfulness pulling his face long. Rasim blurted, "Oh. Sorry," and the yellow-haired Northerner laughed.

"Not at all. It's your ship, and I'm the one in the way. How do passengers do it?" he asked, mystified. "I feel guilty standing around without a job to do. Everyone else is busy with honest work."

"Everybody except the Stonemasters," Rasim said cheerfully. "Go ask the captain for something to do. I'm sure she'll be happy to put those soft Northern hands to good use."

Lorens turned his hands up, revealing sword-made calluses, and raised an eyebrow at Rasim, who turned his sea-roughened left hand up in turn. "Soft for a sailor, Highness. You'll have blisters inside a day."

"And how fast do you think you would have blisters if you took up the sword?"

"Teach me and find out." Rasim clapped his hand over his mouth, eyes large with horror at his own impudence. Lorens let go a shout of laughter that drew half the crew's attention, and offered a sunny bright smile around at all of them. "How many others do you suppose I'd have to train, if I took you under my tutelage?"

"Desimi and Kisia at the very least." Rasim knew it would be more than that, though. Every journeyman who could spare a moment would want to study with the Northern prince, even if they already knew the basics of swordplay. Ilyara's fleet was, after all, a navy: they fought when they had to, though their strength had always been their witchery rather than their skill with blades. But the chance to cross blades with a foreigner, to learn from a prince—that would be more than almost anyone could resist.

And Nasira was going to blame Rasim for any further disruptions to her shipboard routine. He opened his mouth to demur, but Lorens, still smiling, waved him off.

"Go about your duties, sea witch, and perhaps I'll speak to your captain about making soldiers of you all."

FOURTEEN

After the island storm, unseasonably fair weather gave Lorens his chance. From dawn until dusk the yellow-haired prince taught journeymen the basics of Northern swordplay. Even Hassin came to the training sessions when he could, and a time or two Rasim caught Nasira watching them all from the captain's deck, an expression of angry satisfaction marking her thin features. It took him a while to understand, and when he did, he dropped his guard and took one of the blunt sticks they used for practice right in the gut, knocking the wind from him.

Desimi, wielding the offending stick, dropped his own guard in surprise, and though unable to breathe, Rasim lunged forward and slammed his own stick sword into Desimi's belly. They both collapsed, coughing and choking for air. Desimi's stomach un- knotted first and he dragged in a breath deep enough make his eyes water before he wheezed, "What hap- pened? I never get a hit in like that."

Rasim's eyebrows twitched in acknowledgment. For the first time in his life, being small was turning out to be an advantage. He moved faster than the bigger students, and made a smaller target. Swordplay felt natural, the rolling gait of a ship-bound sea witch translating easily to the light, bobbing footwork Lorens made them practice for hours at a time. Even when they pursued other duties, the journeymen ducked and weaved with each other, practicing without thinking about it. It felt like dancing to Rasim, and he loved it.

His stomach finally loosened and he gasped in a huge lungful of air before speaking. "I thought the captain would disapprove, but she doesn't. She's glad we're learning to fight. Because she's going to need us to be an army, when we hunt the slavers."

Surprise cleared all other expression from Desimi's face. He looked toward Nasira, who watched them. Then, as if she'd heard Rasim's deduction, she gave a short, sharp nod, and turned away.

"On your feet!" Lorens hauled them both up, scolding tone failing before curiosity. "What happened? I've never seen Desimi land a hit on you before, Rasim."

"Hah." Rasim rubbed his stomach, glad the last bruises from the island had faded in the weeks since they'd left it behind. "You haven't known us long enough, that's all. I got distracted."

"Distraction will get you killed. Good fight, Desimi, but you can't let yourself be surprised if your opponent stumbles. Press the advantage. You might have slain Rasim, but he took you with him at the end."

"Aye, Highness."

A whistle blast sounded, marking the shift change. Half a dozen eager journeymen dropped their duties and ran for Lorens' training deck. Rasim and Desimi gave up their mock swords to the newcomers and went to pick up the jobs they'd left off. Lorens waited for the new students to gather, then began the same lessons all over again.

"I don't know where he gets the energy." Sesin swung down from the mast to land neatly beside Rasim. "I don't know where you do, either. I think you only get four hours of sleep a day."

"Sometimes less. Milu's still sick and I still get to clean up after him." Rasim made a face, then smiled ruefully at Sesin. "But I sleep *really well* when I do sleep. How are your ribs?"

"Better. Usia says I'll be good as new by the time we dock in the North."

"Will you start training with Lorens then?"

Sesin shook her head. "I'm not like you or Kisia. I see the need, but I've no wish to put myself at either end of a sword." Slow hope built in her eyes. "But Master Usia says I may have a knack for his kind of witchery. When we get home I'm to study with him."

"*Sesin,*" Rasim said in genuine admiration. Healers of moderate skill were common enough among the sea witches, but ones as skilled as Master Usia came along once in a generation. He hadn't taken a student in years, and the most recent one was the guild's master healer, a position Usia had given up for his own love of the sea. Rasim was, in fact, surprised that Usia had joined them on this voyage, given that the rugged old healer had been taking care of Guildmaster Isidri for the past weeks. Usia must believe the ancient Guildmaster really was fine, or he'd have never left her.

Sesin's cheeks rounded into apples with the size of her smile. "I know. I never even dreamed of it, Rasim, but it fills my heart. It's what I want."

Rasim's grin felt broad enough to split his face. "Congratulations. We're beginning to find our places, aren't we?" He gestured around the ship, at the journeymen becoming soldiers, at the captain readying herself to become a general, at the sailors whose whole beings were given over to sailing the *Waifia*. "I never knew how it happened, really. Not once we were assigned to ships or to the shipyard, anyway. I thought we'd be told where we belonged, but it's more that we discover it, isn't it?"

"If we're lucky. But you belong everywhere, Rasim. I see you with all of them. Even Sunmaster Endat, and don't think the captain doesn't know you're still studying with him."

"Not sunwitchery." Rasim shuddered. "None of us are, not even Pynda and Daka. Just diplomatic stories. It's boring. I'd rather climb the rigging in a storm."

"Well, what about the Stonemasters? You spend a lot of time with them."

"I spent a lot of time cleaning up after Milu." Rasim made another face. "Stonemaster Lusa doesn't want to have a thing to do with me, after I got her onto a rowboat in that storm. I'm busy with all of them all the time," he agreed, "but I don't think I belong with any of them, or with all of them, Sesi. I belong here." He put his hand on the *Waifia*'s main mast. "Your heart's with the healers. Mine's with the sea. It's all I ever wanted."

"Sometimes we're lucky enough to get what we want." Sesin smiled, leaving Rasim a little uncertain of what she meant. He swung up the mast to take his lookout point, and caught Hassin's amused glance while on his way up. His ears heated, though he wasn't sure why, and he climbed into the crow's mast feeling somewhat disgruntled.

The mood fell away, though, up in the cold crisp air. He'd told Sesin the truth: the *Waifia* was all he'd ever wanted, and if Kisia didn't want her captaincy ambitions spoken aloud, well, Rasim knew his were no secret. They weren't ever likely to make shore, but he would hold on to the hope and work for the dream until someone took it away.

A playful breeze whisked up the mast, wrapping around it and tugging at the ropes before fading away. Not a natural breeze, either. Rasim felt the light, laughter-like touch of skymastery in it, and peered toward the base of the mast. One of the sky witch journeymen, Zara, walked by it, trailing her fingers against the wood as she passed. The trill of witchery was probably as thoughtless and instinctive to her as making eddies in still water might be to a sea witch. Rasim smiled and settled back down, watching the busy ship below. What with sword lessons and his own duties and stone witches to care for and also trying to stay out of the captain's way, he'd never managed to talk to Skymaster Arret about whether there were guild members who left Ilyara; about whether there *could* be a rogue guild out there. Nor had he thanked them for lifting his voice during the worst of the storm. There never seemed to be a moment, between his own duties and theirs.

Not that their duties looked all that impressive. The Skymasters always took up a place at the stern, to best guide winds into pushing the ship along. Most of the time, they did nothing visible but sit, straight-backed and swaying with the ship's rock. Wind was finicky stuff, gusting and blasting where it wished. Any sea witch knew that, and any sea witch worth her salt knew how to tack the sails to get the most out of the dancing air. They did it constantly, even with sky witch help, and when no Skymasters were there to shape the wind, the sailors persevered without them.

But since the storm, Rasim had been paying attention to the Skymasters, even if he hadn't had time to speak with them. Their magic was constant, far more

constant than any sea witch. It almost always had
that light soft feeling to it, not the weight of sea or
stonewitchery, though in the heart of the storm even
skymastery had carried weight. But they were *always*
doing *something*. Rasim didn't know why, but he was
reluctant to interrupt, fearing the consequences. He
could talk to Master Arret, and thank them all, once
they made port in the Northern capital of Ringenstand.

A familiar yelp rose up from the deck. Rasim
grinned down at Kisia, who hopped and swore as
she nursed a bruised hand. Seawitchery might come
naturally to the baker's daughter, but swordplay did
not. It made her all the more determined to learn.
Lorens seemed to like her for that, and he'd given her
a few lessons alone after she pestered him enough.

That had been the cycle of days since leaving the
storm island: study, fight, work, sleep. And clean up
after Milu, of course. As Rasim watched, Milu
stumbled down to the training deck and picked up a
stick himself. He was using the swordplay to distract
himself from his sickness, and although he hadn't yet
made it through a whole training session, and was
still just as sick after, for a little while every day, at
least, he was able to think about something else.
He'd regained strength in the past few days, and
that, given how fragile he'd become, was a lot.

Moreover, the stars said it was another three days
to Ringenstand and there were signs of nearby land:

birds wheeling in the sky, smudges on the horizon, wood floating in the water. Someone had pointed those signs out to Milu, and now he stayed on deck as much as he could, gripping the ship's rail and staring at the distance like he could hurry landfall through will alone. There was a ship-wide wager going on whether he'd stay in the North or walk home once they made land. Rasim had put coin down on the Stonemaster journeyman braving the ship's journey once more, and reckoned he would win big if he was right.

As the sun fell, a sharp whistle caught Rasim's attention. He swarmed down the mast again and took the meal Usia had prepared down to Missio in the brig. Her expression went flat and cold when he opened the door, but she didn't quite refuse the food. "I'll leave the door open for some air, if you want," he offered. She curled her lip and turned her back on him, hunching on the uncomfortable bunk to eat her food. Rasim sighed and sat beside the door, leaving it open because *he* couldn't bear the idea of her breathing the same thick, smelly air all the time. The brig would be better off with bars, not a door, but no one expected it to be used for weeks on end, and a solid door gave the ship's prow just that much more strength. Still, if Missio was to sail home in there too, Rasim thought he might suggest to Hassin that they temporarily replace the door for the other leg of the journey.

"I've made a rope of my trousers." Missio spoke suddenly, her voice rough and angry. "I could strangle you with it, the way you're sitting with your back to me. Why shouldn't I?"

Rasim's heart jumped, though he tried not to show the thrill of fear when he spoke. "For one thing, the captain would put you off the ship with your feet in chains if you did, and you know it."

"Maybe that would be better than dying in here by inches."

"For another," Rasim said more quietly, "I can protect myself."

Missio snorted. "You're not much of a witch."

"I'm not." But Kisia had seized the very blood in a man's body, had seized the water of it, and used it to squeeze a man's heart until he almost died, like a healer working backward. Rasim found the idea repugnant, but he liked the idea of dying even less. "But I survived the sea serpent and two assassination attempts, including the one you tried. Do you *really* want to make me mad, Missio? I'm not your enemy. I'm just...in the wrong place a lot."

"Northerners are the enemy."

Rasim groaned. Guildmaster Asindo should have checked the sentiments of everyone on the *Waifia* before sending them North. Anybody who thought as Missio did—as Nasira did, for that matter— should have stayed home. Maybe Asindo was trying to teach them that Northerners were people too, but as a boy with Northern blood, Rasim felt strongly Asindo had chosen a bad way to do it.

"Northerners," he said with a little too much emphasis, "lost somebody too, in the Great Fire. Queen Annaken was Prince Lorens's aunt, did you even know that? He knew her. His older sister, who remembers Annaken better, is still broken-hearted over her death. If there's an enemy, Missio—" Rasim pressed his lips shut, suddenly remembering that the suspicions he'd shared with Captain Asindo and King Taishm, were not widely known. The last thing he needed to do was set someone like Missio, who already embraced unreasoning hatred, onto the idea that there might be an internal enemy in Ilyara.

She didn't notice his hesitation, filling it with her own answers. "*Someone* sent five ships of Northern *witches* to Ilyara. You can't tell me they're not the enemy, and anybody with Northern blood is more likely one of them than one of us."

"I was raised Ilyaran," Rasim protested. "Why would I choose the Northlands over my friends and guild?"

"You're friends with Lorens," Missio spat. "Maybe he's promised you gold, or a crown."

Rasim opened his mouth and shut it again. There was no point in arguing, no more than there had ever been in fighting with Desimi. When her taunts failed to get a response, Missio shoved her empty bowl back toward Rasim and turned her back again, dismissing him as if she wasn't the prisoner. Rasim collected the bowl with a sigh, locked the door behind him, and went back to his duties, glad that tomorrow it would be someone else's turn to bring Missio her evening meal. He just hoped she wasn't spewing her poison into everyone else's ears too.

Getting even the most mild fish stew into Milu took well past sunset. The poor stone witch had recovered enough to be apologetic for his illness, but not enough to keep food down easily or eat quickly. Rasim brushed off the apologies, his sympathy for Milu greater than it had been at the beginning of the journey. He'd complained very little, given how sick he was, and every day struggled to overcome his weakness. Rasim admired that, even if he still had messes to clean up several times a day. He was still relieved when exhaustion claimed the other journeyman, after which Rasim collapsed onto deck himself, asleep before he could count to three.

He dreamed of sickeningly sweet smells and difficulty breathing. His head ached, even in the dream, and when he came awake it was with a sharp inhalation that drew a cloying scent deep into his lungs. Dizziness swept him. A wet cloth covered his nose and mouth, pressing the sweet smell into him.

Wet. There was something about wet—he should be able to push it away—send the dampness elsewhere— but his thoughts softened, turning to mush, impossible to follow. He lifted a hand to claw the cloth away and his arms wobbled like the soft dough that Kisia's family made into hearty bread. He dragged another breath, trying to clear his mind, but the sweet scent overpowered him. Consciousness whirled away.

He woke when icy water closed over his head.

FIFTEEN

The cold was incomprehensible, gnawing into his lungs and deadening his muscles instantly. The sea tasted heavily of salt, thick with it, like the Northern lake he'd explored. But this was no lake. It was the ocean, with currents pulling him deeper into the water. It was almost impossible to drown a sea witch, unless that witch was drugged.

Drugged. The idea sluiced through Rasim's foggy mind, clearing it. Drugged, and not well enough, if he'd woken up when he hit the water. Or maybe his witchery knew the element so well it roused him despite the drug. It didn't matter. He was going to freeze soon, in these northern waters this far from shore. Rasim reached for the surface, not with his body but with his magic, seeking to draw air — *cold* air, he had been sleeping on and beneath blankets to keep the chill away — but *air*, necessary for life — down to himself. He didn't want to break the surface, for fear whomever had thrown him overboard was up there, waiting for him to rise. If they even felt his magic working, they could squeeze with their own power, or even simply throw brutal harpoons into the sea until his body was caught by one and his life's blood spilled free.

Air bubbled against his skin, tiny patches that felt far warmer than the water. Rasim gathered more, wrapping himself in it and desperately trying to dry his freezing skin at the same time. He had to stay near the *Waifia*, remain in its wake, or he would certainly die out here anyway, lost at sea. His gut clenched as he wondered if Nasira had decided to rid herself of him after all, or whether Missio's bitter tales had caused others to take matters into their own hands. If he could stay in the ship's wake until dawn—how long away was dawn, how many hours would he have to survive in the freezing sea? Too far, too many, that was certain, but his mind cleared a little more with each breath he dragged in. If he could stay with the ship, come dawn he could seek Hassin's help getting out of the water, and—

—and he didn't know what, then. It was too much to wonder, when shivers wracked his body so hard that his teeth clattered. One thing at a time. Dry off, catch the *Waifia*'s wake, *then* worry about the next steps.

Three more sudden splashes shook the water around him. Befuddled, Rasim reached out with his magic, feeling heavy weights sinking in the water.

One was very close by. He reached out, extending his air blanket to see what else had been thrown overboard, and captured a soaking, terrified Milu in his magic.

For an instant he couldn't even think. Then he yelled and spun around, hanging onto Milu, whose panting breaths sounded like they verged on screams. "Breathe, breathe normally, you're fine!" Rasim shouted. "Did they throw Lusa and Telun over too?"

"Y—yes?" Milu, like Rasim, was groggy and just as clearly had been awakened by the drop into freezing water. Through fear, cold and fogginess, his astonishment at speaking underwater was visible, and for the moment, enough to keep him from fighting Rasim.

Rasim swore. "Just relax. Just relax, I'll keep you from drowning, but—can you swim?" Of course not, he thought as Milu shook his head. "Just *relax*, then."

To his credit, Milu tried as best he could, not fighting as Rasim dragged him through the water in his quest to find the other two Stonemasters. Telun was easy to find, a great hulking panic. His struggles were made worse by a long cloak tangling around him, like he'd worn it to bed because he was cold and now it was determined to drown him. Rasim caught the big journeyman's arm and extended the air bubble further, wishing he could return to the surface long enough to refresh it. Unlike Milu, Telun could not stop panicking enough to hear Rasim's frantic instructions.

Milu, though, reached across Rasim, wrenched Telun out of Rasim's grip, and shouted, "If you don't calm down, he'll have to let you go!" Telun gasped, ceasing to fight for just a moment. Milu wrapped a long gangly arm around Telun's neck and throttled the sturdier boy into unconsciousness.

For a heartbeat or two afterward Rasim could only gape at Milu. The other journeyman gave him a tense smile. "Find Master Lusa."

"Right." Rasim shivered hard, wishing he dared stop and dry all of them. But Lusa wouldn't have time for that, and with as little air as Rasim had drawn down, he wasn't sure they would either. "Hold on." He dove deeper, struggling to retain enough air for all three of them. If he didn't find Lusa very soon, even if he *did* find the Stonemaster, her presence would suffocate all of them. And the heavy weight of witchery in the water was gone, or at least, confined to the journeymen he dragged with him.

But it was easier to move without Telun fighting him. Milu fought through his seasickness, focusing on kicking as well, which helped drive them down far more quickly. But where the journeymen had been thrashing blurs in the water, Lusa was as quiet and solid as a rock, and had sunk that fast too. Rasim couldn't sense her as a disruption, or find anything besides emptiness and salt in the freezing water. He had no idea how long they'd been submerged. It felt like forever already, but he didn't yet feel the false warmth of cold water death coming on, so it couldn't be more than a few minutes.

A few minutes, with the *Waifia* under full sail, was be far too long. He sent one desperate feeler toward the surface, searching for the ship's wake in the currents, but he was too weak or too deep. All he felt was the ocean itself, relentless in its pull. He didn't think they were *that* far beneath the surface, but the darkness was complete, not even any moonlight to help lighten the depths. With a gasp, he turned and began kicking toward the surface again.

Milu caught his breath at the change of direction, then silenced himself. Rasim was grateful: guilt weighed almost as much as the stone witches, but it was no use to Master Lusa if they all died trying to find her.

Familiar magic pushed water aside. Air pocketed and stretched, merging with more air, and in the darkness Kisia whispered, "Who is it?"

Relief broke like a sob in Rasim's throat. "It's Rasim. I've got Milu and Telun. Was it you, not Stonemaster Lusa, they threw in?"

"I don't know. I mean, yes, but I was in deep when the cold finally woke me. I'm still coughing water."

"There were only three splashes." Rasim crushed his eyes shut, hoping he was right. "At least while I was awake. Kisia, we have to surface, we have to find the ship—"

"Someone just *threw us off* the ship! You think we're safe if we go back?"

"I think we'll die if we stay in the water!"

Kisia let go a curse that would have made her mother blush, then fumbled in the dark until she caught Rasim's shoulder. "Oh, Siliaria's tail, you're still wet, you're all still *wet*—" Her witchery rippled over them, squeezing water out of hair, clothes, rolling it off their skin, until it bobbled away and merged with the ocean around them.

Rasim's bone-wracking shudders lessened just a little. Milu gasped in relief, then gathered himself enough to speak. "Rasim's right. We have to surface. We might die on the ship but we'll certainly die out here."

"I wish you had sunwitchery after all," Kisia hissed at Rasim, but together they sprinted for the surface, magic pushing them faster than they could otherwise go.

Starlight glittered on the water, just enough to make shadows of each of them. Kisia gulped air, then embraced Rasim hard before saying, "Give me Telun."

"He weighs a ton, Kees, and he's out of his head with panic—"

"It's madness for you to haul both of them around. I'm taller than you, my arms are longer, which means it's easier for me to hold him, and—"

"And your witchery is stronger than mine," Rasim

finished bitterly. "Milu, let him go."

"If he wakes up again—"

"If he wakes up again I'll convince him to stay calm," Kisia said flatly. "I'll slow the blood to his brain so he's too groggy to fight, if I have to. Give him to me, Milu. Rasim, can you see the *Waifia*?"

"No." Rasim whipped water around himself, creating a spigot to lift him further above the surface. The *Waifia* should have been a shadow against the night, white sails easily visible even in the dark. Sick to his stomach and exhausting himself with the use of witchery, Rasim sank back to the surface to stare bleakly at his closest friend. "Kisia, how long were we under? I thought the water woke me up, and I heard you three hit the water, but the *Waifia* shouldn't—*can't*—be out of sight if we were only under a minute or two."

"I wasn't under long enough to drown, even if I was deep when I woke up." Kisia's voice shook. "Look again, Rasim. It has to be there."

"Could they hide it?" Milu asked in a thin voice. "I don't know about you, but they drugged me. I smelled sweet-sleep as I went unconscious, and it sounds like we all went into the water at pretty much the same time. That means more than one person did this. Could Skymasters hide the ship from us? Make the air...I don't know, foggy? It's too dark for us to see much anyway, so if a fog came up around the *Waifia*...?"

Rasim went even colder, cold all the way to his bones. "I don't know about Skymasters, but most decent sea witches can make fog. But it would be lighter than the night, wouldn't it...? We'd be able to..."

"Not if it came up around more than just the ship." Kisia pointed toward the horizon, where stars blurred and diminished. "The air's cold enough to carry it for miles," she said dully. "We're never going to find the *Waifia*, much less shore. We're still two or three days from land."

"We're three days from Ringenstand," Rasim corrected. "We've seen land closer, on the horizons."

"And how are we going to get there? By flying?"

"Can you make a ship of the water itself?"

Rasim and Kisia both stared at Milu, whose face was drawn and sick in the starlit shadows. "Like a bowl," he said, "Something that can hold us all huddled together. I know we'd still be sitting *on* the water and it'll be freezing, but if we're all piled together at least we'll have our bodies to keep us warmer, right?"

"A water...bowl." Rasim cast a look at Kisia. "Desimi could."

"I swear to the baker's wife, Rasim, if you say that one more time I'm going to drown you myself. We *have* to. Otherwise we're all going to die. We can use the currents to carry us toward land, but—"

Calm dread settled in Rasim's stomach. "But the stars are being hidden by the fog."

"It doesn't matter. I don't know them well enough to navigate by them, not yet."

Offended, Rasim said, "*I* do," sharply enough that despite their danger, Kisia laughed.

"Yeah, I guess you'd better. Which way, before the fog eats the sky?"

Rasim tipped his chin back, staring at the stars through encroaching fog. "There's the north star, and it's so close to overhead in the Northlands to make no difference. The serpent's tongue touches the horizon, in the North." He turned in the water, finding the serpent constellation's tail, then following the line to where its tongue would be, though he couldn't see it anymore. Fog had come up everywhere, whether natural or witched into existence. Even the sky above them was nearly hidden now. "The serpent swallows the rising sun in Northern winters, so that's east and our nearest land from the ship's north-east course was..."

He closed his eyes, trying to be certain before he spoke, but Milu said, "Due west," with absolute conviction. When the others looked at him, he gave them a wan, grim smile. "I'm a Stonemaster journeyman stuck on a ship. I don't care how sick I am. If there's land within twenty miles, I know where it is."

"Twenty miles isn't so far," Kisia whispered.

"Not in a ship with sails," Rasim agreed flatly. "In a bowl of water, though?" And they were *in* a bowl of water now. Kisia had shaped it while he studied

the sky, and the three conscious members of their
group sat cross-legged and leaning on each other
within it. Telun was sprawled over their laps, lumpy
and uncomfortable-looking but not drowned. That,
Rasim thought, was quite a lot, given the circumstances.

He looked up from the unconscious stone witch to
find Kisia's haggard gaze on him. He was supposed
to be the clever one, after all. He was the one who
thought his way out of terrible situations. Except
Milu had suggested both the bowl and recognized
the building fog that hid the *Waifia* from its cast-
aways, which made Rasim not so clever after all.
"There are too many things to do. Hold the bowl,
keep the sky clear enough at least above us so we can
see the stars and navigate, propel the bowl through
the water...Kisia, don't drown me, but we could *probably* do it with Desimi. But with just you and me? It's
too much. It'll fall apart."

Kisia set her jaw. "No. I can hold the bowl. All you
have to do is navigate and create the currents to push
us along. I know it was your idea to do that with the
Waifia, so don't tell me you hadn't thought of it."

"Thinking of it is one thing! Doing it is something
else! It took the whole crew to keep the *Waifia* going,
and I wasn't even part of that!"

"You saved me from the serpent. You threw
witchery *miles*. You have to do it again now. You
have to find that power in yourself, Rasim, or we're

all going to die out here."

"But I *didn't*! I wish I had, Kisia, I wish you were right with your crazy idea about how much magic I have, but I *didn't*! I can't just make power roar out of me when I'm desperate. It doesn't work that way!" He thrust a finger at the sky, frustration pouring out of him in heavy waves. "I can't just say, "Begone, fog!" and have the skies clear! I can't—!"

"Rasim." His name was a low scratchy sound from Kisia's throat as she followed the line of his finger toward the sky. "Rasim, look."

Furious, discouraged, he glared skyward. "*What*? Wh—oh."

Clear skies shone above them.

SIXTEEN

Rasim gaped upward, heart hammering in his chest. The weight of witchery was everywhere, throbbing in his blood. Fog spun away from them in a tunnel, clear path reaching all the way to the stars. He felt the fog's swirl, felt each drop of water in the air, felt its lightness and its weight all at once. He blew a soft breath through pursed lips, and the fog eddied away from that breath, though it was much too far away to actually be affected by it. Magic. Witchery. *Sea*witchery. Rasim's *own* seawitchery. His head spun at the idea, dizzier than it had been even when he'd been drugged.

"I am not doing that." Kisia's voice remained low, even dangerous. "Now take that magic, Rasim al Ilialio, and turn it to the currents around this bowl so we can save ourselves."

He turned his gaze from the sky to Kisia, whose face was set in unforgiving lines. "You sound like Isidri."

"Then listen to me like I *am* Isidri," she snapped. "Push the fog behind us. Imagine pulling it into the sea and propelling us forward with it. Turn it into the current, Rasim, and get us out of here."

"I—"

"Don't you dare say you can't! I *feel* the magic in you, Rasim. It's enough to crush my breath. Now *use* it!"

Rasim caught his own breath, then swallowed his arguments and turned his face to the sky again. It was true, anyway. He felt the weight of witchery within himself, even though it was impossible. And the fog seemed willing to do his bidding, so he exhaled again, like he was pushing more of it away with the breath. Then, his hands clenched, he brought the fog down, back into the sea it had sprung from. Its droplets became one with the greater ocean, but he still felt them each individually, as if they'd built a friendly acquaintance. He encourage them to catch Kisia's water bowl and carry it forward under his guidance, as he navigated by the stars.

After a few minutes, wind caught his hair, a breeze strong enough to make him falter. He turned his attention back to the sea instead of the sky.

Whitecap water spun around the edges of Kisia's bowl. She held her lower lip in her teeth, concentrating on keeping the waves from falling into the bowl, but it wasn't rough seas creating them. It was speed, the strength of Rasim's current great enough to create a wake. He gasped and Milu's gaze flew from Kisia to Rasim. "Stop thinking," the Stonemaster journeyman ordered. "Just feel it, Seamaster. Become the water."

Every guild told their apprentices the same thing: become the water, become the stone, become the sun, become the sky. That, too, was part of the song Daka had sung to him while they were in the island cave. Rasim had never been able to *become* the water, though. *Becoming* the water sounded like somebody should actually turn *in* to water, and that sounded terrifying. He was afraid of the very idea, afraid of losing himself to the oceans.

But now for the first time, he felt it. The rush of blood in his body was the same as the water in the sea, carried by tides and turns. *That* was what they meant, when they said *become the water.* Rasim let go of thought and embraced the water's steady motion, a power that was the same the world over. At the bottom of his soul, it felt familiar: he had experienced it before, after all. The ocean had surged to life, responding to his will, because the fear of losing Kisia to the sea serpent had been greater than his fear of *becoming* the water. He had accepted Siliaria into himself in that moment, seizing everything the sea goddess offered and throwing it farther than he could imagine. He had saved Kisia, and then he had gone deep into the sea himself with the serpent and become reborn.

Rasim's eyes flew open, though he saw nothing. To *become* the water, to be reborn in the heart of the sea: that was to become a Seamaster. Not an apprentice, not a journeyman, but a master, beloved of Siliaria. That was every dream Rasim al Ilialio had ever had, and it awakened in his chest with a roar. Joy exploded within him, so profound that tears streamed down his face. He lifted his arms, shouting to the sky, to the sea and to the stars.

Starlight struck the sea, and from it rose a goddess.

She was everything and nothing Rasim had imagined. Seamasters swore by Siliaria's fins, and fins she had: a dolphin's tail, skin smooth and soft like a human's, not scaled like a fish. Her forearms were finned as well, sleek points that swept off her elbows and looked as dangerous as they did functional.

But she was a woman as well, half of what held up the world. Her watery torso seethed with power, wild hair rushing around a face too wild to be called beautiful. She carried a trident in one hand, favored tool of the Seamasters, and it, like she, changed size with each surge of the waves. Never smaller than inhumanly large, with one breath she took up all of the sky, a sea-silver face staring down at a watery boat full of journeymen, the next, foaming before them as a whale might, standing on its tail in the sea. She dove around them, disappearing and surging up time and again, though it seemed to Rasim he never lost sight of her, either. But then, how could he: she was the sea itself, and he was in the heart of her domain.

Once, in her enormity, she pressed her face deep into their fragile bowl, and came back with her lips peeled away from shockingly pointed teeth. Her mouth opened, sea spray expelling from her throat. She reminded Rasim of nothing so much as a cat encountering something appalling, and after a moment he realized that the Stonemaster journeymen disgusted the sea goddess.

"Your brother Coluth chose these two as his own, lady. They're gifted with his earth-shaping powers, and are needed beyond our borders. They only ask safe travels over your waters. Believe me, they're not trying to...invade." Rasim swallowed on the last word, overwhelmed and embarrassed to be trying to explain things to his goddess. She extended her tongue — long, thin, far too flexible — like she tasted the air, tasted his very words on it, and then opened her mouth further yet. Nothing human — nothing animal, even — could open their mouth that far, but she was a thing of water, constantly shaping and re-forming. Her distaste faded as she inhaled his explanation, and when she looked a second time at Milu and Telun, it was with more interest. Her tongue flickered out again, lashing first Telun, then Milu, on the foreheads.

Milu, sick and miserable as he'd been, shivered with rapture at the goddess's touch. But he ducked his head under her scrutiny, and Telun never opened his eyes at all. After an eternal moment, Siliaria withdrew, her expression pensive. She met Rasim's eyes with her own depthless silver gaze, and he thought he almost recognized the emotion in her wild, stunning features.

Not disappointment. Siliaria was far beyond anything that could feel disappointment, and humans much, much too small to be able *to* disappoint her. Something else. Humor, if the sea itself could laugh, and a sense of deep, unforgiving...*pity*, Rasim thought. Not a human kind of pity, not the feeling of sorrow for a wretched fellow creature, but pity that a challenge had not been met.

Kisia shoved Telun off her lap and staggered awkwardly to her feet, struggling to maintain the water bowl while she moved. Without a thought, Rasim strengthened the witchery holding the bowl's shape. The strain in Kisia's face lessened, blissful awe replacing it. "Siliaria. Goddess." She extended a hand toward Siliaria, not quite pleading. Trembling with hope, but not begging. She was, Rasim thought, *absurdly* brave.

That time Siliaria *did* laugh, a roaring rush of water that sprayed warmth — warmth! — over the four journeymen. Rasim tried to capture that warmth, to make a bubble of water around them that would hold the warmer air in, but Siliaria's presence was too vast and too changeable. She broke through his attempts without noticing they were there, and bent close to Kisia.

Goddess and girl stood nose to nose for the space of a heartbeat, Siliaria as small and contained as she could perhaps ever be. Water whispered, blowing into Kisia's hair and drenching her. Like it amused her, Siliaria lifted a webbed hand and touched Kisia's outstretched hand, fingertip to fingertip.

Water shocked over Kisia, ice-colored and sharp. She dropped into the bowl, wide-eyed, stunned, with her lips parted in wonder. Siliaria laughed again and finally turned her attention back to Rasim.

He had faced the serpent in its element. Its eyes had been black and cold, without emotion. Elemental Siliaria had emotion: Rasim had seen that already, though her fathomless gaze was no *kinder* than the serpent's. It was, she was, he was: there was little more to it than that, except perhaps that he had come into his power there, in the heart of her realm, and it was the only thing he had ever truly wanted. Helpless, Rasim whispered, "Thank you, goddess," and felt it was a silly thing to say.

She changed again, becoming enormous. Becoming the whole of the world, her changeable form splashing around them as falling rain. With only starlight to shine through it, the rain became rainbows, soft and silvery in the night. Beneath them, the sea surged, lifting the water bowl, and threw it forward on a wave that built endlessly as it traveled across the sea. Siliaria danced through the wave, breaking from it in shapes great and small, but through it all her gaze remained fixed on Rasim. His heart beat wildly, joy so great he thought he might go to pieces with it. The power was astounding, but it was the *belonging*, finally belonging, finally having a place, that took his breath away. Siliaria had taken him during the Great Fire and given him to the Seamasters, but not until tonight had he felt like one of them. Like one of Siliaria's children. Like not only had he found where he wanted to be, but where he was also wanted, there in Siliaria's embrace. There was nothing to ask of his goddess, when she had given him everything he could ever dream of.

The tidal wave crashed to a stop, water roaring over itself in endless splashes. The water boat's headlong rush stopped cold too, sea sloshing over it, filling it. Siliaria leaped from the sea in front of them, suddenly human in size. Suddenly beautiful as well, not just overwhelming but in her every aspect stunning. She came to Rasim as she had come to Kisia, but without the laughter. Her webbed fingers slipped into his hair, cold and soft as lapping water. Rasim's heart stopped, his breath a solid thing in his throat, unable to be drawn. Siliaria studied him, her lips so close to his could taste their salt.

She had asked something of Milu with her touch,

and Milu had backed away from that question. It was in her eyes again, in the cool wet fingers in his hair and in the eternal breathlessness of a goddess waiting.

Rasim, dizzy with nervousness, lifted his own hands into Siliaria's endless flowing watery hair, and met her lips with his own. She tasted of sweet fresh water and drew his locked breath into herself, exchanging that breath for one of her own. His heart stuttered and started again, given life by a goddess.

Siliaria, goddess of the ocean, breathed, "*Ssssea-massster*," against Rasim's mouth, and then, in the space of an instant, was gone.

SEVENTEEN

Everything—journeymen, tidal wave, water bowl, fog, *everything*—crashed back into the ocean. Rasim's feet hit bottom and his knees buckled, surprise striking him harder than earth. Kisia went completely underwater and came up again coughing and panicking until she realized Rasim was standing. She got her feet under herself and stood, thigh-deep in surf and gaping.

Dawn burned pale gold on the eastern horizon, sending faint blue shadows against a muddy, rocky shore only a dozen feet away. White-coated mountains swooped up from the shore, riddled with black holes that suggested safe passage, or at least protection from the elements. The air was so cold it felt scrubbed, and Rasim's breath turned to billows of steam on it.

Behind Rasim, Milu struggled to his feet and wheezed. Rasim startled and turned from the view to search for Telun. The big Stonemaster boy was a few yards farther out, also coughing. Rasim waded over, caught his collar, and dragged him in to shore. Kisia followed, water draining from her hair and skin. Milu came last, his long limbs awkward in the water. He dropped to his knees when he reached the muddy beach, squelching his fingers in the muck. It crept up his arms in welcome, the weight of stonewitchery hanging in the air.

Rasim squeezed Telun's collar, sending rivulets of water streaming off him, and shed the wet from his own clothes as well. Before Milu stood, Kisia touched his hair too, sending the last of their damp adventure back into the ocean. All of them were shivering. It was warmer to be dry, but not nearly warm enough. "Get up," Rasim told the Stonemaster lads. "We have to get out of the wind, into one of those caves, before we're too thick-limbed to move."

Kisia swayed, her skin taking on a burnished gleam in the slow-rising sunlight. "Don't you want to talk about..." She waved a hand at the ocean. "About *that*?"

"What happened?" For such a big boy, Telun's voice was thin and very small. Rasim helped him up, but even with help he was clumsy, and his weight sank him deeper into the mud than any of the others.

Milu barked a laugh. "You slept through it, my love, so you're never going to believe it." He shoved himself to his feet, stumbled to Telun, and hugged him hard. "The good news is we're alive and no longer on that wretched ship."

Rasim smiled faintly. "Tsha, Milu, the *Waifia* is a very fine ship. Yes," he said to Kisia, "I want to talk about it. But we won't talk long if we die of exposure, and I'm starting to feel warm."

"Me too," Telun mumbled into Milu's shoulder. "Thank Coluth."

"Thank Siliaria," Rasim and Kisia both said under their breath, and exchanged the briefest smile at that correction. Then Rasim shook his head. "Warm is bad. We're losing feeling. We have to get into those caves *now*."

Milu, without letting go of Telun, extended one hand, palm downward. Mud popped and splorched, making a huge sucking sound as it began quivering beneath their feet. "Come closer," he ordered, sounding nothing like the exhausted, sick youth he'd been for weeks. Kisia and Rasim skittered closer, neither of them fully trusting the shaking muck. "This mud goes down forever," Milu said dreamily. "There's no bedrock for at least half a mile."

"Milu, it's mud," Telun warned, but the gangly boy smiled, hugged Telun tighter, and said, "Hang on."

Mud ripped away from the shore, rising upward like a sea witch water spout. Kisia screamed and collapsed, lying on her belly. Every muscle in Rasim's body clenched. He forced himself to bend his knees, trying desperately to imagine the wobbling mud was nothing more than a rolling ship deck, but a glance down made a lie of that.

They rose on a column of grey clay. It bent toward the mountain faces, more mud rising to support it. The weight of witchery was terrific, and the sea ran to fill the gaping holes left by such massive stone-mastery. Clumps of mud fell away, splattering to the ground, but the great bulk lifted them upward at remarkable speed. By the time Rasim remembered to breathe again, the clay slide had carried them to a cave mouth dozens of yards above the beach. Telun grabbed Kisia and pulled her into the cave, and Milu nodded at Rasim, who forced himself forward to join the other two. Milu came after him, his witchery fading away. Mud collapsed down the mountainside and slid back toward the ocean.

Before they could take a single step into the cave's depths, Telun whacked Milu's shoulder. "*Mud*, Milu?"

Milu laughed. "It worked, didn't it?"

"But *mud*! It's not stone, it's not—"

"But it might someday be, through the pressure of time." Milu grabbed Telun's hand as he threatened another hit and drew him closer, speaking more softly. "It worked, and I won't do it again." Telun relaxed a little, putting his forehead against Milu's shoulder, then nodding.

Kisia, staring between them, wet her lips. "I take it you're not meant to work with mud."

Milu shrugged. "It's not stone, but it's earth. Metal, now, metal is hard to work."

Telun lifted his head to roll his eyes. "He means for most people."

"Shush, Telun." Milu walked several feet into the tunnel, sunrise bleeding into the cave and lighting his way. The weight of stonemastery filled the space again, though Milu wasn't doing anything visible. Rasim glanced at Telun, but he watched Milu with just as much expectation as Rasim or Kisia. After a moment, Milu turned back. "It runs deep, and it would be warmer deeper in, but we have no way of knowing what's back there. I think we're better off staying close to the surface."

"The wind will kill us," Rasim said grimly, but Milu chuckled and shook his head. Stone flowed behind them, closing them away from the tunnel's unknown depths, then sealed up its mouth as well, leaving only a thin arc near the top, for air to come through. Then the space inside the witch-made cave shifted, shrinking until there was barely more than a long arm's length from one side of the cave to the other. It warmed up noticeably as the four Ilyarans crowded together, but Rasim rasped, "Stop. Please. Stop."

Shuddering waves washed over his skin, different from the shivers of cold. His stomach thumped sickly, like his heart had taken up residence in it and neither was happy about it. The walls were too close, pressing on him, and there wasn't enough air in the cave.

"He's got stone sickness. That didn't happen to him in the island cave. Open it up a little, Milu."

Even in the semi-darkness, Rasim saw the sympathy in Milu's eyes before stone flowed back again,
making a little more room. It was still too close, the
mountain's very size threatening to crush him, but it
was better than before. Rasim bit his lip and nodded,
then sat down to bury his face in his knees. Stone
sickness, like sea sickness. He hadn't know there was
such a thing, though it was clear the Stonemasters
were familiar with it. "There was water in the island
cave," he said against his knees. "I know water. It's
not as..."

"Alarming," Kisia offered. It was a nicer word
than *scary*, which is what Rasim had been thinking,
so he nodded. "It's still cold in here, Milu. Really
cold." She had a hard time getting whole sentences
through chattering teeth. Rasim reached for her
hand, pulling her down to huddle with him. Telun,
the biggest and probably warmest of them, hunkered
down too, and a little more heat bloomed from their
shivering bodies.

"Let me concentrate. Maybe I can find sparkstone
somewhere in this mountain." Milu spread his hands
against the walls while Rasim tried to remember
what he knew about warming up.

"Tunics," he finally said, feeling thick. "Take them
off, sit on them. A lot of heat gets lost through the
wood. Rock." He frowned at the cave floor. "Which-
ever. But we always sleep with more blankets under
us than over, on deck. And skin warms skin faster

than cloth." He pulled his shirt off, spreading it out so it would cover the most floor space. Telun and Kisia did the same, and Telun tugged Milu's shirt off him when it was clear the other journeyman was too involved with his witchery to do as he'd been told. He was colder than Rasim, his thin limbs carrying no extra fat, especially after weeks of sea sickness. They made a triangle around him, squishing close. Telun draped his cloak over their heads, making for a lopsided tent that went farther in covering and warming them all than Rasim would have expected.

Once in their puddle of warmth, Kisia peered under Milu's arm at Telun. "Shouldn't you help?"

"Me? No, if Milu can't find it it's not here to be f..." The big journeyman trailed off, considering the shivering, slender young man they crowded around. "Ah. He's been so sick you wouldn't know. It's Milu who has the power, between us. Master Lusa brought him, not me, to work witchery for the Northerners. I've no great strength at stonecraft."

Rasim, rubbing his chest, muttered, "Then why bring you at all?" and then made a face. "I didn't mean it that way."

Telun chortled. "No, I understand. Milu wouldn't go without me. What, ah." His smile disappeared entirely. "What happened to us?"

"Someone threw us overboard. Siliaria rescued us." Rasim thought he sounded ridiculous, but his tone was so flat and matter-of-fact that Telun only blinked.

"Siliaria? The sea goddess?" At Rasim's nod, Telun looked flummoxed. "She's *real*?"

Kisia made a small strange sound. "More real than anything I've ever seen. What, don't you believe in Coluth, Telun?"

"Of course, but...well, no." Telun shrugged his big shoulders. "I mean, we pray to him and we swear by him, but it's not like he drops by for dinner. There's never been any proof to believe *in*. I could swear by my sand lizard, too, but that doesn't make him a god."

Kisia's face, in the shadowed light of their little tent, was still incredulous. Rasim thought he understood, though. Gods and goddesses were from old stories, not things that appeared in everyday life. Cursing someone in Siliaria's name might relieve anger, but no one expected the goddess herself to rise out of the sea and strike the offender down. The idea of them was real enough, but even in the midst of storms, they didn't seem entirely...*real*.

Or they hadn't until last night, anyway. Since Siliaria had come for him, Rasim thought maybe some part of him had always thought she did exist, even if he understood Telun's point of view. "Siliaria is real," he said with quiet conviction. "I'm guessing Coluth and Riorda and Tilarea are too. She saved us. She—"

"*Kissed* you!" Kisia said with the outrage of having just remembered. She sat up straight, bumping the top of their tent around, and thrust an accusing finger around Milu and toward Rasim. "You *kissed* her! A *goddess!*"

Scarlet heat started around Rasim's chest and raced upward until his face felt alight. "It seemed like a good idea. It seemed like she...wanted something. And what did she say to you?" he demanded. "She said something, I just couldn't hear what!"

"She said—" Kisia hunched back down, arms folded around herself. "Never mind. She called you Seamaster, Rasim. I heard that. What does it mean if the goddess of the sea calls you Seamaster?"

"That I'm forever hers," Rasim said, and frowned as Kisia hunched down even more. "I don't know what it means, Kees, except..." He drew a deep breath, tasting the salt water on the air, then sank down as he exhaled. "Except I guess you were right. I guess it was me who saved you when the serpent attacked. I guess I did throw witchery all that way. I remember getting dizzy afterward, but...what?"

Kisia's gaze was on him again, eyes bright. "I knew it was you. I told Captain Asindo. It *felt* like you, like you were catching me. He said it couldn't be, but I *knew* it was. That was the first time I knew how strong you were. That's why I think it was you who set the ropes on fire, too, Rasim. I think you have to balance it, that's all. You were starting to learn sunmastery and it broke down the walls holding back your sea magic. Sun and sea, don't you see? It makes sense. Who knows," she said breathlessly, "maybe we can all work two magics, and we've just never tried because of how the guilds are set up. Maybe we all have complementary witchery in us."

Telun breathed, "Hah. I'd like that. Tilarea did me only one favor by guiding me into Coluth's arms." Milu, although half asleep, made a pleased sound, and Telun smiled at him before speaking to the other two again. "If it's sun and sea, stone and sky, maybe I can find a real gift for skywitchery in myself, rather than being weak at one alone."

"See?" Kisia demanded triumphantly. "That's just like how you are, Rasim. Not very strong except when you really needed to be, but getting better now that you've been studying another magic!"

"Have you ever done unexpected witchery?" Rasim asked Telun dubiously. "Called more power than you imagined you had? I guess I did once or twice..."

"Nah. But until this journey I've never done anything unusual at all. Give me a chance." Telun smiled, and Rasim's heart twisted in sympathy. He knew exactly what it was like to be underrated, and he wasn't sure Telun's big build had done him any favors. At least being physically slight fit Rasim's witchery skills. Telun *looked* like a Stonemaster, like he should be able to move mountains. Fiddling with pebbles might be even harder, in those circumstances.

"Can you feel it now, Rasim? The ocean? You said you never could, before..."

Rasim nodded before Kisia finished the questions. "I can feel all of it, in my blood. It's moving there. It's a...it's not a song, but it's like one. Constant sound, inside me. I can..." His face heated again and Kisia reached over to poke him, curiously. "I can almost hear Siliaria's voice," he mumbled. "Which doesn't make any sense, because she only sounded like the ocean, really, but..."

"Good." Milu opened his eyes. "If you're feeling the ocean, that means you can feel some driftwood in it." He opened his hands, too, revealing chunks of sharp-edged, opaque rock. "I've found sparkstone and we all carry steel knives. Now all we need is something to burn."

"I'm just barely warm," Kisia said in despair.

"I'll go with Rasim," Telun volunteered. "You two wrap up in my cloak. Milu's too thin to keep warm in the wind right now anyway. Close the cave up after us, and shape a chimney from the stone, Milu. We'll be back with wood in no time, and then we can rest beside a fire until we're warmed through."

"Easier said than done," Rasim muttered, but with the stone witch's help, it was easier done than he imagined. Climbing up and down the mountain on his own would have exhausted him, but Telun shaped ladder rungs for them to climb, and rolled the wood they collected up the mountainside in a bowl of stone not unlike the watery one they'd spent the night in. Rasim sent him ahead with the wood, and went fishing.

All his life he'd watched others walk easily into the ocean, carrying warm air with themselves. For the first time he did it as easily, reveling in Siliaria's comforting grasp. Within minutes, he found a large, flat white fish lying quietly on the muddy ocean floor and scooped it up with witchery, carrying it, water and all, to shore. He killed it there and hauled it up to their cave, which was so much warmer than outdoors he started shivering again once inside. The big white fish's skin and bones had to be cooked out rather than cut with a knife, but none of the others complained, especially after Kisia roused herself to go down the shore again and came back with a palmful of fresh sea salt. Finally warm, full, and feeling safe, they dropped into sleep in their small protected cave. What to do next could wait another day.

A steady banging from within the mountain disturbed Rasim's dreams. He opened his eyes in confusion as the back wall of their cave shattered and a monstrously hairy creature stepped through. A wide grin split the hair, turning the monster into a man, and in the same moment, irons were clamped around Rasim's ankles.

They were all taken prisoner before any of them were fully awake.

EIGHTEEN

"Wait—!" Rasim coughed the word first in Ilyaran, then in the Northern tongue, which at least stopped the enormous man who'd chained him. Then he grunted and grinned at the others of his kind, all large, all grimy with earth.

"Good of—" He said something Rasim didn't understand, but thought might be the name of their god— "to give us workers who speak a civilized tongue. Keep those two—" More words Rasim didn't know, but four of the other men seized Milu and Telun. Their noses were pinched closed and their heads wrenched back, mouths open, as someone upended jugs of thick liquid into their mouths.

Or tried, at least. Rasim splayed his fingers, calling witchery, and held the liquid in its place. Kisia, now wide awake, kicked his shin and gave his hand a sharp look. He flinched and closed his fingers again, trying not to let it be obvious what was keeping the drug—because Rasim was certain it was a drug — from flowing.

Stonemastery surged. Rock spiked from the cave walls, slamming through one of their captors. He screamed and died. Others were luckier, only knocked aside by the magical onslaught, but more spikes burst out of the walls and floor, making most of their captors scatter.

Another order barked through the little cave. Men spun in place, avoiding the living stone, and hit both Milu and Telun on the heads hard enough that the cracks echoed. Kisia shrieked and this time Rasim didn't care if the Northerners knew he called magic. He reached for the endless strength of the sea so nearby, fully intending to drown every last one of their captors.

Something cracked against the back of his head, too, and the world went black.

His mouth tasted metallic and thick, when he came to again. His head throbbed in time to his heartbeat, and he didn't need to feel it to know a fist-sized lump graced it. He did anyway, finding the tender spot and hissing with pain as it squished beneath his probing touch. His hair was caked around it, sticky with blood. He was lucky they hadn't broken his skull.

It took a while to even be surprised that his hands weren't bound. It took longer yet to wonder about his feet. He fumbled them around enough to determine they were chained. His thoughts seemed very slow, each one an effort. Sitting up was dizzying. His stomach swirled and dipped. Rasim fell sideways, spewing onto the floor. All that white fish wasted, except the bile was thin and watery, not chunky. He had been unconscious a long time.

Someone appeared. A woman this time. Not his original captor. She was tall too, though. All the Northerners seemed to be. Her hair was so dirty he couldn't tell its color. So was her face, for that matter, but she had to be Northern because her eyes were sky-colored. She spoke, and Rasim knew he should understand her. He had studied the Northern language for weeks. But it made no sense. All he could do was stare blankly at her until she gave up trying. Then she gave him something to drink: sweet, faintly alcoholic, thick. Not mead like Lorens drank. Not enough to use as a weapon, either, unless she drank some and he could clog her throat with it.

Kisia had squeezed someone's heart once. Rasim shuddered at the idea. He could. He had the power now, Siliaria's gift. But he lacked the will. Kisia would scoff. Desimi would scorn him. It didn't matter. He couldn't do it, not coldly. Maybe if the woman came at him with a knife.

But she didn't. She waited to see if the drink stayed down. It did. Rasim knew he should struggle somehow, but his limbs were slow-moving. As slow as his thoughts. He waited. Didn't throw up. Didn't fight. Didn't talk. Didn't listen when the woman spoke again, because he couldn't understand anyway.

Not until she pulled him to his feet. Not until she drove him out of the chamber — rock, now that he thought to notice it. Lit by torches. Smoke followed an air stream upward, outward. They were still underground. Chains clanked around Rasim's ankles. He stumbled. His head hurt more than ever now that he was moving. The movement and the pain cleared it some, though. He could think a little more easily, at least. It wasn't just being hit on the head that was slowing his thoughts. He'd been drugged, like when he'd been thrown off the *Waifia*.

The woman drove him downhill, away from the air currents. Clanging began in his ears, making the pain worse. His stomach surged, sickness rising again, but he clenched his teeth and pushed it down. She would only feed him more, and the thickness in his skull had cleared enough to let him realize the drug was probably in the drink. If he was Usia or Sesin, he might be able to purge the stuff from his system, but as it was —

He tripped and stumbled down another tunnel, landing awkwardly at someone's feet. Big feet, bare feet. Rasim twisted, looking up.

The man who'd captured them stood above him, arms akimbo and that smile splitting his wild beard.

"Are you worthless like the girl, or a stone shaper like the lads?"

Rasim blinked, startled to understand him. His head *was* clearing, even if he'd been newly drugged again. Or maybe she hadn't drugged him a second time, judging coherence more useful than obedience. "We're all useful."

Their captor rocked back on his heels, huge eyebrows lifting and making a space for his eyes. Light-colored eyes, just like most Northerners. Like Rasim himself, for that matter. "You *do* speak our language. How are you useful?"

"The girl and I can clean water, make it drinkable."

This time the man spoke to others, too fast for Rasim to follow. All he caught was "Ilyaran witches," and hoped the debate wasn't about how best to kill them.

"Keep them separate." The woman spoke more slowly, but not, Rasim thought, so he would understand her. She was thinking aloud, that was all. Considering their options. "Let them see each other once in a while so they all know they're all still alive. The fear of risking their friends will keep them quiet, maybe even without the mindkiller drug. We can mine more with witches helping. Maybe even buy out our—" She used another word Rasim didn't know.

"Hah." The man—men, there were several now, most of them looking at Rasim like they'd never seen an Ilyaran before—they all barked sounds of disbelief and laughter, but the woman shrugged and kicked Rasim with her toe.

"Laugh if you want, but the other lads are stone shapers and this one's a water witch. How much time will we save if this one and the girl are—" She became unintelligible again, but the gist was clear enough. Ilyaran stone and sea witches working a mine could increase its productivity enormously. Rasim's chest felt too small for the dreadful thudding of his heart.

Stonemasters *did*, of course, work mines around Ilyara. Rasim knew nothing about the practice, but he was certain the constant banging of metal against stone inside this mountain didn't happen in Ilyaran mines. It wouldn't have to: Milu had shown how easy it was for a stone witch to reshape the tunnels. For someone of his talent, finding precious metals or salt or whatever they might need to mine would be a matter of sensing the stone until it changed to something else, and then moving the stone to reveal the goal. There would be no debris like lay under Rasim's cheek now, nor any need for miners to do nothing but move that mess out of the way.

Oh. Rasim's face wrinkled. That was what they wanted Kisia and him for, then. Bringing water up— there had to be some reachable by witchery—to sluice the tunnels clear. That way they could use all their miners to dig out new ore, save for those few who would need to watch over Milu and Telun as *they* worked.

If there was a renegade band of Ilyaran witches somewhere on the continent, Rasim hoped they were having more luck than *he* was, because every non-guild encounter he'd had with foreigners put him in chains or the threat of them. He *knew* other people used slaves, and knew as well that Ilyara's vast witching talent allowed them not to. He just hadn't realized how appealing Ilyaran witches were *as* slaves until he'd left the safety of the guild. Now that he did know, it was hard to imagine rogue witches surviving the outside world in safety.

His head was *much* clearer, if he could think about such things. He sat up stiffly and wished he dared prod the lump on his head again. But he didn't want to draw attention to it, in case he might later be able to heal it somewhat. It would never do for these Northerners to learn seawitchery could help the body to heal.

"Where do you think you're going?" The big man, the original captor, growled.

Rasim swallowed down pain and fear, trying to sound clear-headed and calm. "I want to see my friends. I need to know they're all right."

The woman muttered, "Told you," but the man eyed first her, then Rasim before growling, "And what'll you do if you don't see them?" in a deep mocking tone.

Cold anger filled Rasim's chest, though he tried not to let it show. There would be a way out of this soon enough. Sunmaster Endat would disapprove of him getting into fights with opportunistic Northerners, even if these particular Northerners were definitely at fault. Rasim had not, after all, captured himself. But Queen Jaana was making peace overtures after rebel Northerners had attacked Ilyara, and Rasim was *not* going to make that worse. He almost stomped his foot, as if the physical emphasis would help him keep his temper. "I certainly won't work for you."

"Everyone works, when it's work or death." The woman spoke again, voice deep and grim.

Rasim lifted his chin and met her eyes, wishing the throbbing in his head would stop making his vision swim. He wasn't sure where he should focus, and chose the middle-most of the three blurred female forms he could see. "Killing me would be a mistake. First, we witches are *useful* to you, if we're agreeable. You said that yourself. But second, and maybe more importantly, we're here at Queen Jaana's request."

"In the mines?" The woman guffawed, her laughter bouncing off the walls.

The echoes pierced Rasim's head, making him dizzy again, but he drew a careful breath and kept speaking in an even tone. "In the North. You're isolated here, aren't you? But you're probably not entirely alone, even in winter. Send a message. Ask if there are Ilyarans in the North, visiting the queen. Then decide for yourselves what to do with us."

"And in the meantime?"

Kisia was going to kill him. Rasim's hands shook and his head hurt terribly, but he remembered the endless dry, dull pages he'd read while studying with the Sunmasters, and spoke with careful confidence. "Take the chains off, and we'll work for you until word comes from the capitol."

"Willingly," the woman scoffed.

Rasim turned his palms up long enough to suggest a shrug. Then he put them down again, hoping the pair he negotiated with hadn't noticed their trembling. "We're sea and stone witches. We can't fly away, so until someone comes, we may as well be helpful."

The man's eyes bugged. "Can witches fly?"

Only the most absurdly powerful Skymasters even dared attempt riding the wind. No one had tried even in Isidri's lifetime, much less Rasim's, so he shook his head gingerly, trying not to make it hurt more, and tried for a faint smile. "No. So we're all the less likely to fly away."

Rumblings sounded from the others, who had faded far enough into the shadows that Rasim had almost forgotten they were there. The speakers frowned between Rasim and the others, then stepped away to talk quietly and quickly enough that Rasim couldn't follow their conversations. Finally someone —not the two who had been talking—spoke up. "How are we to know you won't witch us to death if we take the iron off you?"

"How are you to know that anyway?" It wasn't the diplomatic answer Master Endat would have wanted, but Rasim's head hurt and he was becoming exasperated. "What does iron have to do with it?"

A silence rippled around the cavern. "Everybody knows witchery don't work with iron," someone else said as if it was obvious.

Rasim stared at them in the dim light, then looked at his bound ankles. In his thirteen years with the Seamasters, he'd never heard any such thing, but the Sunmasters had drilled enough sense into him to not admit *that*, at least. Instead he looked up, trying to keep his expression mild. "Then how do you expect us to do slave labor for you, if we can't work our witchery while bound by iron?"

Another more uncomfortable silence rose up, and in that instant, Rasim recognized his mistake. He'd been too clever, he'd made someone important look foolish, and—

—a fist came at him, and for the second time that day the world went dark.

NINETEEN

The chains around his ankles were different when he awakened. Heavier, with a different sound when he moved, and gleaming when light caught them. No one was watching over him this time, and though his head still hurt, the dizziness had passed. He examined the chains and almost laughed. Silver. It had to be a rare slave who was worthy of wrought silver chains. Of course, Ilyaran witches *were* rare slaves, almost unheard of.

Almost. Somewhere, at least some of Nasira's crew had survived as slaves, and now Rasim and the other journeymen had joined them in spirit, if not in body. Anger finally flared in Rasim's belly. He had genuinely meant the offer he'd made to the big-bearded miner. There was no reason for them to be at odds, and no reason for the Ilyarans not to help mine the mountain while they waited for rescue. Or there hadn't been, anyway. What could have been washed away as a misunderstanding had reached a tide mark now, a line they couldn't go beyond.

At least they were still alive. Rasim felt confident they *all* were. Their captors wouldn't have bothered replacing iron with silver if they were going to kill him, and if they didn't kill *him*, they weren't going to kill the others. Not right away, at least, and in the meantime Rasim couldn't imagine how they thought they would make the journeymen work for them.

"On your feet, Ilyaran." The woman again, her voice low and commanding as she stepped into the chamber he lay in. The same one he'd been in before, probably. Now that he noticed, there was a bloodstain on the thin pillow where his head had pressed against it. Usia would never allow them to sleep in muck like that. Rasim began a defiant protest, but the woman said, "On your feet," again, and this time Rasim got up.

He didn't *mean* to. He had no intention of doing so. But his legs swung over the edge of the hard bed, chains rattling, and he stood as if it had always been his plan. The woman curled her lip in satisfaction. "Get water from the stone."

That was an old saying in Ilyara, that not even a seamaster could get water from a stone, but Rasim walked to the nearest wall and put his hand on it anyway. Astonishment bubbled through him as he did. He still didn't *mean* to, didn't *want* to, but his body acted without his mind's consent. He put a palm on the cool stone, feeling dampness there. Condensation from temperature differences, maybe from runoff within the mountain itself. There was a lot of it, running all through the mountain. He could probably find his way out by following it, except he couldn't make his body respond to the idea. Instead he pulled water off the wall until his palm was full, then turned to the woman like a puppy eager for praise.

"Good. Can you do more than that?"

Rasim shouted *No!* inside his head, but nodded. Horror wrapped around his guts, chilling them, and his eyes widened.

The woman laughed. "Not so cocky now, are you? You're on mindkiller, boy. You can't even use your water witchery unless someone tells you to, so there's no escaping now. You'll work until our—" She used an unfamiliar phrase again, but his incomprehension must have shown in his eyes, because she tried a second time: "We're debt slaves, lad, in debt to Radolf of the Southern Wide because our own master was a fool."

Radolf. The Southern Wide. Rasim knew there were noble families and fiefdoms within the Northlands, because unlike Ilyara, the Northlands were too large for a single monarch to hold without help. Queen Jaana held rank over them, but only met with their council once a year. Disappointment flashed through Rasim. He had imagined the Northern monarchs to be more civilized than to allow slavery, though there was no reason to believe that except he liked Inga and Lorens. Head aching, he tried to remember where the Southern Wide was, on the Northlands maps. Farther east than its name implied, on the outer reaches of the Northlands territories. Even through his headache, Rasim was fairly certain the Southern Wide was mostly a mountain range sweeping south through the ocean, making it the Northlands' most southerly holdings.

"Get to clearing tunnels, boy. We have a lot of gold to find before we're clear of debt."

Rasim's feet carried him down the tunnels, following where the woman led. Deeper in the mountain he felt water more strongly, and the moment a crack let him reach for it, he did. He still didn't *mean* to, but he extended his hands, calling water to rise from the mountain's depths. It seeped, then spilled, through the fissured wall. The woman's jaw dropped, though she tried to hide it. He saw a flash of fear in her face as she realized how much power he might command, followed hard by relief at the knowledge that he couldn't command it without her permission.

Because despite everything he wanted, water poured out, pooled without making a mess of the floor, then swept down the tunnels, gathering dust and small stones as it went. A sense of the damp walls told him where a bottomless natural chasm lay, and the water ran that way, cleaning up as it went. It was master-level witchery, and his heart would sing if he had chosen to use it this way. Instead it felt like a violation. Magic wasn't supposed to be forced, or worked by others through a witch as the conduit, and that was what the woman was doing. *She* was commanding his power, even if she couldn't work it herself.

Rasim shuddered at the idea of an army of Ilyaran witches all fed the mindkiller drug, all unable to call witchery except in the ways they were told to. He *had* to escape, had to rescue his friends, and then they had to find Nasira and warn her. If other slavers used mindkiller, then the very sailors she intended to save might unwillingly turn against her. He bowed his head, pretending resignation and obedience, but his thoughts tore down every stream and rivulet of hope he could imagine.

There weren't many. He was too hungry to refuse food when it was finally given to him, and though he stared grimly at the cup of thick fortifying drink, he couldn't make the liquid respond any more than he might have made stone itself respond. The woman stood over him and chortled while he tried, then ordered him to drink, and he could no more refuse that than any other demand she'd placed on him.

He slept twice, the throbbing in his head lessened each time he woke. After the second sleep—he had no idea if days were passing or not—he felt a touch of water witchery from elsewhere in the mine. Kisia, no doubt doing the same tasks he was set to. If Kisia was alive, the Stonemaster journeymen certainly were. Stonewitchery was far more useful to miners than water witchery. Rasim held that idea close, taking comfort from it. He'd have been more comforted still if his own witchery was as weak as it had been before Siliaria's intervention, because if they kept him alive and busy with so little power, Kisia would be in no danger at all. Now, though, he was afraid he was stronger than she, and that she might be exhausted or killed through being forced to keep up with him.

The third morning, after a tasteless breakfast under the woman's sneering watch, an argument rose up from somewhere in the mine's depths. One voice was the big-bearded captor's, coming clearer as the woman hauled Rasim with her when she went to find out what the problem was.

Rock had slipped. A huge chunk, weighing more than Rasim could even imagine, was wedged into the mouth of a tunnel, blocking access. The miners who needed into the passage wanted the stone witches to fix it, but Big Beard was using them elsewhere. Good news, as far as Rasim was concerned: it verified his friends were still alive. He stood passively as the woman waded into the argument too, though he saw an easy solution.

They were near one of the deep water vents in the mountain, and water could move anything, even stone. It wouldn't even take that much to slick the surfaces get the wedge moving, though it would require careful handling because the fallen rock was easily big enough to crush people. But the woman hadn't commanded him to help, and he couldn't use witchery without an order. Siliaria herself would have Rasim's ears before he volunteered.

His mind fogged, spinning around something he'd thought, but unable to quite touch on it. Something about forbidden witchery.

That was it. The woman had said he couldn't use his *water* witchery without being commanded to.

Kisia was certain Rasim had set fire to the *Waifia's* ropes.

Rasim's stomach dropped and he stared at the wedge like he might set it on fire by scowling hard enough. Kisia was wrong, he *knew* she was wrong, but...he'd known she was wrong when she'd believed his magic had saved her when the serpent attacked, too. And *he* had been wrong then. Maybe she was right. Maybe the two magics complemented each other. Maybe he'd mastered seawitchery because he'd touched sunmastery.

Not that sun witchery would do him any good down here. He needed *stone*witchery, this time, and the idea that he could master a third magic was absurd. But it was something to try. It couldn't hurt, and it would keep him occupied and less resentful of his captivity while they awaited rescue.

If rescue was even coming. Rasim barely saw the

Northerners anymore, his gaze entirely focused on the wedged stone, like *it* was what lay between himself and freedom. The miners obviously had no intention of letting the Ilyarans go free until they'd worked off their debts. There was no reason, then, for them to have sent word to see if the Ilyarans might truly be there at Queen Jaana's request. And as far as anyone inboard the *Waifia* was concerned, Rasim and the others had been lost at sea. Someone —Rasim truly had no idea who—would be held accountable for that, but dead was dead: Nasira had no reason to search for them.

"There are people in there! Get your cursed stone shapers and get them out!" The shout brought Rasim out of his thoughts. A chill swept over him. Big Beard refusing to use the Stonemasters for a laborious but menial task like moving the wedge was one thing, but risking lives was another.

Big Beard gave Rasim a canny glance, as if trying to hide something, and shook his head at the shouting man. "Too far. If they've got water back there—"

"They don't! They were ending their shift, Hans!"

Too far. Rasim worried at that, trying to understand what it meant. Telun and Milu were of the most use in the mine.

No. They were of the most use in *mines*, but not necessarily this one. And it was clear Big Beard— Hans—would use them in any way he could to lighten his own load. Like offering them to his lord Radolf, maybe, or selling them on to real slavers instead of opportunistic miners. Rasim's jaw set, as stony as the walls around him. If Kisia had been sent away or sold, he would tear the North apart to find her.

"You." The woman thrust a finger at him. "You use your witchery to get them out. Don't tell me you can't. I see it in your eyes."

Rasim met her eyes with all the fury in his own. She flinched, then snarled like they were desert dogs fighting for dominance. But his feet were already moving, his magic stirring despite himself. The mindkiller was a terrible drug, leaving him free to think but unable to act without a command. There were so many ways to abuse it, not least the way it was being used on him. He went to the wedge, crouched, and examined the broken bottom of stone against the rough floor.

There were enough rough edges that water could seep under. That was good. Without them, even a seamaster would have real difficulty moving the vast chunk of rock. It could be done, but eroding stone took a long time even if water moved witch-fast. Rasim cleared a few shards away, pressing his fingertips against the wedged rock. "How big is it?"

He was startled at his voice: rough, dry, unused for days. The Northerners seemed equally surprised. One finally responded: "Three feet deep, and maybe eight wide at the top. You can see how it narrows a little."

"Is there enough room for it to fall backward if the tip is moved forward far enough?"

Hesitation preceded this answer, too. "Maybe."

It would be worse if he tried pushing it that way and it stuck even more thoroughly. Rasim stood up, studying the tunnel they stood in. It was neither tall nor wide itself, but it was larger than the tunnel mouth in which the stone had wedged. "This is dangerous," he said, more to himself than the Northerners. "You need Stonemasters. Do you have a way to communicate with the people trapped on the other side?"

The one who'd appointed himself speaker shuffled forward and nodded. "We tap out messages to each other."

"Then tell them to get to high ground, if they can." Rasim, hands clenched with anger, turned to Big Beard. "Empty the mine. Get everyone to high ground."

Belligerence split the big beard. "I can't do that!"

"Then bring the Stonemasters." Rasim stared Big Beard down, unrelenting until the large man snarled defeat. Rasim's gaze fogged with anger. "Where are they?"

"Sold."

"*What*?" Someone else—the man who'd wanted to use Milu and Telun to clear the tunnel—spoke the word that leaped into Rasim's throat. Rasim crushed his eyes shut, trying to contain the rage that built in him as his suspicions were confirmed. He was deep inside a mountain, well away from the sea, but he felt it rising in his blood along with his anger. It would be as easy to draw water all the way up from the inlet as it would be to pull it from the depths of the mountain. Maybe easier. Probably *safer*, because raising it from the inside the mountain would mean the stone itself would crack from the pressure of the rising water.

"Clear the mine," he repeated under the growing argument between Big Beard and the new men. "Clear it, or command me not to work this witchery, because if I do and you're still here, you're all going to die."

That silenced them. Rasim opened his eyes. The woman looked fearful. Big Beard's whiskers bristled with anger. The other man seemed nearly as furious as Rasim himself. That man knocked a warning against the stone, and waited until a response came through before nodding to Rasim. "They'll go as high as they can. I've no right to ask, but try to be careful with their lives, please." His gaze skittered to Big Beard and the woman. "I don't care so much about theirs. I'll get the others out. How long do I have?"

Rasim struggled to contain the impulse to just drown the whole mine now. "That depends on what he's done with the girl. The other water witch."

"Sold her too," Hans said defiantly, but the woman hissed and spat.

"He didn't, not yet. She's a pretty thing, if you like strange dark skin and eyes. Figured he could get more for her if he brought her to a slave city himself, once his debts are paid off. She's working the mine like you are now."

Relief and rage tangled together so strongly Rasim barely stayed on his feet. "Bring her here. Two of us at once can control the water better than I can alone. It'll give you time to empty the mine," he said to the third Northman, who nodded vigorously and ran without looking back.

"No." Big Beard thrust his hairy jaw out. "Let the magic go, witch. I don't want you saving those men. They're not worth it," he said to the woman. "Who knows what happens if we put two witches together? They might burn out the mindkiller."

A guttural scream of frustration ripped Rasim's throat as his witchery faded at Big Beard's order. Fingers clawed, he flung himself at the slaver, only to be slammed to the stone by the silver chains around his ankles. His body, his mind, they were almost his own to command, but *only* because he hadn't been forbidden to think or move. Big Beard danced back a step or two, guffawing, and Rasim bellowed anger at the rock.

"Go after Lars," Big Beard told the woman. "We'll tell everyone else that he was caught on the other side of the rockfall too, and that nobody's answering. Just make sure nobody else sees him."

"We could use all those men if we've no stone shapers to help us pay off our debt," the woman protested, but she did as she was told.

When they were alone, Big Beard kicked Rasim in the ribs. "Get up."

Grunting, furious, unable to fight, Rasim did, and threw a look of loathing at Big Beard. The miner laughed again. "I'll take you with me, when the slave ships arrive. These fools don't know it, but my own debt is paid. The rest of them can rot."

Rasim rasped, "How long? How long before they get here?"

"Two days," Big Beard said. "You won't say a word about any of this to anyone, either. You won't say a word at all."

Rasim's tongue thickened, swelling until it filled his mouth. He tried once to curse, and choked on the words. The mindkiller drug could do that too, then. The miner laughed once more at Rasim's hate-filled gaze, then kicked him into motion. "Get back to work, witch."

Head bent, eyes blinded with anger, Rasim did as he was told.

Two days. He had two days to find Kisia, and escape.

TWENTY

The Sunmasters had given him a candle flame to
study. Not, Master Endat had said, so he could master
sunwitchery, but as a point to focus on. He was to
think of nothing but the flame, its quick always-
changing, never-ending dance. It was meant to calm,
to help distractions fade away, to make him serene
and ready for diplomatic engagements. But Rasim
was surrounded by stone here, and in the wake of Big
Beard's brutality, he couldn't keep the idea of the
flame in his head.

He focused on the stone instead, pretending he
could see into it, through it, the way he could see
through flame. It helped calm him, though it also
made him far too aware of the mountain pressing
down on him. He gathered water and sluiced tunnels
under the woman's watch, trying to empty his mind
of anything but the idea of stone. If he could calm his
thoughts, he could be clever, and clever would get
them out of there.

By the time the woman brought his noon meal, he could look at her without fury blinding him, but she never came close enough for him to even try overcoming her physically. That would be easiest, if not cleverest, and she knew it as well as Rasim did. He refused his lunch, hoping she might try to force it in him, but she only snorted and dragged him back to work. The mindkiller drug was either not in his food, or lasted long enough that a missed meal wouldn't matter. He stumbled along after her, still thinking about stone. He'd watched it shift, gaining depth like it was clear water, when Milu had shaped it. If he could sit down, concentrate...perhaps at night, when he was supposed to be sleeping. A night's missed sleep would be a small price to pay for getting out of the mines unchained.

And it didn't matter that no one mastered witchery overnight. He *had* to, as he'd *had* to call great seawitchery to save Kisia from the serpent. It was as simple as that. Kisia was depending on him again, and he wouldn't let her down. He watched each tunnel mouth as they passed them, trying to gain a sense of the stone. The woman snarled, "Keep your face forward," and against his will, Rasim obediently looked where they were going, and nowhere else.

Instead of the huff of satisfaction he'd come to expect from her, a dull crack echoed off the walls. Rasim spun—his face *was* forward, if his whole body turned around—and saw her fall, blood leaking from her head. Behind her, a chunk of timber still upraised from delivering the blow, stood the miner Lars. Rasim and he both stared at the woman's form before meeting each other's eyes.

Confusion made Rasim as dizzy as any drug might. He hadn't imagined an ally of any sort in the tunnels, least of all the brown-haired miner he'd told to clear the mine. The miner said, "What's your name?" and Rasim shook his head, pointing to his throat. "What, you don't have a na—oh, Hans wouldn't let you talk, would he? You can talk now."

Rasim cleared his throat, his first question crackling out. "Aren't you dead?"

The miner laughed, though it was a thin dry sound. "Not for lack of trying on Hans's part. I heard him telling her to go after me, so I went deep into the tunnels instead of going to warn the men to clear the mine. She's afraid of the dark, so she would never go where she didn't have to."

"But—but Hans—"

"She must've lied to him. He doesn't like getting his hands dirty, and he's not too smart. He'd believe her if she said she'd finished me. Can you do what you said?" The Northman's pale skin became even paler. "Can you rescue those men from the mine shaft?"

Rasim looked at the woman's silent body, then at Lars. "You'd better hope I can."

Lars managed another thin smile. "Yes. I'd have asked you before I hit her, but I didn't think she would give me a chance. Get them out, Ilyaran, and your freedom is your own. My wife is in there," he said more quietly. "Tell me you can save her."

"I can." Rasim finally dared to try moving and found he *could* move. Of course he could: Lars had said *get them out*. It was a command, of sorts. Enough that Rasim could interpret it as one, at least, and take his actions into his own hands. He took a few steps to the side of the tunnel and pressing his fingers against the wall. It felt soft, malleable, like all his concentration had paid off and the stone was willing to respond to him after all. A quick, hysterical laugh rose in his chest. He choked it off, afraid Lars would think he'd lost his mind. Rasim wasn't sure he *hadn't*, not if he was imagining the stone answered his touch. He looked at his ankles, at the heavy silver chains. "Can you get these off me?"

"Sooner or later." Lars knelt, digging through the woman's tunic, and came up with a set of clanging keys. Rasim did laugh that time, even if it was hysterical. He hadn't realized the woman had keys on her. If he'd only been able to jump her, he could have been free days earlier.

And the people behind the caved-in tunnel mouth would have died, with no witches to save them. Rasim squished his hand against the wall, feeling wetness shift and flow through his fingers. There had to be a waterfall somewhere nearby, a trickle greater than the slow condensation the caves seemed to create naturally. Lars unlocked the cuffs, silver falling away with startling clanks. Rasim rose up on his toes, feeling like a Skymaster brave enough to risk flight. He hadn't realized how heavy the chains were until they were gone.

"Take care of your ankles," Lars advised. "They'll be bruised worse than you know."

"Are there other slaves here? Besides me and Kisia?"

Lars shook his head as he stood up. His back stooped, like he'd been bending over in tunnels for a long time. "We're debt slaves here, and there's nowhere much to run. Our lord Radolf's men watch the only pass, and there are wolves, big cats, and bears to keep anyone from trying overland in the summers."

Which suggested no one would even think of it in the winter, like it was now. Rasim put his heels back on the ground, but picked his feet up over and over, reveling in their weightlessness without really realizing he was doing it. "Big Beard—Hans—said there are slaver ships on the way. How did he sell Telun and Milu, if you're so isolated?"

"Probably brought them to Radolf's men at the pass. We've had a lot of storms. You might get lucky. They might still be there." Lars hesitated. "We'd fight for you, if you took us with."

That put Rasim's feet on the ground and kept them there. The stoop-shouldered Northman was at least twice again Rasim's age, and had just freed him. It would be natural for the Northerner to take the lead. "How long have you been a miner?"

"Since I was a lad. The debt was my parents'." Lars shrugged. "It's near enough all I know."

"Queen Jaana allows this?"

Lars chuckled, but not like it was funny. "The queen doesn't pay much attention to what happens on the far borders, Ilyaran. She has her own business to attend to."

Rasim thrust his jaw out. "Children being made slaves to work off their parents' debts *should* be her business, and I'm going to tell her so."

This time Lars's laughter sounded amused. "Are you? I'll fight through snow and claw to see that happen. But later," he added, humor diminishing. "Will you help them? We should act before Hans notices Silje is missing." He nodded at the prone woman.

"Is there an antidote to the mindkiller? I can't use my witchery right."

"You've only been on it a week. It'll wear off inside a day or so. For now, I could...tell you how to use it."

"You mean order me. And I'd have to do it, and you knew that all along," Rasim said quietly. "But you didn't order me."

"I might not be wearing chains, Ilyaran, but I know the weight of someone else's mastery."

"Rasim," Rasim said. "My name is Rasim. Help me find Kisia. Clear the mine. Then tell me to save your wife, Northman, and I'll do my best."

Relief made Lars's cheeks flush. "And after?"

"Let's worry about that after." Rasim shook his fingers loose of the wall, finding them cold. He tucked them under his arm and frowned at the woman on the floor. "What are we going to do about her?"

Lars sighed, bent, and scooped her into an over-the-shoulder carry. "I can't just leave her. That would be murder. Even if she doesn't much deserve to live."

"Let the god of stone and mountains decide that. This is his domain, after all." Rasim ground his teeth together. "Same with Hans, if you can find him. But get the others first. Don't face Hans alone. He's dangerous."

"I won't. The girl is in his chamber. We'll go there first, and tell anyone we see on the way to leave or come with us. Safety in numbers, right?"

"Right." It was easy to run without the chains. Every step made Rasim feel like he would rise impossibly high into the sky. Or it would, he thought as he ducked under a low-roofed tunnel, if they could reach the sky. They moved quickly, Lars stopping often to tell other miners to spread the word and get out. Someone took Silje off Lars's shoulders and left with her. Half a dozen others joined Rasim and Lars as they made their way to Hans's chambers. The big-bearded Northman was not, Rasim judged, popular.

Lars pushed the rough-woven blanket that made up Hans's door out of the way, then stopped two steps into the big-bearded man's room, uncertain. "She's not—"

Kisia dropped from above onto him. She fell backward, sliding down his shoulders until her chained ankles caught around his neck. Then she surged, flinging her body around so the chain twisted, choking him. He fell with a shout, fingers scrabbling at his throat and behind his back as he tried to find his attacker.

"Kisia! *Kisia!*" Rasim flung himself into the room, trying to unwind the chain, trying to calm her, trying not to laugh in relief and admiration. "Kisia, it's me! It's Rasim! Let him go!"

Kisia twisted again, choking Lars that much more thoroughly, but this time she was only trying to see Rasim. Her eyes widened in astonishment and she relaxed, no longer *trying* to choke Lars. He rasped in a breath and got his fingers under the chains, giving himself room to breathe. Rasim patted the miner's shirt frantically, looking for the keys, and unlocked Kisia's ankles with shaking hands. Lars fell over one direction and Kisia the other, into Rasim's arms. "Rasim. Oh, thank Siliaria. I thought it was Hans. I thought my only chance was to choke him before he could tell me not to—"

Rasim hugged her until they were both breathless. "You're the bravest person I know. That was amazing. That was—"

Lars croaked, "Deadly. Gods on the mountaintops, I'll fight with you until my dying day, if this is what your soldiers are like, Ilyaran."

"Hah. She's not even a soldier," Rasim said, then translated it all to Kisia, who sniffed.

"I'm better than a soldier. I'm a Seamaster." Then her face wrinkled. "Are you—is he all right, Rasim? I'm sorry. I thought he was—"

"Hans," Rasim said. "I think he's fine. Lars—" He translated again and a smile split Lars's beard.

"I'm all right. Tell her I'm glad I *wasn't* Hans."

Kisia said, "But who is he?" after Rasim translated again. "Wait. Wait, he's the one whose people got trapped in the cave-in. Rasim, what's going on?" Kisia sat up in Rasim's arms, looking from one face to another.

"I'm going to flood the tunnels. I'm going to get those people out."

"Nobody here has done you any favors, Rasim!"

Rasim gave Kisia a tight smile and jerked a thumb toward Lars. "He did. He freed me. Besides, Desimi says part of the reason I'm so annoying is because I do the right thing even when it's inconvenient. I'd hate to disappoint him."

Kisia's chin dropped to her chest and she chuckled. "I guess that's what I like about you. All right. Let's do it."

Rasim grinned. "That easy, is it?"

Kisia nodded and Rasim grinned again, this time at Lars. "Get out of here. Get the rest of the miners out. Is an hour enough time?"

"We'll make it enough." Lars staggered to his feet. "Can you find your way back to the cave-in, or should I guide you?"

"I've been studying the rock," Rasim said drolly. "I can find it. All right, go."

Lars nodded, then took a deep breath. "Water witch, clear the cave-in."

A compulsion rose in Rasim. He nodded once. Lars gave him a nervous, hopeful smile, then gathered the others and ran. Rasim, feet itching to carry him to the cave-in, turned to Kisia. "Can you stand against the tide?"

"A week ago I'd have been asking *you* that. Now let's go. I want you to show me what Siliaria's chosen can really do." Kisia's eyes sparkled.

Rasim choked. "Siliaria's *chosen*?"

"Well, I'd call you Siliaria's son, but she better not be kissing her son like that, is all I'm saying."

Rasim's ears heated until they hurt, and he was grateful to leave the conversation behind as they followed the mine shafts deep into the mountain again. As they ran, he built witchery in his mind, imagining the twists and turns that led to the outside world and to the cold grey inlet water that had brought them to the Northern shores. It was such a long way to reach, but he could hear the ocean whispering in his blood. Siliaria had named him Seamaster, and her waters were his to command.

He dug deep, asking for water all the way from the inlet's clay-thickened bottom. It stirred sluggishly, responding slowly, but it didn't have to be fast. Not yet. And the depths were cold, cold enough that he felt it even high in the mountain. Rasim knew he would be left exhausted when this work was done. But lives would be saved, and that was important.

It took longer than he expected to return to the cave-in. Water had crept out of its sea bed by then, crawling toward Rasim's command. It now licked the mine's mouth, cold and curious. Men and women had come from it in great numbers, but the water said now they were few, and then, after a little while, said there were no more. It was time. Rasim touched the stone they needed to move, then pulled away from it, standing at a safe distance. He didn't want it falling on them, and it would take all of his — their — concentration to keep their feet once the water came in. Nervous, excited, Rasim looked at Kisia. "Ready?"

She nodded, her eyes wide and fixed on the tunnel mouth they'd just come through. Rasim stretched out his hands, palms up, then curled his fingers toward himself and whispered, "Come," to the waiting inlet.

Its weight should have been staggering. Instead, as the water rose, Rasim felt like he was floating in it, weightless, free of all constraints. The air turned cold and misty, even this far ahead of the seawall. Beside him, Kisia gasped in delight. Rasim grabbed her hand, surprised she wasn't floating too. Her witchery joined his, less powerful but equally focused. They called the sea to them, urging it on. Waves splashed down the wrong tunnels, but the bulk of water came onward, roaring, rolling, making the air taste of salt. Rasim closed his eyes, seeing the water like a blade, forming a relentless arrowhead that would drive against the bottom of the wedged stone so hard that it would fall. It would work. His confidence soared.

Kisia's power suddenly cut out and she slammed herself against him, knocking him aside. Rasim's eyes flew open again.

Hans, damp with sea water and sweat, flashed by them, narrowly missing Kisia's ribs with a blade as she and Rasim crashed sideways. Hans spun again, showing an ugly grin through his big beard. "If I can't have your slave price in my pocket, nobody will."

"You're mad." Even as Rasim and Kisia scrambled backward, Rasim felt the onslaught of water as it poured down the tunnels behind them. "You can't be here, Hans. You're going to get killed."

"You won't kill me. You're soft enough that even in chains, you would have saved those fools." Hans sneered at the caved-in tunnel. "You're not going to stand there as a free man and let me drown."

Kisia swallowed her opinion loudly enough that Rasim heard the gulp. He more than half agreed with whatever she'd been going to say, even without hearing it. *She* certainly wouldn't lose sleep over Hans's death, and the truth was, neither would Rasim. He spoke slowly, wondering what he would say. "If you drown, it won't be because I let you. It'll be because you're stupid and cruel. You've been warned. The whole mine has been warned. If you die, it's because you chose to come here and try to stop me, kill me, instead of saving your own life."

"You're on mindkiller. You have to do what I say, and I say to stop using magic!"

He did. He couldn't stop himself. The power released, but Rasim kept speaking, soft and sad. "You don't understand. It's too late, Hans. The sea is coming. Listen." He turned his head a fraction of an inch and saw Hans lift his own gaze to the tunnel behind the Ilyarans. Even through the beard, the Northman visibly paled. He whirled, already running, trying to escape the inevitable.

Kisia shrieked, "Rasim, save us!" and the water crashed through.

TWENTY-ONE

Nothing, not Desimi, not Hans, not even the sea serpent, had ever hit Rasim has hard as the water did. He flew forward, stunned by the power he'd unleashed. In a panic, he grabbed a pocket of water and threw it in front of them, barely softening the impact as he and Kisia bashed into the nearest wall and slammed back again. The water was freezing, silt-filled and grey and impossible to see through. Kisia's arms were still wrapped around Rasim. He twisted, seizing her as they were thrown back and forth again.

A boom reverberated through the tunnel, shaking the water. Rasim caught the vibrations, cushioning himself and Kisia with them. He hurt everywhere, worse than falling down the island crevasse, but she had said *save us!* and he was on mindkiller, forced to do what he was told.

The surges were already fading. He'd let the sea-draining witchery go, and water by nature took the easiest path, falling back into its sea bed, draining into deeper tunnels. Rasim rode the fading waves, Kisia held in his arms. The moment air pockets appeared in the tunnel he reached for them, seizing the air and bringing it down to surround them. Kisia gasped against his chest and he coughed water, shocked to have inhaled any. Then the worst of the witched water was gone and they settled into puddles on the rocky floor, shivering and wheezing.

Only when Rasim tried prying his eyes open did he realize there was no light at all. His breath caught. Kisia sat up, though she didn't move away. "Rasi?"

"I'm fine. We're fine. I just...I didn't think. The water put the torches out. I don't know how we're going to get out of here in the dark." Rasim's shoulders slumped. "I'm tired, Kees."

"And freezing," Kisia said in a business-like tone. Her witchery came to life, stripping the water from their clothes. After a moment, sounding satisfied, she said, "There. Now at least we're dry while lost in a mountain."

Rasim arched an eyebrow at her dubiously, and though he knew she couldn't see it, she laughed. "I thought that would make you eyeball me."

"How do you even know?"

"From the way you shifted. Can you still feel the inlet?"

"I can hardly feel the end of my nose."

Kisia's fingertips found his nose and tweaked it.

"It's right there."

"Ow!"

"Tsha, Sunburn, that didn't hurt."

"Sunburn?" Despite himself, Rasim smiled. "Really?"

"All right. The last surges came from the way our feet are pointing, so that's probably where the water was coming from, which means that way is out. Crawl," Kisia advised. "We're in the main tunnels, so there shouldn't be open shafts, but that was before you threw an ocean through here." She took Rasim's hand and tugged him along a few crawling steps until they got into a rhythm of moving slowly down the lightless tunnel together. Then she spoke again, her voice much gentler. "That was impressive, Rasim. A lot more impressive than saving me from the serpent. I'm not sure even Isidri could have done that."

Rasim snorted in disbelief. "Isidri thawed the entire Ilyaran harbor. She could've done this standing on her head. I just hope it worked."

Light glimmered ahead of them, so faint Rasim thought he was imagining it until Kisia whispered, "Do you see something?" hopefully. Then she lifted her voice, shouting, "Hello?"

It echoed down the tunnels, louder and sharper than was natural. After a few seconds, another shout responded, bouncing around just as noisily: "*Lars?*"

Kisia breathed, "Heh," and Rasim smiled agreement before yelling, "Friends of his!"

Within minutes, five bedraggled miners appeared

carrying torches and expressions of hopeful uncertainty. Rasim and Kisia stood, shading their eyes against the light for a moment. There were two women. Rasim squinted at both of them. "Are either of you Lars's wife?"

The slighter of the two nodded. Rasim sighed in relief. "He's waiting for you outside."

"You're the water witches," Lars's wife whispered. "I'm Sondra. You cleared the cave-in?"

Suddenly self-conscious, Rasim nodded. Sondra closed her eyes, then took a few rushing steps forward and hugged both the sea witches. "Thank you. Thank you. We thought we would die in there, even after Lars's message to go to high ground. We were about to give up when the water came. Thank you."

"You're welcome," Kisia said, understanding a hug even if she didn't understand the repeated words. When it became clear Rasim was too embarrassed to speak, she added, "You can repay us by getting us out of here," and whether she understood or not, Sondra led the way.

The purple Northern sunset was unbelievably bright after days in the tunnels, and the deep blue shadowed snow only increased its brilliance. Rasim's eyes watered, but he couldn't stop looking from sea to sky and back again. The tide was full, reaching for the seaweed-littered high mark as if he hadn't drawn harbors-full of water from the inlet. Between tide marks and the mountains, the miners had been busy setting up tents and starting driftwood fires for warmth. A shout greeted their appearance, and Lars threw back one of the tent doors, hope and fear at war on his bearded features.

Joy won out as he saw Sondra. His roar was loud enough to shake the air, loud enough that another miner, eyeing the snow-covered mountains, cuffed him and muttered warnings about snowslides. Rasim, though, smiled wearily as Sondra ran to meet her husband, their embrace making his exhaustion worthwhile. He hobbled to a fire and hunkered down, trying not to think about how much his body ached. Kisia bit her lip in concentration, mumbling something about Usia's scoldings. After a while her witchery touched him, soothing the worst bangs and bruises. Half-asleep, Rasim startled awake and blinked at her. "You can heal?"

Kisia looked embarrassed and proud. "Not very well, but Usia said anybody who can squeeze a man's heart like I did to Roscord can learn the healing witchery if they want. I told him I'd rather sail or fight, but I can't just let you sit here turning as purple as the sky."

"You're all bruised up too," Rasim pointed out.

Kisia looked at the bruises blackening on her arms even though her skin was much darker than Rasim's, and shrugged. "You put yourself between me and the walls. You took the worst of it. I'll try to deal with these after you're patched up."

"It is," Lars said unexpectedly, "after, water witch. Rasim."

Both journeymen looked up at the stoop-shouldered Northman. Kisia, despite having just been fussing over Rasim's injuries, elbowed him in the ribs. "What'd he say?"

"He said it was afte...oh. After. Yes." Rasim switched to the Northern tongue. "It is after. And we have to decide what to do, but we're not doing anything without rest, Lars. Whether we risk trying to take the slaver's ships or whether we go through the mountain pass, we need sleep first. And food. Real food, not that slop from the mines. Kisia," he said, switching back to Ilyaran, "would you mind going fishing? I could, but..."

"You'd drown," Kisia said dryly. "How many do we have to feed?"

Rasim asked and wrinkled his nose at the answer. "Seventy or a hundred. You'd better catch a whale."

"No way. Whales talk." Kisia got up, wincing and stretching. "I'll fish," she informed Lars, and pointed at the fire. "You cook."

Lars laughed when Rasim translated, but nodded agreeably. Kisia, satisfied, went fishing. Without her support, Rasim tipped over, and didn't awaken until morning.

#

Sunlight filtered through the cloth tent he slept in, and Rasim's first thought was gratitude at seeing daylight again. His second was of the gurgling hunger in his stomach, and the third, as he crawled over other sleeping bodies to squeeze out of the tent, was a conviction that they should go north and not wait on the slave ships. Too much could go wrong in trying to take a ship away, and the Northern miners were unlikely to know anything at all about sailing. Better to risk a fight with Lord Radolf's men, because at least the miners knew how to swing a pick.

Sondra and Lars, along with a handful of others, were already awake and making stew of the fish left over from the night before. Rasim went to the water and took handsful of it, wicking wetness away until only salt was left, and brought that as his offering for the stew. Sondra had already added edible seaweed, giving it more body, and the aroma was enough to set Rasim drooling.

"You made a decision while you slept." Lars ladled stew into large, shallow stone bowls from the mine and sat down beside Rasim to eat.

Rasim nodded, too hungry to talk. He was less exhausted than he'd expected after yesterday's witchery, but he felt he could eat the entire cauldron's worth of stew and need more. He'd already eaten more than his share when he realized Sondra was ladling him up a fifth bowl. Embarrassed, he shook his head.

"You didn't eat yesterday," Sondra said. "You're welcome to as much as you need."

"I remember how much I ate when I was your age," Lars said wryly, when Rasim hesitated. "Go on, lad. You need it."

Rasim mumbled his thanks and ate another two bowls' worth before he began to feel sated. By that time, Kisia had come blinking and sleepy-eyed out of a tent, though she woke up with a smile when she saw Rasim was there and eating. "Good. I was afraid you might be sick, like Isidri's been."

"Guildmaster Isidri is a hundred years old," Rasim said, vaguely offended. "I'm only thirteen."

"Yeah, but you've been asleep since I went fishing," Kisia said.

"Desimi can sleep twelve hours even if he hasn't been dragging a harbor's worth of water around!"

Kisia paused in the midst of getting herself some of the stew. "That was two days ago, Rasi. You've been unconscious a day and a half."

All the food in Rasim's stomach suddenly felt heavy, making him nauseous with surprise. "I have been?" Sondra's comment abruptly made sense: she said he hadn't eaten yesterday. "Oh. ...oh. Oh. That's...I thought I should feel more exhausted, after that much magic. I guess...I guess that makes sense, then."

"So I was worried," Kisia emphasized as she sat down with her stew. "But while you were sleeping

I've been thinking. Hans sold Telun and Milu north, to the men who watch the pass—"

Knots untied in Rasim's stomach. He beamed at Kisia, who shifted in surprise. "What?"

"I wasn't sure if that's what he done with them. Lars thought he might have, and I'd already decided we had to go north to check, but—how do you even know?"

Kisia rolled her eyes. "Hans bragged to me about it."

Rasim's voice broke in surprise. "Hans spoke Ilyaran?"

Kisia blinked. "He did. I wonder where he learned it. I didn't even think about it, because I understood him. Anyway, he was so proud of himself. He wanted to take his earnings and pay to sail south with the slavers and you and me. He was going to sell us and set up a comfortable warm life, he said. I guess he never thought that slavers would take his money and put him in chains too. He wasn't very smart."

"I guess he wasn't. I still wish..."

"What, that you could have saved him? You said it yourself, Rasim. He killed himself by following us down there. You gave him more of a chance than I would. Than most people would. Forget him. Let's go find the Stonemasters."

Lars had watched the whole conversation, light eyes bright with curiosity. "I can see I'll have to learn your liquid language, water witch, if I'm going to pledge my arm to yours."

Sondra nodded, making it clear she and Lars had discussed the idea already, but Rasim's mouth quirked in half-pleased dismay. King Taishm had sent the *Waifia* north so the Sunmasters could renew treaties with the Northern queen, not so Rasim could gather a rag-tag army of bent-backed miners. Worse, Rasim even had Donnan the pirate queen's word that she would come with an army at Rasim's call, too. If Rasim wasn't careful, *he* was going to look like the bad guy plotting against the Ilyaran throne. "You learn Ilyaran," he finally said, "and teach Kisia the Northern tongue. How far is the northern pass?"

Lars's gaze cleared as his unspoken questions were answered. "Less than a day's journey, even in winter. That's our destination, then?"

Rasim shook his head. "It's a way-point. Our destination is the capital. We're going to Ringenstand."

Knowing they would have a chance to strike at the master who had imprisoned them provided plenty of motivation to march for every miner who had come out of the mountain. Knowing that staying at the mining beach would mean facing well-equipped slavers motivated them even more, and with their shared determination, it turned out the northern pass was only a half day's journey. Lars set a grueling pace across the half-frozen clay and stone beaches, but no one complained.

More than once they happened on streams too wide to leap. The first time, Lars's face turned grim: the aftereffects of wading through icy water would slow them considerably. Without discussing it, Rasim and Kisia both turned their witchery on the stream, walling it off from itself to create a clear passage. Lars's eyes popped before his big laugh bounced off the mountains. After that, the mood lightened even if they kept a hard pace. It seemed that the Northerners felt having witches helping out meant they would unquestionably succeed in their goals. Rasim, feeling rather more conservative, didn't argue, though more than once he caught Kisia's slightly worried glance coming his way. He tried not to meet that look, afraid his feeble plans would fall apart if they were questioned.

They came around a bend and the mountain garrison was suddenly in front of them. Rasim startled and fell back, holding up a hand to keep the masses from spilling around the bend. The garrison looked like it had been hewn directly out of the stone, its harsh edges showing pickax and hammer work, not the flowing grace of a Stonemaster's magic. There were parts of the base that curved, stone glittering like scales in the diffuse Northern light. Other chunks simply jutted upward, looking like giants had made steps of the mountainside. Snow lay in massive heaps on huge battlements, making the garrison seem more, not less, intimidating. It was far, far larger than Rasim imagined necessary to keep a hundred slaves on this side of the mountains. "There's a pass behind that?"

"This is one of the easiest places to cross into the heartland. The old kings built this garrison to keep slavers out. They still come to trade in the winter months, but the pass hasn't been breached in hundreds of years."

"Nobody mentioned that part." Rasim frowned at the garrison. Nothing could stand forever, but without the right equipment, he couldn't see how they might break in. They would have to take a different approach. "Does anybody have an extra set of chains? You're going to have to bring Kisia and me in, Lars. Tell them you and Hans fought over us and he lost, and that you want to trade us for passage back to the heartland for you and your wife. Once we're inside I'll...figure something else out."

Lars eyed Kisia, and asked in his own language, "Is this how his plans always work?"

Rasim translated and Kisia laughed. "Ask him if he can come up with a better one." When Lars shook his head, Kisia looked smug. "Nobody else ever can, either. But tell him he'd better not lock those chains."

"He won't. Sondra, you need to look—"

"Terrified and abject?" The sallow Northwoman smiled faintly. "I can do that."

"All right. We'll open the gates for the rest of you," Rasim said to the others with a confidence he didn't feel. To his astonishment, smiles and nods of belief met the assurance. He tried to hide the surprise, but as Lars chained them and drove them around the corner, he also murmured, "Yesterday they were debt slaves, water witch, and today they're free men because the ocean reached into the mountain to save them. If you say you'll come back for them, of course they believe it."

"Then I'd better not be wrong." Rasim fell silent as they approached the garrison. It was even larger up close, the rocky walls extending eight or ten times his height. No one bothered to pace the tops, either confident of their security or so rarely approached that it was a waste of time.

Lars wound them past sea-thrown stones that made up a hard-to-breach barrier of their own before a hinged crack in the garrison walls a passageway. The Northman reached into a divot and hauled on a chain that set a thin, sour bell to ringing. All of them shivered with cold and stamped their feet by the time the doors swung open.

No one stood on the other side. Rubble lay everywhere, like someone had come through smashing inner walls with a vast hammer. Doors were torn off their hinges, shutters dangled uselessly from windows. It looked like it had been abandoned for decades and left to fall to pieces, but as Rasim's wide gaze took in more, he realized there were huddled, still forms on the ground. Bodies, wearing soldiers' insignia on the heavy fur cloaks that kept winter cold off them. *Had* kept the cold off: they would never need the cloaks again.

"Something's wrong." Rasim's voice, barely a whisper, still cracked when he spoke. "Something terrible has—!"

An enormous stone snake burst from an inner door and lunged at them with gaping jaws.

TWENTY-TWO

They screamed and scattered, flinging themselves in every direction to avoid the snake. Its scales hissed across the icy-slicked ground and tore into the stone, dust rising from its passage. It turned with far more speed than something its size should be able to, huge jaws slamming together, enormous fangs driving holes into the garrison's stone floor. Rasim felt its breath chase him as it narrowly missed his legs. He hit the ground, rolled, and leaped to his feet again, running without knowing where he was going. He tore up a set of stairs carved from the stone, expecting the snake's breath to blow over him again.

Worse: it *didn't*. That meant the vast beast had turned on one of the others as its quarry. Rasim flung himself back down the stairs, not thinking.

Lars lay on top of Sondra, protecting her as they cowered in a corner. Kisia was nowhere to be seen. The snake struck at Lars, but its blunt nose bashed into the outer stone walls they were tucked between.

It reared back, hissing with outrage, and struck again, to the same effect. Then it turned at great speed and went the other way, mouth open, tongue darting out as it searched for easier targets.

It was every bit as large as the sea serpent Rasim had once faced, and serpentine as well, but the resemblance ended there. The serpent's face had been eel-like, elongated, narrow, whiskered: the stone snake's was blunter, wider, and its jaws opened much, much farther than the serpent's had. Its scales crackled when it moved, the sound of stone breaking and reforming faster than the eye could see, but its debris hung in the air and littered the earth. It was as dark and striated as the mountains themselves, with streaks of reddish-orange, like rusted iron, along its body. Dirt clotted under some scales, and in places scraggly plants still hung on. It had *been* the mountain, and now the mountain had come alive.

Rasim's hands went cold as he thought of the scale-like appearance of the lower walls outside the garrison. He twisted, staring upward at the mountains towering above them. The sea serpent had been a single creature, but if the snake *was* the mountain, if the scales outside the fort were a part of the beast that hadn't yet awakened, then it might unwind from deeper and deeper within the stone, never ending. It might drag the mountains along on its back, and tear the world apart, if they couldn't stop it.

Rasim clenched his fists, willing warmth back into

them. There was not a snake in Ilyara that could survive having its head struck off. Even a snake born of stone couldn't be *that* different from the hooded, poisonous creatures that slithered down Ilyaran streets.

The only problem was cutting the head off a snake whose spine stood twice Rasim's height from the ground.

It reared up again, hissing mouth spread wide. Then it doubled, diving. Stone ripped and tore as the earth itself swallowed the snake. It *did* have an end, thank Siliaria: it had a tail that whipped the air and drove the beast deeper into the ground. Rubble clattered and spilled across the suddenly empty earth, the hole sealing itself over as the snake disappeared into it. Rasim swayed, staring at the undisturbed rock in befuddlement.

As fast as it had disappeared, the snake returned, this time surging upward beneath Lars and Sondra. Sondra's scream shattered the air, but only the snake's lower jaw protruded from the ground beneath them. The garrison walls shuddered and shook with its impact, and for an instant it was as though Rasim could see *through* the rock.

"It's witched!" Rasim's voice broke with comprehension. "The garrison, it's witched somehow! The snake can't get out of it! It—it hit its face when it—!" A giggle dissolved his ability to explain. He could *see* it as clearly as if it the walls were water. The snake clearly knew it couldn't pass the garrison walls, and had tried to judge its spacing, but its vast head was too large. It couldn't come up beneath Lars and Sondra in their protected corner without bashing its nose into the impenetrable walls. As Rasim giggled, the snake sank away again into the earth's depths. "Stay there," Rasim shouted to the Northerners. "Just stay there. It can't get to you!"

Though they obviously didn't think it was funny, both Northerners nodded. Rasim knew they were right, but laughing and being able to think was far better than fear and frozen indecision. And they'd agreed to stay put, even if they didn't know why he was laughing. That was enough. That was one thing Rasim didn't have to worry about.

The snake burst out of the stone in front of him, hungry jaws wide again. Rasim jumped sideways, so close to the closing jaws his arm brushed the strangely soft stony skin at the side of its mouth. Behind him, the entire stairwell he'd been standing in collapsed under the snake's bite: *it* wasn't magicked the way the garrison walls were. He had to reach them for safety, and from there, find Kisia. He was on his feet, running, before the plan had fully formed.

There were crags and buttresses all along the garrison walls, places for sentries to hide from the wind as they watched for trespassers beyond the walls. Rasim flung himself into one as the snake turned again, dust billowing from its mouth. Its eyes were depthless brown, not black like every other snake Rasim had ever seen. The color of good earth, that's what they were. The color of earth that would grow food and give life. It seemed strange that a creature bent on eating them would have eyes like that. The beast struck at him repeatedly, though it never came close enough to smash its nose against the witched walls. It didn't have to, though, to keep Rasim pinned there. He started forward once or twice, only to be driven back again immediately.

Kisia appeared from behind the snake's coiled body, running at top speed. She bent and scooped up a dead soldier's sword without missing a step, moving so smoothly she might have been dancing in the sea. She sprang from a low stone to a higher one, her lithe form darting higher and higher in great bounds. Then she was in the air, sword held in both hands, raised above her head as she fell an impossible distance toward the snake's head.

Panicked laughter burst in Rasim's chest. He had taken that very leap from the *Waifia*'s mast when he fought the sea serpent. He wondered if anyone had seen him as clearly as he now saw Kisia, clearly enough to appreciate the beauty and grace of her pose as she fell. She was perfect, brave, heroic, and completely crazy.

The cold metal sword blade shattered into a thousand pieces as it slammed against the snake's stone skull.

It bellowed and flung its head back. Kisia went

flying again, thrown across the yard. She tumbled end over end, so quickly Rasim couldn't possibly follow her with his eyes, but somehow he saw her white-faced terror, and the way she sealed her lips so she wouldn't scream. Rasim shouted, flinging his hands out as if he could catch her. Witchery surged within him, but the sea was too far away to answer in time.

A huge stone hand formed out of the rock wall and caught her gently in its grasp.

For an instant, silence hung over the garrison. Then Kisia leaped onto the stone hand's fingers and punched the air with her fist. "*Yeah!*"

The snake whipped around and struck at the stone hand. Kisia howled and slide inside its protection. The snake's jaws closed around it and it thrashed, trying to crush or absorb the hand, but like the witchery-infused outer walls, it couldn't pass through the witch-shaped stone. Rasim heard Kisia's shouts and wondered if she still had the sword stub, whether she was jabbing the roof of the snake's mouth, or was just disgusted at being half swallowed. He had to trust the stone hand would hold, and that the snake would be distracted long enough for him to find a way to defeat it.

A familiar, unexpected voice called, "Rasim! Up here!"

Rasim spun, searching the parapets. Telun, pale with concentration, waved at him from atop the tall stone walls.

Relief took the strength from Rasim's legs. His knees buckled and he hit the earth, fingers digging into broken shards of stone. The weight of stonemastery suddenly seemed evident, permeating the garrison walls. No wonder the snake couldn't dive through them. No wonder the stone had shaped itself to save Kisia. He looked up, asking, "Milu?" so raspily he doubted Telun would hear him.

The other journeyman nodded anyway. Relief as strong as the first wave hammered Rasim down even farther, until his forehead touched the ground and his lungs were full of rock dust. He hadn't known how badly he was worried about the Stonemaster journeymen until he learned they were safe.

Not that the garrison was really *safe*. Still, somehow, knowing that Milu and Telun were alive gave Rasim strength. And Kisia was alive, and she would tease him mercilessly if he didn't get up. He had slain a sea serpent. He and three other Ilyaran witches could handle a stone snake in the far, frozen North.

Frozen. *Ice.* Isidri could freeze the very water, a vanishingly rare skill among Seamasters. But stone shattered under ice's pressures, and they had no other weapon that might work. Not unless the Stonemasters could shape a sword of stone that would penetrate the snake's hard skull.

That sounded like a much better idea than risking them all on the chance Rasim could now make ice from salt water. He filled his lungs and bellowed, "*Shape a sword!*" at Telun, whose round face went blank, then bright with understanding.

"It'll take me a few minutes! Milu is—" Telun waved his hands and disappeared, leaving Rasim staring upward in bewilderment. Either Milu was hurt and unable to work the stonewitchery, or—more likely, Rasim thought—the gangly journeyman was the one holding the snake within the garrison walls.

A snap echoed through the garrison. Rasim whirled. The rock behind the stone hand was beginning to crack. The snake's great strength would break it down sooner rather than later.

There wasn't time to wait for Telun's stone sword. Rasim swore, then lifted his voice. "Lars! Sondra! Get to high ground!"

He caught a glimpse of them darting out of the protective cubby, their eyes wide with expectation. Later he might think their expressions funny: they knew what had happened *last* time he told them to get to high ground. Right now he only hoped he could live up to the witchery he'd performed in the mines, and then outshine it.

The power came easily, thanks to Siliaria's blessing. It felt far more natural than it ever had, through all the years that he'd struggled to command magic in the guild. It flowed now like his breath, like his blood, pulsing and pulling with the ocean's tides. He didn't need nearly as much power now as he'd needed in the mines. He just needed enough to seep into the snake's head, to pour it into its throat and to seek membranes around the eyes, vulnerable spots where encroaching water, turned to ice, could shatter the stone skull.

And yet it was harder than pulling the inlet into the mines had been. There, he had gathered water but not separated it from itself. Here he was trying to make a bubble of water, a river in the air like the Seamasters had done to stop the recent fire in Ilyara. Water was *heavy*, when not carried on an earth bed.

A kind of embarrassment close to anger suddenly swept through Rasim. He didn't have to *lift* the water. He'd seen, outside the garrison walls, how the tide had carried huge stones right up to the door, shifting bits of sand beneath them until they moved. If the tide came that far on its own, it could creep high enough to come through the door, with his encouragement. It could swim up the snake's body, coating it, getting beneath scales as they shifted and broke, and in time it would rise to the creature's massive head.

A very *short* amount of time. It had taken most of an hour to work the witchery that drowned the mine. Kisia had nothing like that much time: the stone was shattering now, breaking away in great chunks, and any snake could swallow something larger than its own head. The stone hand might not be digestible, but Kisia, trapped inside it, was. Rasim extended his hands, one toward the inlet tongue outside the garrison, and the other toward the snake's twisty body.

The water was already so cold, so cold. Ice floated in it, great heavy chunks that melted on bottom and froze anew on top as the water and air worked their conflicting powers on it. Rasim grasped the idea of freezing, holding on to the so-cold crystals as they formed. They were *only* water, he told himself, water in a different form, but only water, and a Seamaster worked with water. He had seen Isidri do it. He knew it could be done. He would do it, with Siliaria's grace, just this once. Just enough to save his friends. It was all he asked. All he needed. The sea spilled into the garrison, slicking the rock floor, freezing Rasim's unprotected feet.

It reached the snake's tail, washing over it, and began to turn to frost.

A squeak of excitement tightened Rasim's throat. He kept the inlet flowing toward him, beckoning it with one hand, pointing it, guiding it, with the other. It ran up the snake's body more quickly, turning its many colors to a blurry white. It crept beneath scales, stiffening and slowing them, and finally reached the beast's vast skull.

Much too late, he saw that the high ground Lars had chosen was, for some inexplicable reason, the snake's head. It coated with ice beneath the North-man's feet, but he flung himself on his belly, fingers dug into growing frost. He slid over the side of its mouth, toes buried in the thickening ice as well, to help him to keep from sliding the terrible distance to the ground. He let go with one hand. Bile rose in Rasim's throat, barely kept in check by his teeth. Above him, Lars flipped sideways, suddenly holding on with only one hand, and swung into the snake's maw. Rasim let go a cry of dismay and choked it off a breath later as Lars swung free again.

Kisia clung to the Northman's free hand. A wild, panicked grin split her face.

But the slick surface was too much. Lars's hand slipped along the snake's face, fingers clawing the ice, but he couldn't get a grip. They fell, both screaming. Above them, the triumphant serpent ripped the stone hand free of the wall and swallowed it before slamming to the ground repeatedly, like it was breaking the hand to pieces inside itself. Like it was trying to shake the ice that slowed it away.

A stone slide rippled from the wall and caught Kisia and Lars both. Their screams turned to surprise, and then Kisia's laughter shouted across the garrison again as they whipped toward the earth. A hollow opened up at the slide's foot and they fell inside, protected by magic-worked stone.

Rasim turned an incredulous gaze upward, to where he'd last seen Telun. Milu stood there with Telun now, one hand extended and utter weariness on his face. Telun said something that made Milu smile wanly, and another slide appeared in front of

Rasim. A stone sword, as striated and colorful as the snake, rattled down the slide and landed at his feet.

Ocean water, still rising around his feet, became ice that lifted him and sent him sailing across the garrison floor to the flailing, freezing snake. Rasim lifted the sword to strike, then hesitated. Only its eyes were unfrosted now, and they were dull with cold, just as any desert snake's might be. The frost thickened and the snake's motions slowed, growing ever-weaker.

"Telun. Milu." Rasim hardly knew his own voice, nor the sorrowful strength that carried it across the garrison. "Can you sink it back into the stone? Put it back to sleep beneath the garrison, now that it's calm?"

Surprise filled their answer: "Yes, but why?"

Rasim stepped away, letting the weight of witchery go, and leaned heavily on the unused sword. "Because it can't hurt us now, and it shouldn't have to die if it's already been defeated. It's not evil, just big and hungry. And its eyes are the earth." He closed his own eyes. "We shouldn't kill the earth."

Trembling, he dropped the sword and left the snake to slumber.

TWENTY-THREE

"Telun and Milu need to rest." Kisia came to the door of the chamber Rasim had taken for his own. He had been there for hours, too cold and tired to watch as the Stonemasters sank the snake back into the stone. He had gotten up once for the necessary, and had stopped on the way to look into the garrison's shattered courtyard. The snake's sinuous body made a wide, twisting path across the ground, its differently colored stone easy to see from above. The sight made Rasim's chest hurt, and he'd returned to his room to shiver and wonder why he felt such sadness over the beast's near death. It, after all, had attacked *them*.

When he didn't answer, Kisia came into the chamber and hunkered down beside him, right in front of the fire. "They were given mindkiller, too, but either not as much or their magic makes it not work as well on them. They tried to free themselves. Milu thinks they probably woke the stone snake with their witchery. It went after everyone else, but not them."

A raw breath exploded from Rasim's chest. "Then I was right not to kill it. We disturbed it. A lot of people died because of that."

"Slavers and soldiers who were happy to keep slaves," Kisia said with a curled lip.

Rasim looked at her, feeling as dull as the snake's eyes had been. "Maybe nobody ever offered them a better way. Maybe they were just bad, but maybe they could have learned better. I don't like killing people, Kisia. It's not right."

She pursed her mouth, but didn't argue. "Anyway, Milu and Telun are exhausted. Almost as tired as you are. You look like Isidri now, Rasim. You look that sick. We're going to stay here tonight," she said like she was challenging him to disagree. "We'll find clothes to travel in and we'll leave tomorrow or the next day, after we've all had enough to eat and have slept and warmed up. Then we'll go, but going overland isn't an option."

Rasim inhaled and Kisia said, "I found maps," sharply, as if defying a protest Rasim hadn't yet made. "This peninsula sweeps down from the mainland into the sea for hundreds of miles, Ras. There are passes and passageways marked through them, but they're only usable in the summer, and even then it's a months-long journey. So I've been searching the grounds. There's a ship that hardly deserves the name, one of their silly one-masted ones, but some of the miners know how to sail it, and with two Seamasters aboard we should make the capital in three or four days."

"All right."

Kisia's eyebrows rose and she glanced around like Rasim might have been talking to someone else. "That's it? All right?"

"It's a good plan. Why wouldn't it be all right?"

"Because you're the one who plans things."

"Only because I usually think of things faster than most people, Kees, and I'm too tired to think right now. Ice is hard." He felt foolish as soon as he'd said it, but it was true. No wonder Isidri had been so wrecked after thawing the harbor. He was ninety years younger than she was, and he could barely stay sitting upright after icing the snake.

Kisia's smile appeared, softer than usual. "It is. If you don't mind, I'll sleep in here too. It's warm, and..." She drew a deep breath. "And I don't trust the Northerners. I'd rather be with you. Telun and Milu are next door."

Rasim nodded. Kisia did too, and got up. "All right. I'll bring you food in a little while. Sondra and Lars raided the larder. There's meat, not just fish, and they're baking bread. It smells wonderful. I'll tell you if anything needs your attention." She went to the door, pausing there to look back. "Rasim?"

He looked up tiredly. Kisia smiled. "You saved me again. Thank you."

Laughter jolted out of him. "You just about killed

that snake single-handedly, Kees. I don't think you need much saving."

"Still, *I* didn't shape the stone that caught me." Kisia waved and left Rasim looking after her in bemusement. He didn't think he'd shaped the giant stone hand, either, but the only thing worse than arguing with Kisia was arguing with her and later discovering she was right. He would ask Milu privately. Tomorrow, after they'd all slept.

Or, as it turned out, two mornings later, when they had indeed all slept, and eaten, and after Kisia had prepared the one-masted ship to sail. Rasim had barely left his room for the two days, glad to do nothing but eat and rest. By the second morning he felt well enough to come down to shore, where Kisia climbed the ship's rigging and shouted orders at Northerners who understood well enough to do as they were told.

Milu stood on the beach too, his brown face as pale as it could be, and wry. "I cannot tell you how much I do not want to get on that boat."

"Ship," Rasim corrected cheerfully. "Would you rather stay here?"

"Almost. But it's days past when the slave ships were supposed to arrive, and if we have to sail, I'd rather do it before they get here. Maybe a storm took them," Milu said with an unusual viciousness.

"Or maybe they saw the mess we left at the mines and decided it wasn't worth the trouble. Thank you," Rasim said abruptly, feeling awkward. "For burying the snake instead of killing it."

Milu glanced at him, surprised. "Not at all. You were right. We disturbed it, and...I didn't want it to die," he confessed. "There's a mind in there. I could almost feel it, thinking slowly, the way stone...does." He made a face. "Not that stone really thinks, but..."

"No, I know what you mean. Water is like that too. Alive, in its own way. Anyway, thank you. And thank you for saving Kisia."

"After that display with the hand, I figured I'd better catch her when she fell again or I'd have you to answer to." Milu sighed. "And I owe you enough for cleaning up after me on the *Waifia*. I'll try not to be so much trouble on this journey. I'd better go get something to throw up in, in fact." He left without realizing he'd stunned Rasim into silence.

He had implied that the stone hand hadn't been his doing at all, but Rasim's. Which was either impossible, or everything the guilds thought they knew about mastery really *was* wrong. No one studied more than one magic, or at least no one but the royal family. It was unlikely many—or any— Seamasters had spent as many long, mind-numbing hours trying to understand stone's structure at all, never mind after watching a master stone witch at work, as Rasim had. The masters would have said there was no point, that everyone *knew* a witch could only master one magic, but if no one had *tried*, then they didn't really know it, they just *believed* it.

"But why wouldn't anyone try?" Rasim asked Kisia's ship. It rocked, offering no answers, but Rasim came to one on his own, after a moment. The guilds had been created centuries ago by the royal family — the only people who *could* use more than one kind of witchery. If they wanted to remain in uncontested power, convincing others that only royal blood could master many magics was very, very clever. It might have been difficult in the first years, but over time any royal matchmaker could find men and women able to use more than one magic and marry them into the royals, until no one thought to test the tale's truth. It would make a lie of the legends, of the song about Sunchild and all the others, and of the royal family's descendence from the gods, but that was a *story*, not history.

A band of Northerners at his side, an army of Islanders at his call, and now a dangerous insight into Ilyaran magic. Even Rasim could envision himself as an enemy of Taishm's rule, with those things in hand, and he didn't even *want* to be king. If any others in the King's Guild came to these same conclusions, or found themselves supported by foreign nations, Ilyara could fall into civil war breathtakingly quickly.

Rasim closed his hands into fists, admitting the possibility that Kisia and Milu were right. He would *never* work stonewitchery again, if it was true that he could. The last thing he wanted was to upset the balance of power in Ilyara, never mind anywhere else. He would ask to leave the King's Guild when they returned to Ilyara, and go back to the Sea- masters where he belonged. And if Kisia ever asked him about it, he would just have to lie. Maybe he had worked stonewitchery once, to save her, but that was all he had ever worked a great seamastery for, too, before Siliaria's blessing. If Coluth came calling, Rasim would look away the same way Milu had when Siliaria had examined him.

"Hey!" Kisia leaped off the ship and snapped her fingers under Rasim's nose. "Hey, Sunburn! I've been calling you for five minutes. We're ready to cast off, and you're standing here like a statue."

Rasim startled, then caught Kisia's hand to stop her snapping. "Sorry. I was thinking. What do you need me to do..." He hesitated, genuinely not wanting to tease her. "...Captain?"

A grin crooked the corner of her mouth. "Come aboard, First Mate, and translate. We've gotten by so far, but once we're at sea I don't want to be relying on pointing and arguing over the word for some- thing. We sail on the tide, and I, for one, can't *wait* to see Missio's face when we turn up alive."

#

After shipboard fires, storms, island adventures, slavery, and stone snakes, Rasim did not expect the sail to Ringenstand to go smoothly. Nor did it, from Milu's point of view: the bony Stonemaster youth spent the entire journey hanging over the rail or flat on his face on the deck, too wrung out to even weep. Telun, much more comfortable on shipboard this time, took over cleaning up after his partner while Rasim ran from one end of the ship to the other, always moving, translating, giving orders, and wondering how Hassin kept up enough energy to work this hard *and* to be favored by admiring women. But the exhausting work made the time pass quickly, and despite Milu's misery, the journey went smoothly.

Only when they neared the capital's harbor did he begin to think about making an entrance. It was very clear they were approaching the right harbor: unlike the more modest cove at Hongrunn, where Rasim had last entered the Northlands, the capital's harbor was guarded by massive, stunning statues that rose up fifty times a man's height, carved out of the mountains themselves.

"They did that without stonemastery?" Kisia asked in awe as the statues became clearer. A man and a woman stood on either side of the harbor's mouth, both holding the same kinds of heavy swords Lorens had been teaching the journeymen to fight with. They were both armored, though neither wore helms, and both held their inside hands outward a little, as if welcoming sailors while also warning them that the people within were not to be trifled with.

"I don't know." Rasim stood beside her on the captain's deck, his gaze drawn upward just as hers was. "Princess Inga said they used to have magic here. Maybe they used to have stonemasters. Kisia, how are we going to...I mean, we're..." He gestured at them, and then at the impossible statues.

"You mean we're dressed like riff-raff, sailing a beaten-up old ship one step shy of the salvage yard, with a crew of slaves and puking journeymen, so how are we going to make a good impression on the Northlands queen and her court?"

"Yeah." Rasim smiled faintly. "That's exactly what I mean."

"I don't think we're really going to have to worry about it." Kisia pointed ahead of them, between the feet of the massive statues.

The entire Northern fleet sailed out to greet them, the *Waifia* at its head.

TWENTY-FOUR

"Drop anchor." Even as he spoke, Rasim sent a tendril of witchery deep, searching for the seabed floor. Kisia gave him a look of faint disgust that made him sheepish as he discovered what she already knew: the sea floor was much too deep here to anchor. Instead, Kisia swung up onto a rail, gaining attention before shouting orders to turn into the wind and hold position while the fleet approached.

For a moment, Rasim wondered why the *Waifia* didn't leap ahead of the single-sailed ships in a rush to greet them. Then, aloud, he said, "Oh. They don't know it's us. How could they?" in embarrassment, before frowning in confusion. "Why are they even coming out, if they don't know it's us?".

Kisia flashed him a broad grin. "I don't know, but why don't you let them know who it is?"

Pure reckless joy rose in Rasim's breast. He ran to the prow, grinning, and flung his fingertips toward the water, toward the oncoming ships, and called power.

Mermaids — called Siliaria's daughters — leaped
from the sea, made of magic and water. They
sparkled in the soft sunlight, diving and splashing,
their watery laughter burbling across the sea's surface. Rasim climbed higher on the prow, then scrambled over it to perch precariously on the figurehead,
laughing as he shaped water into all the dreams and
stories told by young sailors. Small ships appeared
alongside the racing mermaids, who dove over the
ships and captured sea witches to dance across the
water with them. Some became mermaids and mer-
men themselves, embracing the sea with all their
hearts. Embracing Siliaria, Rasim thought, because
that was how it had felt to be graced by the goddess:
as if he had finally, truly become part of the sea himself. His creations rode fanciful creatures, seahorses
as tall as a mast or sea-glittering dolphins that
sprayed rainbowed mist into the air.

Then *real* dolphins burst up, disrupting the witchery
and chasing it down, greeting their watery brethren
with delight. Rasim threw his hands skyward, cheering
and laughing as the *Waifia* finally did leap ahead of the
other ships, drawn to the witchery on display. They
were still a half mile away when Hassin's voice roared
across the distance: "*Rasim!*"

Rasim bellowed, "*Hassin!*" in return, knowing the
Waifia's first mate would never hear him, but it ap-
peared chaos was breaking out aboard the *Waifia*.
Half a dozen water spigots whirled to life, witches

leaping from shipboard to ride the waves. For the
first time in his life, Rasim flung down the power to
ride the water too, and went to join them.

Hassin's water spout raced ahead of the others,
crashing into Rasim's before he'd gone very far from
Kisia's Northern ship. The handsome first mate's
magic actually wobbled, almost tossing him into the
sea before Rasim lunged and caught him in a mind-
less, shouting hug. Hassin pounded Rasim's back,
shouting in return, the noise so great neither could
be understood. Within a minute, the others had
caught up, half a dozen whirlpools bashing into each
other, vying for dominance, dizzying their witches,
and finally dumping all of them in icy waters. For
once every sea witch got wet, all too busy shouting
and questioning and pounding on one another to
fend off the cold water. Even Desimi was in the
mess, grabbing Rasim around the neck and knuck-
ling his head as he shoved him under the surface.
Rasim came up spluttering and seized Desimi in
turn, returning the treatment. The bigger boy bellowed in half-real outraged astonishment, and on it
went until they were all blue and chattering with
cold. Only then did anyone have the presence of
mind to get out of the water, witchery working together to lift all of them at once and deposit them on
Kisia's deck.

She stood arms akimbo and trying to look stern
through a smile that threatened to split her head.

"Look at all of you," she said in the most severe voice she could manage. "Soaked to the bone. What kind of seamaster—"

Hassin and Desimi jumped on her, dragging her to the deck and soaking her to the skin while they returned to roaring greetings and shouting questions no one had any real desire to answer. It wasn't until the *Waifia* pulled alongside Kisia's ship that any semblance of decorum was restored, but even Hassin was still dripping as Nasira's crew threw clawed ropes over and hauled the ships side to side. Nasira climbed onto the rail, narrow braid lashing over her shoulder as she looked down at the sopping first mate who had just abandoned his ship, and then one by one examined the others.

She came to Rasim and Kisia last, with all the hardness Rasim remembered in her eyes. His jubilation faded more the longer she stared at him, until she finally startled him by grinning broadly. "Well. I can see *this* is going to take a lot of explaining. I'm glad to see you alive, journeymen." Her gaze found Telun and Milu as well, and she nodded to them too. "You too, lads, but I'll thank you to stay on this lump of a ship while we get this sorted out."

"*Telun? Milu?*" Stonemaster Lusa burst up from below decks, her round face so hopeful it made Rasim's heart hurt. No more comfortable with the sea than her journeymen were, Lusa nonetheless scrambled over the rail and all but fell onto Kisia's ship, then ran the short distance to catch her journeymen in an encompassing hug. For the first time in three days, Milu's color turned normal as they shared the embrace. Rasim's eyes stung with happiness and Kisia elbowed him in the ribs, beaming and pointing at the Stonemasters, like he couldn't see them himself.

When Lusa finally drew back and composed herself, she said what the *Waifia*'s crew were all obviously thinking: "We thought you were dead. What happened?"

To his dismay, the other three journeymen looked at Rasim. He dropped his chin to his chest, looking for an easy answer, and found none. "Someone drugged us and threw us overboard. The cold water woke me up, so we survived, and..." There was too much to explain, he decided, and skipped to, "And now we're here." The rest could be told later, perhaps when Captain Nasira's jaw wasn't quite so tight. Rasim shivered, which reminded him he was wet. He squeezed water off himself with his magic, and that made Nasira's jaw tighten even more.

"You just water-danced, journeyman. As skillfully as a master. What *happened*?"

Rasim flushed, knowing no one would believe the truth, and not having tried to come up with an excuse as to why he'd finally come into the seamastery he'd always longed for. Silence drew out while he struggled to speak.

"Siliaria kissed him."

Every eye on two ships turned to Kisia, who looked almost nonchalant. "Rasim would never tell you,
because you wouldn't believe him and that would
upset him, but I don't really care if you believe me,
because I know what's true. Siliaria came to us in the
fog, tested Milu, called me sister, kissed Rasim, and
brought us to shore before we died of exposure. And
now Rasim is a seamaster, as strong as Guildmaster
Isidri. I watched him turn salt water to ice to save
our lives. Where," she said, her tone changing to
sharp demand, "is Missio? I want to see her face
when she sees we survived."

Disbelief faded to discomfort at Kisia's last
question. Even Nasira, whose face was drawn and
thoughtful as she studied the journeymen, shook her
head. "Missio disappeared into Ringenstand a few
hours after we docked. No one has seen since."

Rasim stared at the *Waifia*'s captain. "She's a dark
brown *Ilyaran* in a city of snow-colored *Northerners*.
How can she hide?"

One of Nasira's eyebrows edged up. "She obviously has help."

"Or she's dead." Rasim clapped his hands over his
own mouth, appalled at the suggestion.

Nasira's eyes narrowed, but she didn't respond
beyond that. Instead she frowned at the open sea,
then back at the narrow harbor mouth and its mountain guardians. "The Northern queen was..." She
chose the next word carefully: "Disappointed. Not to

meet you. She kept us in the capital days longer than we might have expected, trying to understand what had happened to you. We should return and present you, now that you've reappeared." Her frown pinched a line between her eyebrows as she glanced at Rasim. "You have an uncanny ability to return from the dead, journeyman. Cats have fewer lives than you do."

Rasim, forgetting his rank relative to the queen's — or his captain's, for that matter — spoke frankly. "I'd like to have a talk with her, too. But you're — are you sailing for Hongrunn? To try to fix the water supply?"

Nasira nodded once. Rasim gestured to the sea. "Then I think we should go do that, before things get any worse there. I can come back here another time — "

Nasira snorted, making Rasim listen to himself. It did, on the face of it, seem unlikely that a Seamaster journeyman should have such an easy expectation of returning to the Northlands. Six months ago he'd never dreamed he might visit the North once, never mind return. On the other hand... "I've been North twice in three months," he said in his own defense. "Besides, the queen doesn't know I'm here, so she won't miss me if we just sail straight to Hongrunn. I can come back again after we've found the *Sinaz*'s crew who've been enslaved."

The captain's eyes glittered, telling Rasim that he'd found the point with which Nasira could be persuaded. Still, she looked beyond him at the ship full of miners and arched her thin eyebrows. "And these? Do we send them to Ringenstand or take them to Hongrunn?"

"With all due respect, ma'am," Lars said in his own language, "we'll go with Rasim."

Rasim turned to him in surprise, then smiled in even greater surprise. Pynda, the bigger Sunmaster journeyman, had come aboard Kisia's ship while Rasim wasn't paying attention, and now stood at Lars's side, where she had clearly been translating their conversation. Nasira, over Rasim's head, said, "You will, will you?" and the miner met her gaze levelly.

"It's him that got us out of the mines, ma'am. It's him I've sworn to follow, and for better or worse, these 'uns have chosen me to lead. I think a fair lot of them will stay in Hongrunn." He glanced over his shoulder to see how many of his countrymen nodded, while Pynda translated. Then he looked back at Nasira. "But we'll all of us go as far as that, at least."

"Whatever we do," Milu said as he finally extracted himself from Lusa's hugs, "could we do it now? The less time I'm on this boa — *ship*. The less time I'm on this ship, the happier I'll be."

Nasira laughed, surprising Rasim as much as Lars's speech had. "The less time you're on my ship the happier I'll be too, Stonemaster. All right." She whistled sharply, as if everyone wasn't paying attention to her anyway. "We'll cast off. I need volunteers to help man the Northern ship. Your men might mean well," she told Lars, "but you need sailors to keep that tub in time with the rest of the fleet."

Then she eyed Kisia and spoke with an unexpectedly droll formality. "Captain, I relieve you of your command, and elevate First Mate Hassin in your place. Don't priss your mouth at me, girl. There's not a first-year journeyman in the fleet who's ever captained a ship before, so your name will be sung in yet another song of our histories."

"I don't *care* about the histories. I just want—"

As unexpectedly, Nasira cut her off with a short motion of one hand, and a nod. "I know what you want. But you're back under Seamaster law now, and Hassin's your captain. Don't spoil what you've done by sulking, Journeyman. You're better than that." She stepped back to the *Waifia*'s rail and leaped down to the deck, calling out orders that Hassin echoed on his own ship. A dozen sea witches joined Hassin's crew, and by the time the rest of the Northern fleet caught up to them, they were under sail again.

Kisia, far from pouting over her loss of rank, took up the job of relating the events of the past several days. She had to tell it all six or eight times, as sailors came in and out of earshot, but Rasim was glad to leave her to it. She was right: no one would believe him if he'd told it as the central figure, but wide gazes and whispered comments said they almost believed it coming from Kisia.

Desimi, wearing his King's Guard pearl, listened to

the story on and off throughout the afternoon, and as the sun lingered on the horizon, cornered Rasim to sneer half-heartedly at him. "It wasn't enough to slay a serpent and save a king? You had to go and tell Siliaria herself your name?"

Rasim, lost in work and glad of it, stopped to wipe sweat away, then flicked a finger toward Desimi's pearl. "You got a mark of honor out of all that. I just got more work. I guess she took pity on me."

"Pity's about all you're worth." Desimi stumped off, but Rasim grinned after him, remembering how the bigger boy had pounded his back, glad to see him alive. He wouldn't know what to do if Desimi stopped insulting him, but there was no hatred in the taunts anymore. Happy, tired, and content, Rasim finished his duties and went to sleep, dreamlessly, on the open deck.

TWENTY-FIVE

Two days under full sail saw them at Hongrunn's harbor. Rasim, smiling, watched the approach from the prow. Last time he'd come here, he'd dived off a pirate ship's mast and entered the city through a sewer. A well-protected sewer, as it turned out. He wondered if giant Gontur still guarded that particular city entryway.

This time a procession awaited them at the docks. To Rasim's astonishment, at its head was Inga, Lorens's older sister and mistress of Hongrunn. Her solemn, inviting expression turned to amazement as she recognized Rasim. All protocol was abandoned as the Northern princess hitched up her skirts and ran up the gangplank the moment it touched the dock. "Ilyaran! Word had come that you were dead!"

She threw herself at Rasim, seizing him in a hug that sent him staggering halfway across the deck. He hadn't gotten any taller, nor Inga any shorter: she had a considerable size advantage. Rasim laughed, trying to get their feet back under them, and felt his face heat when she kissed his cheeks. "Lorens will be so happy! My mother will be glad too. Oh, I must write to them immediately. Almost immediately."

As quickly as she'd lost decorum, Inga found it again. She turned to Hassin with perfect controlled formality and smiled. "Welcome to Hongrunn. I am Inga Jaanadottir, heir to the Northern throne. I apologize for my outburst, but Rasim al Ilialio has been a good friend to the North, and we were distraught to hear of his death."

Humor washed over Hassin's handsome face. "I understand completely, Highness. We were equally glad to have him returned to us. I'm Hassin al Ilialio, First Mate of the *Waifia* and temporarily captaining this ship. If I might have the honor of introducing you to Captain Nasira...?" He offered his arm and Inga accepted it as he guided her down the dock.

The two of them walking side by side made Rasim catch his breath. They were as opposite and equal as they could be. Hassin's long dark hair in its tightly controlled que contrasted perfectly with Inga's equally long, but wheat-blonde hair falling down her back in loose waves. She wore a pale green gown under a thick fur coat; Hassin wore rough sailor's garb in darker green. Her fingertips, resting against his exposed forearm, were cloud-white against his earth-brown skin. Neither of them was more or less beautiful than the other, as if they'd been cast in stone and made to match.

That, Rasim thought, might have been what his own parents looked like, except with their colors reversed. His mother had almost certainly been the Ilyaran of the pair, as Northern men sailed south more frequently than the women did. If either of them had had half the beauty of Inga and Hassin as they walked together, it was no wonder they had caught each other's eyes, and had a child.

He wasn't the only one who noticed, either. Kisia pressed her fingers against her mouth, eyes wide as she watched them depart the ship. She cast Rasim a quick look, then jerked her gaze forward again as if guilty for thinking about an orphan's parentage. Others didn't seem to follow her line of thought, but the whole ship, the whole *dock*, became quiet with appreciation as they crossed to the *Waifia*.

Rasim was too far away to hear the formalities, but they didn't matter. What mattered was that soon Stonemaster Lusa and her journeymen would go up to the mountain lake and, with Seamaster assistance, stop salt from pouring into it. Then the sea witches would purify the lake water again, and a city would thrive. Rasim smiled at the idea, then elbowed Kisia. "I got to see some of the city when I was here last. We should go look around while we're here."

"That sounds great, but I don't know if you'll get to." Kisia nodded toward Hassin and Inga, who had turned back. When they caught Rasim's eye, they beckoned him forward. Rasim furled his eyebrows at

Kisia, trying to get her to come along, but she lifted her own eyebrows and shook her head no. Nearby, Desimi snorted. Rasim shot him a dirty look, then hurried toward the Northern princess.

"I expected you to come with us," Inga chided him. "Who else will guide your Stonemasters to the bottom of the lake?"

Rasim's mouth fell open. He closed it again with a pop, but his jaw seemed to have come loose: it dropped again instantly. "*Me?* Highness, that, I'm, I mean—!"

"Of course you." Inga looked amused. "Why do you think my mother requested you in particular? Aside from your talent for building bridges between nations, I mean. You know more about our affliction than anyone."

"My talent for—" Rasim swallowed his incredulity and cast a glance around, hoping Desimi hadn't heard that.

He hadn't, but Sunmaster Endat, standing a few yards away with his arms folded across his chest, had. He looked rather forbidding, especially flanked by solemn-faced Pynda and Daka, but then his lips quirked in a faint smile. He unfolded one arm just enough to thump his closed fist over his heart in a small salute of recognition. Rasim gave him a weak smile in return and tried not to roll his eyes. The idea that he built bridges between nations was ridiculous. He just ended up in the wrong place at the right time a lot.

Inga clearly expected him to finish his sentence. Rasim cleared his throat. "If you want me to help with the salt fountain I will, but I'm not much..."

Kisia had scolded him for saying those words too often, and now Rasim found how ingrained they were: *I'm not much of a witch.* It was hard not to say it, even if it wasn't true anymore. Even if Kisia was right, and it had never been true, except in his own mind. "I mean, of course I will, Highness."

Inga's smile lit up. "I hoped you would agree. I have one more favor to ask, Rasim."

"Sure. It can't be anything too awful," Rasim said cheerfully. "I already know your sewers are clean."

Inga laughed. "So they are. No, this is less potentially smelly than that, I think. I'd like to join you when you go to the bottom of the lake. I'd like you, specifically, to take me."

"You—what? Me? Really?" Rasim stuttered through the words, undone by Inga's hopeful gaze. He shot a nervous glance at Captain Nasira, and was rewarded for it: she lurched forward, her expression at war with itself. She looked like she *wanted* to smack Inga silly, but was forced to put on a polite, concerned face instead.

"I'm sorry, Highness. I think I misunderstood. Did you just suggest the heir to the Northern throne should dive three hundred feet into a half-frozen lake with nothing but a Seamaster journeyman to protect her?"

"I did." Inga smiled beautifully. "I think it's important that I understand what's truly happening in this lake, and in my mother's country. Rasim has alerted us to a possibility that seems ever-more likely, especially in light of the misadventures he's recently been through. Someone wishes the Northlands harm. I must see what they've wrought, so I can best report to my mother and so we might plan for our future."

Nasira cast a desperate look at Endat, who stepped forward with slow, stately intent and bowed to Inga. "I have every faith that you will be safe in Rasim's hands."

Relief swept Nasira's face, then changed to dismay with comic speed as she heard what Endat had said, rather than what she'd hoped he would say. Inga, however — well, if she wasn't a princess, Rasim would say she was smug. He bet princesses weren't ever smug, though, so it was probably just satisfaction turning her lips up in a smile. "First thing in the morning, then?" she asked serenely. "I'm sure your crew needs rest, and we would like to properly welcome you with food and drink."

Nasira glowered at Rasim, who bit his lip to keep from protesting that Inga's idea couldn't possibly be blamed on him. He already knew the captain could carry unfounded grudges. Antagonizing her by pointing out he wasn't at fault wouldn't help. He still wanted to, and was relieved when she took her gimlet glare from him and fastened it to first the weak afternoon sun, then on Inga herself.

Inga flicked an eyebrow upward at Nasira's unspoken ferocity, but the captain was having none of that. She was accustomed to her own command, and royalty or not, Inga was on her ship. It would, Rasim reckoned, take a lot more than a pointed eyebrow to squelch her temper. Not even Master Endat noisily clearing his throat reduced Nasira's scowl a whit. "Not that the light will penetrate that deep anyway, but the air's as warm now as it's going to be, isn't it? We may as well get it done and celebrate with a feast after."

"The air will have cooled by the time we surface again," Inga said cautiously. "If we went in the morning, we would be returning to the warmest part of the day."

"It's not like I intend any of us to get wet anyway." Nasira, having been thwarted in keeping the princess on dry land, was clearly not going to back down on this.

Inga gave Rasim a glance as cautious as her words had been. "When Rasim made his exploratory dive, he returned to us soaked to the bone."

"Rasim," Nasira muttered, "isn't much of a witch."

Rasim couldn't help looking for Kisia, though she was on an entirely different ship and in no danger of hearing Nasira's comment. Still, he imagined Kisia bristling on his behalf, and grinned at both princess and captain. "I'm more of one than I used to be. We won't get wet, Ing—um, Highness."

Inga nodded. Nasira's face became expressionless. Rasim winced, realizing too late that the princess had just accepted a journeyman's word over a captain's. He would *never* get into Nasira's good graces if he kept on like this. "Maybe we should go," he said miserably, and thought, but didn't say, *before I make things any worse.*

"Indeed." Inga smiled as if nothing untoward had happened. Nasira, still flat-faced and now cold-voiced as well, called out orders. Nearly all of Nasira's crew went ashore, leaving only a handful on board, but others gathered together as well. Lusa and the two Stonemaster journeymen joined the group quietly, as if trying not to draw attention to themselves. Milu stared fixedly at the shore only a few yards away, like he could will himself onto its motionless surface if only he tried hard enough. The Skymasters joined them, followed by all three Sunmasters.

Rasim blurted, "But there's light down there!"

Inga, overhearing, stepped closer and examined the gathering crowd. "So you said. Why do you mention it?"

"That's Sunmaster Endat and his journeymen, Pynda and Daka. We don't need their witchery for light, that's all."

"But for warmth, perhaps?"

"Oh." Rasim didn't know how he could be called clever so often and still be so foolish sometimes. "I didn't think of that. But the air will go faster if they're using sunwitchery. Oh. That's why the Skymasters are with us too. That's good. It'll go faster if we're not cold."

"I look forward to watching your guilds work together." Inga took Rasim's hand and together they joined the group as some of its last members.

"All right, Highness." Nasira finally joined the gathering herself, eyes hard and determined. "Bring us to this poisoned lake of yours."

TWENTY-SIX

The lake water, black in shadow and pale blue where it reflected the sky, was saltier by far than it had been only a few months earlier. The shore was crusted with ice and salt now, crystals of both breaking under Ilyaran feet. And, excepting Inga, they *were* all Ilyaran: even Inga's guards had been made to stay behind, an order which had displeased them immensely. But Rasim thought he understood why. Someone had sabotaged the lake; someone had tried to kill him and his friends. That someone might be a trusted guard, or a curious bystander. There was no way to tell. But whomever it was could be of great danger to the witches. They would be vulnerable as they entered and left the water, even if only for a few seconds. It was smart to keep everyone away.

That, of course, assumed that all of the witches were trustworthy. Since *someone* had taught the Northerners magic, even that wasn't a given. Rasim held back a groan. He would work himself into believing the whole world was an enemy, if he wasn't careful.

"I used to swim in this lake as a child." Inga's comment, soft with reminiscence, broke into Rasim's thoughts. "Before it was salty, and in the summer, though even then it was very cold. Once in a while my father would have great tubs brought up here in the winter, and would have them filled with very hot water. We would bathe in the steaming water, then leap into the icy lake." She shivered and laughed all at once. "It was invigorating. I hadn't thought of that in many years."

"You'll be able to do it again soon," Rasim promised. "I'll get the Sunmasters to build bonfires beneath the tubs, so the water will be as hot as you remember."

"I'll hold you to that, Ilyaran." Inga's smile made her look hardly older than Rasim, though she was at least twice his age. "Now, what should I wear to dive into the lake?"

Rasim looked at her robes and long skirts, then shook his head. "That should be fine. They'll help keep you warm down there, because it's cold even if we're not wet."

"It won't be too cold," dreamy-eyed Daka promised from nearby. She had a spark of fire living between her palms already, its glow making golden shadows against her skin. "We'll keep you warm."

Desimi muttered something impolite as he stomped past the Sunmaster journeyman and straight into the water. It peeled back from him, never touching his clothes or skin as he struck out in a strong swim. Several others followed, Hassin among the very last.

He paused at Rasim's side, nodding toward the witchery that Desimi began to work near the lake's center. "We're going to funnel air all the way to the bottom. The seamasters will keep the whirlpool open and stabilize the water where we have to work, while the sky witches will help keep the air fresh and the sun witches keep us warm. Since we're doing all the work to keep the funnel open, there's no point in those of you going to the bottom wasting energy swimming down. Enjoy the drop."

Grinning, he left Rasim standing beside a wide-eyed Inga, who demanded, "Enjoy the *drop*?"

Rasim met her gaze with equally wide eyes, though his attempt at innocence was ruined by fighting off laughter. "Don't worry. It's not really a *drop.* It's more like a giant swirl. We do it all the time in the harbor. Well, not *all* the time. Most of the fleet has to be gone or the currents knock the ships together."

"Do *what*?"

"Ride the whirlpool to the bottom and then ride another one back up. It's fun! C'mon!" Rasim caught Inga's hand and pulled her toward the water. She hung back, clearly dismayed, but as others passed them, she began to relax. Rasim called his witchery, guiding water just far enough away from them to keep them warm and dry as they surfed toward the growing whirlpool. Ahead of them, Kisia whipped around its funnel and disappeared into the depths with a gleeful shriek. Desimi, holding the mouth of the whirlpool open to the sky, glared ferociously after her. Rasim clapped a hand over his mouth, trying not to laugh. No wonder the bigger boy had gone into the water so sulkily. Everyone else got to ride the whirlpool, but Desimi was stuck at the surface. For once, his great witchery talent was working against him.

Shrieks of laughter — and of pure terror, when the Stonemasters made the drop — echoed out of the cold water as the *Waifia*'s crew headed for the bottom of the lake. Inga, nervously, said, "Are you sure this is a good idea?" as the whipping water began to draw them in.

Rasim grinned wildly at her. "It was *your* idea, Highness!"

"But I didn't know — !" Her protest came too late. The whirlpool seized them. They swung around at dizzying speeds, drawn deeper into the water. Rasim folded his arms around Inga, streamlining them both, and howled with delight as they lashed through foaming salt water. He had never in his life made it to the bottom of the Ilyaran harbor without losing control of his witchery and getting drenched. This time, though, the magic was his to command. He and the Northern princess spun faster and faster, until Inga gave up being afraid and began giggling breathlessly.

The whirlpool narrowed, but not as much as a natural one would. Rasim felt witchery at work, the heaviness of seamastery holding the funnel wider than it wished to be, and indeed, slowing its mad rush in circles. It was still ridiculously, hysterically fast. Above the roar of water, other gleeful—and terrified—shouts could sometimes be heard. The water darkened around them, making the descent feel all the more dangerous, though they were in the hands of a dozen or more sea witches. There was more real danger of drowning in a cup of sakka than in the Northern lake.

Then they were slowing, the whirlpool's strength spent into broader, heavier eddies that rippled through the lake's depths. The last little distance *was* a drop, all the way to the stony lake bed. Rasim landed neatly, but Inga collapsed sideways, clutching her head. Rasim knelt and touched her ears, finding the madly sloshing water inside them and stabilizing it.

Inga's eyes stopped whirling and she clapped her hands over her ears, still swaying. "Oh my. Stopping my head spinning was almost as bad as the—I'm talking. We're underwater and I'm talking! And breathing!" She clutched Rasim's shoulder in astonishment. "Rasim, *look.*"

Seamasters stood shoulder to shoulder, heads

down and eyes closed in concentration. Water domed above them, drips forming and falling to the lake bed, but its crushing weight was held aloft. The three Sunmasters were evenly spaced around the small dome, arms spread and wreathed with flame. Warmth wobbled the air, almost visible as the Skymasters kept it moving, kept it fresh, always exchanging it with the air from the surface.

To one side of the dome, the salt fountain rose from the lake floor. It glowed with a soft white light of its own, just as it had when Rasim had first seen it. It was as if the salt itself was illuminated somehow, its light only fading as it drifted farther into the lake waters. Now, without those waters to absorb it, the salt was piling rapidly onto the drying rock and slipped over the fountain's sides. With the light offered by the Sunmasters, Rasim saw that the fountain itself was beautiful, which he hadn't noticed on his first journey to the lake's bottom. It looked like a wine jug, with a delicate round belly and a thin, narrow spout. A giant's wine jug, to be sure: it stood at least twice Rasim's height, and salt spilled from its spout with a soft hiss. The Stonemasters, ankle-deep in salt, examined it.

"A salt bed lies beneath the lake's floor." Master Lusa's voice echoed strangely against the water, though she didn't sound afraid. Not even Milu looked disturbed at the weight of water above them. Maybe it was the focus of witchery, of doing their duty, that made it bearable. "The witchery done here is tremendous. This," she gestured at the fountain itself, with its swollen belly and slender spout, "this isn't really necessary. There's a bewitched crack in the lake floor, beneath the bottom of this..." She reared back, protecting her eyes from falling salt as she examined the fountain. "This *jug*. The belly fills up and it's forced out the top, but the only reason to have the jug is for the beauty of it."

"But no one was ever meant to see it." Inga took a nervous step forward, making certain Rasim stayed beside her.

Lusa shrugged. "Any witch has a certain vanity about what she does, Highness. No matter if no one would see it. You want to leave something you're proud of behind. Maybe something someone else would recognize, if they *did* see it."

"And do you?" Inga's nerves fell away with the regal demand, but the Stonemaster gave her a sour look.

"Not yet. Stone holds the memory of who's shaped it, but I haven't begun my own work yet. I might be able to tell you more when we're done. What I don't understand," she said, turning back to the fountain, "is how the magic continues in perpetuity. It's not natural for the salt to fountain upward, not unless there's something beneath it pushing it upward."

"Or unless someone is still down here working the witchery." Rasim regretted the words as soon as he'd said them. Everyone, even the intensely-concentrating seamasters, looked sickened at the idea.

Inga paled in the sunmasters' golden light. "Is that possible?"

Lusa snorted. "Of course not. No one would survive down here for as long as these waters have been being poisoned."

"Guildmaster...Isidri..." Kisia spoke from the far side of the fountain, startling Rasim. He had thought she was helping keep the whirlpool open, not down on the lake bed like he was. He stretched out his hand, finally thinking to add his own magic to the power keeping the water domed above them. Kisia relaxed just enough to speak more clearly. "Guild-master Isidri remembers when other countries had witchery, or at least remembers old stories of it. Their magic wasn't all like ours."

"Like the Northern fleet turning the harbor to ice," Rasim said quietly. Inga glanced at him. He shrugged. "Ilyarans have a hard time turning water to ice. We work with pure elements. Once you change water to ice, it's kind of...something else. It's still water, but it's not water the way we sea witches know it. But whomever taught the Northerners magic — well, they could do ice really easily. Maybe some witches can shape...I don't know. Wood, maybe. Or..." He nodded at the lake floor. "Maybe somebody can shape... *people*. Make them so they can live like this, and keep using their witchery."

Inga's eyes went dark, but she nodded. Lusa, though, made a dismissive sound. "Or maybe there's water or hot rock trying to get up from below that salt bed, and it's pushing the salt into the fountain. I can certainly feel layers of metal between the rock and the salt itself, so there's no reason to think that deeper down there might not be other things. It's nothing to close it up, Highness. Purifying the lake, though, that's going to take a while. I don't envy Nasira's crew the job."

"The sooner you get this done," Nasira muttered from near Kisia.

Lusa chuckled and clicked her fingers at Telun and Milu. "You two, move back."

"Master—"

"Hush, Milu. This is a master's work. I'm much more likely to recognize the witch's touch than you are, but it'll be easier if I don't have the two of you working witchery alongside me. Besides, the day I can't close a crack in the stone is the day I take *al Colutar* from my name." She winked and waded through salt to kneel beside the fountain. "The bottom of this big jug is the crack itself. Captain Nasira, maybe you and your witches can bring it to the surface for us when we're done, to have a good look at and maybe put in her Highness's council chambers to be admired."

Nasira made a skeptical sound that echoed around the watery dome. A low chuckle followed. Telun and Milu, both smiling ruefully, fell back a little distance, then joined the circle of sea witches after Kisia beckoned to them.

Lusa clucked appreciatively. "Good lads. A moment, and then..." She laid her hands on the fountain, stonewitchery's usual weight seeming much less significant to Rasim, compared to the pressure of water from above.

The fountain rippled faintly with her touch, as if welcoming her, and something *clicked* at the back of Rasim's mind, a heaviness that felt wrong. He caught Inga's hand, holding it hard enough to make her grunt in surprise. "Rasim?"

"Something's not right. Something—"

The lake floor beneath Lusa's feet swelled, rock rolling back to expose dull silver metal. Lusa took a few startled, dancing steps. "What the—get back." The Stonemaster's voice sharpened. "Everyone get back."

Startled but obedient, the sea witches edged back. Their grip on the magic intensified. Milu and Telun started forward. Kisia grabbed them both, hauling them away. Telun began a protest, but Kisia tweaked the big boy's ear. "She meant you too!"

Water droplets, forgotten about until now, splashed against the dull metal and sizzled.

Lusa's voice was soft and swift with concentration. "Reshaping the stone to seal the crack triggered something. A cascade of other magic, though I've never heard of a master who could do that. And the metal is reacting to water. Nasira, the water drops, can you — "

Holes opened up in the stone under their feet. Water gushed upward and spilled across the lake floor. The uncovered metal's hissing got louder, half drowning the shouts that filled the little dome. Telun and Milu tried frantically to close the holes as sea witches slammed water spigots aside. Stonemaster Lusa's voice rose above all of them: "Get out of here, go, go, *go!*" Her witchery flowed at a terrible pace, stone walls rising around herself and the exposed metal lake bed.

An orange flash of fire seared Rasim's vision in the instant before a vast concussive blast shattered the sea-witched water dome of safety apart.

TWENTY-SEVEN

Panicked, Rasim clung to all the air he could. It lost its heat almost instantly, no longer warmed by sunwitchery. Screams rang in his ears, high and thin compared to the ringing caused by the blast. His own throat didn't hurt: *he* wasn't the one screaming.

"*Inga!*" Rasim squeezed, hoping desperately he still held the princess's hand.

The screams stopped, and through the shrill noise in his ears he heard gasping sobs. "Rasim? Rasim, what happened? I can't see!"

"I don't know. Neither can I. Quiet." He crushed his eyes closed. It was easier that way, because at least he didn't think he *should* be able to see. Breathing through his teeth, trying not to let fear get the best of him, he stretched his witchery beyond their little bubble of safety.

Fire burned in the water, huge rocking explosions slamming waves against him. They should have been tumbling tail over toes, but he'd stabilized them without realizing it. Siliaria's grace, saving him again. It had saved others as well: he could feel pockets of air like his own, bouncing across the cold lake bottom or fleeing for the surface. Siliaria's grace and Stonemaster Lusa's bravery. She had saved them from the worst of the blast, warned them in time to hold their air and save themselves. She could not have survived the explosion, and even if she had, the lake's depths would have crushed her already.

As it was crushing others. There were bodies in the water, thrashing against the huge rolling blasts. Rasim imagined the water itself as a battering tool, the way he'd used it in the mines. He smashed it through itself, focusing his witchery as strongly as he could and trying to snatch some of the dying sailors off the lake bottom.

Too late, even when he acted as quickly as he could. They went still before he reached them, their souls in Siliaria's hands. "We have to go up. See who's survived." Rasim's voice cracked. "Are you all right, Inga?"

"I am." Inga sounded completely in control. Grateful, Rasim told himself that if *she* was calm, he had no reason to be afraid either.

New explosions smashed the water, so loud he thought he would never hear properly again. Swells lifted them, tossing them around the lake, and huge belches of gas rose upward. Rasim followed them, fighting the urge to go too fast. Air got squeezed somehow, when it went deep in the water. It had to stretch back to its right shape everywhere, even inside their lungs, before they reached the surface, or it could wrack a body with terrible, killing pain. It didn't always happen, but if there was a choice, it was better to surface slowly, even for a sea witch.

The water and metal were still reacting when they finally came up. Steam billowed wildly above the lake, turning the early Northern sunset into fire that glowed across the sky. All over the lake, others surfaced too. Even at the distance, most looked as ragged as Rasim felt: battered and bruised, even if the water had muffled the explosions' effects. He couldn't make out many faces, though, and still had no idea who might have been left on the lake bottom.

Skymaster Arret had survived, at least. He was nearby, elevated out of the water on a spigot that Captain Nasira held in place. Arret stood with his arms spread and head lowered. Grim concentration made deep lines in his face.

"What is he doing?" Inga asked. Rasim shook his head, but someone—Desimi! Rasim had never been so glad to see the other boy in his life!—Desimi took a few hard strokes their direction and answered the question.

"Poison air came up with that explosion. We lost the whirlpool to the blast, before the bad air came up. I dove to see what happened. Arret was coming up fast with Nasira. Way too fast, but I guess a sky witch doesn't have to worry about the air squeezing. They stopped to tell me not to surface and to find anybody else I could and to stop them for at least five minutes, so Arret could clear the air. But I've already found three bodies." Desimi's eyes looked much older than his thirteen years. "How many died down there? What happened?"

"We don't know yet." Inga spoke again, her calm as soothing as a blanket. "We'll find out. Rasim, bring me back to shore. I'll stay there, out of the way, until we know the worst of it."

"You shouldn't be alone, Highness."

"This wasn't a personal attack." Inga lifted her chin, determined. "No one could possibly know that I would be with the people who tried to fix our lake. This was intended to destroy *you*, Rasim. To destroy you and any witches who might discover something at the bottom of this lake. We need to learn who's survived, and what they may have learned."

"Bring her to shore," Desimi said, the words clipped. "I'll let the captain know you're alive."

"Desimi." Rasim swallowed. "Have you seen Kisia yet?"

Desimi's face went blank and he shook his head no. He swam away without saying anything else. Rasim pressed his lips together, then nodded and took himself to shore with Inga, who gathered her robes, regal and unafraid. "Go back into the lake," she said gently. "Find your friends."

"I'm going to find a Skymaster," Rasim said through gritted teeth. "We have to make sure the air you breathe stays clean. It might not have been a personal attack, but if someone is trying to destabilize the Northlands like they're trying to ruin Ilyara, I think accidentally murdering the crown princess would count as a success in their minds."

Surprisingly, Inga smiled and offered a shallow bow. "That, I will not argue with. Thank you for your wisdom, Rasim al Ilialio."

Jaw clenched so hard it ached, Rasim struck back out into the water. If he'd been *wise* he would have expected some kind of trap at the bottom of the lake, although like Lusa, he had never heard of anyone setting one magic to trigger at the use of another. That didn't mean it wasn't possible. He should have thought that anyone able and willing to work the salt fountain witchery would have also been prepared to protect it at all costs.

He wanted, suddenly and intensely, to return to the Sunmaster archives in Ilyara. Surely *somewhere* in them — or in the royal papers, or maybe even in Isidri's long memory — *somewhere* there must be notes, comments, proof of these kinds of magics being worked before. Histories of those who had left the guilds, who might have taught others the Ilyaran witcheries, or whose talents were remarkable in strength and might also be unusual in cleverness. There had to be answers somewhere. Rasim was determined to find them.

Even in the fading light it was easy to find the
Skymaster and Captain Nasira. Rasim swam to the
captain's side, reluctant to disturb her witchery but
needing to know: "Did the other skymasters survive?
Inga is on shore and I want to be sure—"

"Arret whispered it to them already." Nasira
nodded sharply at the shore, making Rasim squint
against the dim light. Inga's tall, slender form was
easy to pick out, her robes bright and her hair
brighter. Someone with dark skin and hair had
joined her. Rasim was too tired to even try feeling for
skywitchery at that distance, but he trusted that it
was indeed one of Master Arret's apprentices.
Relieved, he glanced back at Nasira, really seeing her
for the first time.

Blood dried around a gash on the captain's cheek,
but even more shockingly, her whip-thin braid was
gone, burned away all the way to her nape. What
hair remained was very straight and slicked back
from her face, though whether with blood or water,
Rasim wasn't certain. Her jaw was as tight as his, her
lips bloodless as she concentrated on holding the
Skymaster aloft so he could do his own duties. The
water trembled around her, almost seeping through
her clothes. From the current whirling around them,
Rasim knew she kept herself from sinking through
witchery alone. Most of the time, sea witches would
use a combination of magic and treading water. A
cold chill went through Rasim's belly. "Captain, how

badly are you hurt?"

"I'm fine."

The short, chopped words were so obviously un-
true that Rasim barked laughter. "You're not either.
Are you bleeding?"

Nasira gave him a scathing look. Rasim curled his
lip in return and, if she wouldn't answer, determined
to see for himself. He sank into the cold water, closing
air above his head so he could breathe, then gasped as
he realized the black water here wasn't *just* reflecting
the darkening skies. Blood flowed slowly and steadily
from Nasira's torso, puncture wounds that were
probably even worse than they looked.

Rasim popped back to the surface bellowing,
"*Desimi!*" as loudly as he could. Even the Skymaster
flinched at the strength of Rasim's shout, giving him
a startled glance. Within seconds, water surged
around them, announcing Desimi's speedy arrival.

So furious with Nasira that he could hardly see
straight, Rasim growled, "Get the captain to shore.
Send someone for Usia, if he's not already on the
way up here. And *sit on her* if you have to, to keep
her down!" he shouted as Desimi cast uncertain
looks between his captain and his age-mate, then
followed Rasim's orders over Nasira's protests. A
moment later, the infuriated captain was being
rushed to shore on a wave of Desimi's making, and
Rasim took over Nasira's waterworking, keeping the
Skymaster elevated so he could clear the air.

"If you can spare someone to send me to shore, the immediate danger over the lake is past, I think," Arret called down. "But this gas may have rolled down the passes toward the city. I need to follow it, to make sure no one dies."

"Will the lake burp up the bad air again?"

"I don't know, but Cara can stay behind to watch for it. I believe the city is in more danger than the lake, now."

Rasim nodded and filled his lungs again. "Hassin! Kisia!" Neither of them appeared, but another bleak-faced sailor came out of the dark to bring the Skymaster journeyman, Cara, to shore. More and more witches were going that way now, the search on the water coming to an end.

Firelight suddenly came to life on the shore, roaring bonfires that assured Rasim at least one of the Sunmasters had survived. People began gathering around them as their light cast a yellow glare over the water. By their light, Rasim searched for swimmers with witchery and vision alike. Within minutes the lake was still, and he still hadn't seen Kisia. Cold with fear, he finally returned to shore to search around the bonfires.

Usia was there already, shadowed by Sesin. Rasim's heart lurched with relief as the pretty healer's apprentice smiled at him, but her smile faded again as she returned to work. Nasira lay close to one of the fires, shivering but awake, which had to be a good sign. But too many faces he knew were missing, and he realized anyone hurt worse than Nasira was probably already dead. At least a third of the crew were gone, and he still hadn't found Hassin or Kisia. By the time he reached the last fire, tears streamed down his face, burning hot against the cold evening air.

Inga, of all people, knelt by the last fire, murmuring something to one of the sailors lying beside it. She looked up, and even with the heat of the fire and its golden hues, Rasim thought he saw her blush. Then he saw who she knelt by, and gave a shaky laugh. Hassin, despite tightly wrapped ribs, was trying to get up on an elbow so he could flirt more successfully with the Northern princess. Inga, laughing, slipped her fur cloak over his shoulders, its paleness a stark contrast to his brown Ilyaran skin.

"Rasim." Kisia came around the fire and tripped over her own feet, falling into Rasim's arms. She was much warmer than he was, and his heart felt like it would break with relief. She held on for a long minute, then looked at him with a wavering smile. "Rasim, I've had enough adventures. Can we go home yet?"

He laughed again, weakly. "I don't think so. We have to... oh, Siliaria. Telun? Milu? Did either of them...?"

"They're all right, but Daka is missing."

Rasim stared at Kisia's dark eyes, made darker by the shadows and flickering light, without really understanding. Delicate, flighty Daka seemed like she would have been able to just rise up, fly away safely like fire licking at the stars. He couldn't imagine that she'd died at the bottom of a half-frozen Northern lake. "Who made the bonfires, then?" he finally asked, feeling stupid.

"Master Endat. Pynda's here, but she can't even talk. She just sits and looks into the fire. Rasim, what *happened* down there?"

"It was a trap. Someone used magic in ways we don't even think about."

"But who? Why? Look how many people they killed. Who would do that?"

"I don't know, Kisia. They were already trying to kill, or drive out, a whole city's worth of people. Here, Ilyara—" Rasim swallowed sharply as a thought struck him. "I wonder if there's something about these locations. Something special, to make someone want to have control over them? Because otherwise why not choose Ringenstand, if they want to attack the Northlands?"

"Roscord wanted control over the Islands, too," Kisia said almost instantly. "Compass points. South, east, north. Think of the maps, Rasim. Where do you end up if you draw a line from each of these places inward?"

"The continent." Rasim closed his eyes, imagining

the bulky continent's protruding shape above Ilyara and west of the Islands. "It would be somewhere in the middle of the continent, away from the seas. I don't know much about the midlands. But if you go west from the middle of the continent the same distance as Ilyara and Hongrunn are, you find—" He caught his breath as his eyes popped open. "Senreyla, where the Dynerian horse clans meet every five years to call a new council. I *have* studied them a little, with the Sunmasters. The horse clans are due to meet in the spring. Kisia, we have to—to *warn* them!"

"Of what?"

"I don't know, but something bad is going to happen there, I'm sure of it. They need to be prepared."

"Rasim." Inga rose from beside Hassin and put her hands on Rasim and Kisia's shoulders. "Rasim, let it go for now."

Rasim gave Inga a wild stare. "I can't! We have to do something, we have to help—!"

"We have to mourn," Inga said very gently. "And when we are done mourning, we must celebrate. Your people have paid a great cost to help mine, Ilyaran, but in doing so you have saved a city. You'll be honored in the Northlands until memory fades to history and history into legend."

"But—!"

"No." Inga's gentle voice became firmer. "Rasim, listen to me. You are desperate to act, and I understand. I felt the same way when Annaken died in the Ilyaran fire, and I believe you felt this way when you thought all your fleet was drowned at sea. When I first met you, you would not let yourself stop moving or acting, for fear you would think too much about what you had lost." She gestured to the lake, to the bonfires, to the depleted number of sea witches. "Tonight, perhaps, is even worse than those hard days, because tonight there is no doubt that too many have died. Stop a while and remember them, Rasim. Stop a while and be grateful we survived. There will be time to ride to Senreyla in the spring."

TWENTY-EIGHT

He would not—*could* not—wait until spring. But neither could Rasim leave Hongrunn the same night of the lake explosions, no matter how much he might want to. That thought helped him in the days following, as the sea witches did what they had come to the Northlands to do.

It had not, Inga had told them a thousand times, been necessary. Certainly not so soon, she had said, and not in such quantities: the city could survive easily on purified barrels and mountain run-off. But it *had* been necessary, not just for the city, but for the seamasters' hearts. They had come to know every drop of water in the deep lake, dredging it with magic over the course of five long, hard days. Rasim, like all of the uninjured witches, barely slept in those days. They dropped when exhaustion took them, and returned to work the moment strength returned.

They had taken more than salt from its waters. They had found bodies as well, their crewmates preserved in the icy lake. Not all the dead were rescued—some, Telun said dully, must have simply been destroyed by the explosions—but enough were. Enough to ease Rasim's spirit, and the spirits of those around him. Earlier that morning they had taken the *Waifia* out of Hongrunn's harbor, out to the open ocean, and given Siliaria back her dead.

There would be a wake tonight, a roaring party full of tall tales and shared memories of their friends, but until then, Rasim wanted to be alone. So he'd climbed the mountain again, glancing back once in a while to see if he was followed. People were easy to see against the glaring white snow and slippery black ice paths, but no one else seemed to have the same thought he did. No surprise, really: they'd spent five full days and nights on the mountain. Climbing it again was the last thing on most of their minds. Rasim was grateful. The silence of snow and winter air was unlike anything he'd ever encountered in Ilyara, and he wanted its peace.

The half-frozen air over the lake smelled different: clearer, sharper, without the tang of salt. The water moved differently, too, less sluggish and visibly less brackish. Rasim crouched and sank his palm into it, bringing up a handful to sip. It was perfect, fresh and clean and cold enough to hurt his teeth. The harsh, fresh agony of it suited his mood as he stood up from the lakeside and began to walk along the shore.

There wasn't *much* shore, truth be told. A few hundred narrow feet where the Northerners had made their beach approach, but mountains plunged straight into the lake in most places, without so much as a passable strand or climbable hill in sight. For anyone but a water witch, it was a daunting aspect. Rasim called witchery, wrapping himself in a swirl of lake water, and let it carry him around a bend or two, until he found another small patch of beach. He stepped free of the water and knelt, brushing snow away with bare fingers until he'd scraped down to frozen stone.

It was foolish. He shouldn't do it. He shouldn't even try it, because if it was *possible*, then the trouble he was in knew no bounds. But he did it anyway, just to see if he could.

He had spent a week in the darkness of the mine. A week surrounded by an element not his own. A week surrounded by stone, washing it, cleaning it, trying to see inside it, as if, like water, it could be transparent. And for a moment, fighting the stone snake, he'd felt that he understood the stone as well as he understood water. Eyes closed, he searched for the calm depth of stone that he remembered from the mines. It was more unchanging than water, though of course everything changed with time. Still, stone was in no hurry to change, even when he tried whispering and coaxing it into new shapes. It didn't rush, it didn't spill, it didn't seem to do much of anything, even when Rasim thought he felt the weight of witchery alive in the air around him. He had a vision in mind, an idea he wanted to make happen, but the stone's quiet presence had none of water's excitement or life to it, no sense of anything happening. Finally, feeling silly, he opened his eyes again and looked around.

Stone figures stood all around him.

Triumph so sharp it was almost terror spiked through Rasim. His hands, already cold from the winter air, became icier while his cheeks burned with excitement. His chest felt so full he thought it would burst, or that he might lift up and fly from the speed of his heartbeat. It was *impossible*, but he'd done it. Mastered stonewitchery, felt its quiet magic working around him—he *had* felt it, too, just hadn't realized it was working!—and had built the thing he had dreamed.

It was rough, nothing like what Telun or Milu, never mind Stonemaster Lusa, might have done. But there, written in stone, were the faces of those who had gone into the lake and not come out again. They were taller than in life, more slender, almost airy, despite the element they were shaped from. They stood in a circle around a more delicate, elongated version of the salt fountain, which had ripples in it. A statue of Stonemaster Lusa touched it. Above all of them, dancing on graceful reeds of stone, were patches of dome, like the water dome they had held beneath the lake. Droplets even formed on the undersides of the domes, reminiscent of water.

It wouldn't last. The harsh winters, with their snow and cold, would shatter the sculptures as time passed. But it didn't have to last. It was a memorial, and memories faded. His would last at least as long as the sculptures, and that was enough.

More than enough, since he wasn't supposed to be able to do something like this at all. Rasim flashed a pained grin at the sculptures and at the sky. He wasn't going to tell anyone, not ever, but knowing he could do it was a bright burning delight inside him.

It was the only warm thing about him, he realized. He was *freezing*. He shivered all over, then breathed a quiet, steaming laugh into the cold air, and turned his palms up. *Fire.* Dancing, light, impatient, afraid of its own death. Fire, glowing deep and dark in the heart of an ember, patiently waiting to ignite again. *Anything,* he thought hopefully, anything to warm his frozen fingers.

Nothing. Rasim shivered again and grinned at his half-numb fingertips. Nothing, and that was *good*. It was best for Kisia to be wrong sometimes, and besides, if *he* hadn't set the *Waifia's* ropes on fire, maybe it had been Kisia after all. Maybe he wasn't the only Ilyaran witch able to work more than one magic at all. Maybe Taishm and Isidri were right, and it was only tradition that kept all of them from being much more than they were. Shivering more, Rasim rubbed his chest and hurried back the way he'd come. Water witchery carried him to shore, and then he concentrated on where to put his feet until a splash startled him into looking up.

Kisia sat on the shore, tossing rocks into the lake. Rasim cast a guilty look back at the stoneworking he'd done, though it was well-hidden behind a curve of mountain. When he looked back, Kisia was watching him with one corner of her mouth turned up. Squirming like he'd been caught doing something wrong, Rasim hurried the rest of the way to her. She stayed where she was, idly tossing rocks into the water, until he got close enough to see a smirk of knowledge dancing in her eyes.

He bit back the impulse to ask what she'd seen, and somehow, like she knew he was silencing himself, her grin got bigger. She stood up, but all she said was, "There you are. Come on. The sun is setting, and they won't want to start the wake without you." She offered her hand.

Rasim took it, surprised that steam didn't rise from their clasped fingers, hers were so much warmer than his. "Desimi," he said, "will always be glad to start a party without me."

"True. Let's not give him the satisfaction. Come on." Kisia tugged Rasim's hand, drawing him toward the path they'd climbed to reach the lake. "Captain Nasira has some things to say."

Rasim winced as they slipped and slid their way down the ice-covered stone. "I bet she does." They spent the rest of the journey in silence, concentrating on where their feet went so they wouldn't end up sliding down the hill like children playing on the sand dunes outside of Ilyara. Not until they'd passed the tree line and found more solid footing on snow-covered earth just outside of the city did Kisia say, "You saved her life, you know."

"She was mad enough about it, too."

"The rest of us aren't." Kisia waved up at one of the big yellow-haired guards who stood watch on Hongrunn's enormous fortified walls. He waved back, gesturing them through the portcullis gate that they closed at dusk every day, as if trouble might come rolling down the mountainside in the middle of the night. And maybe it did in the summer months, for all Rasim knew, but he couldn't imagine anybody hearty enough to attack over the mountains in a ferocious Northern winter.

They scurried through the streets, nodding greetings to Northerners who no longer looked twice at the brown-skinned Ilyarans in their midst. The city still struck Rasim as it had when he'd first visited, grim and grey on the outside but surprisingly warm and welcoming behind heavy oak doors and thick stone walls. The *Waifia*'s crew had been given space in a block of inns and taverns that faced a central square and were backed up by alleys narrower and more treacherous than anything in Ilyara. Some of the apprentices and younger journeymen had been racing down those sharply angled alleys on foot, on sheets of metal, on wooden blocks—anything they could find. The first broken arm had been considered a sign of pride, until Usia refused to heal it, or any other injuries sustained through what he called *youthful idiocy*.

Now the square had been filled with bonfires: small ones at each corner, and a larger one in the middle, all tended by Sunmaster Endat. Pynda sat to the side on a stone bench, watching the largest blaze with no light in her eyes; she had not called her power since Daka's death, and there were whispers that she no longer could. Rasim didn't believe that, although he believed she might choose to never do so again.

Sea witches had already gathered, swaying to music played on hidden drums and on Ilyaran pipes, as well as on Northern instruments Rasim didn't know. Others danced, and some carried the leather flasks of honey mead favored by Northerners. A few had clearly drunk heavily of the mead already, though no one was quite staggering yet. Even those who looked close to it straightened up, sobering, as Hassin escorted Captain Nasira toward the largest fire. She stopped well short of it, and in its flickering golden light Rasim saw sweat beading on her forehead and upper lip. He wondered if it was the fire, or the injury she was still recovering from, that made her stop. Her chin-length hair, shorter than any master sea witch Rasim had ever seen, was tucked behind her ears.

"We've cleared the lake's waters," Nasira said abruptly. Hoarsely; her throat had taken damage in the poison air, and Usia said only time would really heal it. She was easily heard, though. Skymaster Arret had to be nearby, helping her voice carry, but Rasim didn't see him. The music faded to near silence as she spoke, and dancers and drinkers alike came together to listen.

"We've given our dead into Siliaria's arms. We've sang our songs for them, and we've wept for them. Tonight we sing again for ourselves, and laugh, and weep, and remember. Tomorrow we'll begin to look for answers."

Her gaze swept the gathered sea witches, and a chill shot down Rasim's spine as she met his eyes momentarily. Then her attention moved on, her voice rising steadily. "We'll look for our stolen guildmates. We'll search for those who poisoned Hongrunn's lake, and perhaps even for those who began the Great Fire in Ilyara. We will find answers," she promised, and closed her eyes, as if the effort of that promise was almost too great for her. But she opened them again, looking to each of her crew with the same piercing regard she'd turned on Rasim. "But that's for tomorrow. Tonight, we celebrate and mourn together, as a guild. As a family." She lifted a fist in a salute to the crew and gave a short laugh as someone tossed a mead skin toward her uplifted hand. She caught it, pulled the cork with her teeth, and drained a long sip to the cheers of her crew. The music began again, and in moments the square was filled with dancing bodies, their warmth carrying the heat of the fire through the cold night.

Someone handed Kisia a skin of mead. She took a sip and offered it to Rasim, who felt Desimi join them as he took a drink of his own. He handed the skin on, passing it to Desimi, and for a little while they stood together in silence, watching sparks rise toward the stars. Finally, under the cover of all the noise, Rasim said, "You were on the ship after we were thrown off, Desimi."

The bigger boy grunted. Rasim took it as invitation to continue. "Who let Missio out of the brig? Who dumped us overboard?"

Desimi spun toward him, genuine anger darkening his eyes. Startled, Rasim took a step back, hands lifted, then gasped a half-laugh. "Siliaria's *fins*, Desi, I didn't mean was it you. I didn't think that at all."

Tension remained bunched along Desimi's square jaw. "Some people did."

"Well, you haven't exactly been Rasim's best friend," Kisia said acerbically. "Who *was* it?"

"I don't know." Desimi, sullen but placated, hunched his shoulders and looked back at the biggest fire. It flickered as dancing bodies passed in front of it. Milu and Telun were among them, leaning on each other with tears on their faces. "We forgot about Missio for a while when we landed in

Ringenstand. By the time someone remembered to get her, she was gone. It could have been someone on the ship, or someone from the city."

"How could someone in the city know she was in the brig?" Kisia asked.

Desimi, sounding a bit like Guildmaster Isidri, said, "I don't know, Kees, maybe somebody *told* them? Probably whoever dumped you and the Stonemasters."

"Someone with access to sweet-sleep," Rasim said.

Kisia snorted. "Master Usia, maybe?" Both the boys looked at her in horror and she snorted again. "He'd be best at it, but it comes from seaweed. Any sea witch could have made some. Who else doesn't like you, Rasim?"

"I don't know. I think the list is longer than I realized."

This time Desimi snorted. Rasim aimed a half-hearted kick at his shin. "Whoever it was didn't like *you*, either, Kisia. Or the Stonemasters."

"Or they knew I'd never let Nasira sail on, once I found out you were gone."

"You're a first-year journeyman," Desimi said, about as half-heartedly as Rasim's kick. "Who would think you could make a captain do what you wanted? And nobody on the *Waifia* liked the Stonemasters."

"You should be with your friends," said a voice behind them. Rasim felt a hand on his shoulder and looked back to see Prince Lorens and Princess Inga joining them. "What's got you on the edges and so solemn?"

"We're trying to solve the mysteries of the world," Kisia said, lightly enough that Lorens laughed, even though it was perfectly true.

"Perhaps not tonight," Inga suggested. "We wondered if we might join you."

Rasim smiled. "I can't imagine anyone telling you no."

"Well…" Inga stepped aside, gesturing out of the square. Northerners stood beyond her, dozens and dozens of them, all carrying lit candles that gave their pale faces a gentle unearthly glow. "Not just Lorens and me. Tonight is our Longest Night, Rasim. It's our tradition here in Hongrunn, and across the Northlands, to carry candles on the longest, darkest night of the year, and to go to the eastern shore with them to show the sun the way back home. It's also the night we believe our ancestors and dead loved ones come closest to this world again. We carry the light to show them the way, too. If we could join your mourning tonight, and have you join our vigil in the morning—" For once, Inga seemed unsure of herself, as if she thought she might be intruding. "We would be honored."

"It would be *our* honor." Captain Nasira spoke from behind Rasim, who hadn't even realized he'd turned away from the bonfires. Hassin stood a step or two behind her, smiling at Inga. When relief flashed across her face, he put his hand out, and the Northern princess took it, her bright hair and gown a beacon even as they slipped into the crowd. Lorens offered his arm to Nasira, whose mouth creased with as much amusement as seemed possible for her, and they, too, went into the throng of dancing sea witches. Little by little, person by person, the candle-bearing Northerners joined them, until only Desimi, Kisia and Rasim lingered on the edges.

"She's right, you know," Rasim finally said. "It's waited this long. Tomorrow's soon enough. It'll be easier to see answers in the daylight, anyway."

"You can ask your ancestors why you're such a troublemaker on the way," Desimi said sourly. Rasim gaped at him in protest. Kisia, borrowing a candle from one of the Northerners, laughed, handing Rasim the candle. It went out as he took it, and she lifted her eyebrows in challenge.

Rasim blinked at her a moment, baffled, then felt his mouth twitch. "I'll try at dawn. With all my ancestors standing with me."

Kisia pointed a finger at him. "I'll hold you to it."

"Maybe if he has enough mead he can use two magics." Desimi slapped the skin back into Rasim's free hand. "Not otherwise."

Rasim promptly handed the drink back. "Better not risk it. I'd hate to show you up, King's Man."

"Not a chance, Sunburn."

"Sunburn," Kisia said again, incredulously. "*Really*?"

Desimi shrugged enormously and stomped off into the crowd, Kisia trailing along in his wake, although she glanced back to see if Rasim was joining them. He hesitated a moment longer, studying the candle's wick, wondering if he might, just *might*, see a glimmer of flame there, if he imagined hard enough.

"Rasim?"

He looked up guiltily, shoved the candle in a pocket, and shouted, "Coming!" as he ran to join the party.

to be continued in

SKYMASTER

Acknowledgments

Thanks are particularly due to my extraordinarily patient nephew, who asked, age 9, when I was going to write some books for little boys, and who is still waiting, age 16, for the last in the series. This year, kiddo. This year!

My hat is off to cover artist Aleksandar Sotirovski, whose paintings are bringing these books to life. My appreciation for editor K.B. Spangler knows no bounds, because she made me fix all the problems with this book. And I always owe one to the war room, where writers all over the world tell me to get my work done.

All my love to Ted and Henry and Dad, and to my sister Deirdre, who thinks these might be her favorites of my books, and to her sons, Breic and Seirid, without whom I'd have never written these at all. The same goes to my mom, who taught me the lullaby that eventually became the Guildmaster Saga.

About the Author

There are those who say CE Murphy began her writing career when she ran away from home at age five to write copy for the circus that had come to town. Her own recollection is that she wrote her first serious work for a school magazine at age six, which is almost as good. She has since gone on to write in science fiction & fantasy, romance, graphic novels, and loves writing middle grade with the Guildmaster Saga.

She was born and raised in Alaska, but now lives with her family in Ireland, which is a magical place where it rains a lot but nothing one could seriously regard as winter ever actually arrives.

CE Murphy can be found online at:
mizkit.com
@ce_murphy
fb.com/cemurphywriter
& her newsletter, at

tinyletter.com/ce_murphy,

which is by far the best place to get up-to-date info on what's out next.

Special Thanks

Special thanks are due to the following Kickstarter backers for this book, who have helped make it a reality. I actually couldn't do this all without you. Thank you so much.

Melinda Skye, Big Al, AlixMV, Ambar, Amy Matosky Amy Stromquist, Andreja River, Andrew Foxx, Andrew J Clark IV, Andy Funk, Antiqueight, aphie, Barbara Hasebe, Beth Lobdell, Brian Nisbet, Brook Freeman, Bryant Durrell. Auntie Makeel, Carl Rigney, Carol J. Guess, Charlotte and Eddie Calvert, Christina Biles, Christine Swendsesid, Chrysoula Tzavelas, Colin Soule, Conrad "Tuftears" Wong, Damien Edward Waters, Deborah Mitchell, Deborah Nicol, Desiree L. L., Diane Nowell, DJ and Nette Ford, Don Whiteside, Donal Cunningham, Douglas McGill, E Jourdan Lewis, Edward Ellis, Eleri Hamilton, Elizabeth Bennefeld, Ellen Million, Emily Poole, Erica Of The Mighty Thumbs, Esther MacCallum-Stewart, Evenstar Deane, Fossa, Gabe Krabbe, Gareth Kavanagh, Gemma, Genevieve Cogman, Genista, Georgie, Hamish Laws, Heather Franklyn Roney, Heather Knutsen, Histalonia, Hoose Family, Image, Silkie and the Weasels, In memory of Ruth Duggan, Jaime Robertson, James Post, Jared Michrina, Jen Cabbage, Jennifer Berk, Jennifer Chun, Jessica Bay, Jonathan Lupa, Kalandryl, Karyl Fulkerson, Kat Feete, Kate Barton, Kate Kirby, Kate Larking, Kathleen, Kathleen Hanrahan, Kathy Jolly, Kathy Rogers Katrina Lehto, Kerry, Kerry aka Trouble, Kes Yocum, Konstanze Tants, Kristi Chadwick, Kristy Kearney,

Kyna Foster, Lali, Laura Wallace, Lauri M. Weaver,
Leah Moore, Liam K., Lilly Ibelo, Linda Pierce
Lisa Stewart, Liza Olmsted, Lori Lum, Louise
Lowenspets, Lynn Shulak, M A Vespry, M. Moellering,
Marguerite Smith, Marion McDowell, Marjorie Taylor,
Marsha S., Mary Anne Walker, Max Kaehn, Melinda
Gonzalez, Michael Bernardi, Michael Feldhusen,
Michelle Carlson, Michelle Curtis, Naomi Twery,
Nathaniel Lanza, Neal Levin, Niamh, Nicolai Buch-
Andersen, Pádraig Ó Méalóid, Pam Blome, Pat Knuth,
Pat Roos, Paul Anthony Shortt, Paul Bulmer, Paul
Knappenberger, Paul-Gabriel Wiener, Quinn Clancy,
Rachel and Edie Gollub, Rachel Caine, Rachel Coleman,
Rachel Sahtout, Richard Lambert, Robert Tienken, Sally
Kennett, Sara Harville, Sarah Brooks, Sarah E. Troedson,
Scott Shanks, Sean Collins, Sharēssa Elliott, Sharon
Karpierz, Shel Kennon, Sherry Menton, Sidney
Whitaker, Sonia, Sumi Funayama, Susan Carlson, Susan
Shaffer, SusanB, Suvana, Tammy Graves, Tara Lynch
and Robert Lynch <3, Tara Teich, Tasha Turner, Team
Milian, Ted Locke, The Brooks de Vita Family, Tina
Connell, TK Vincent, Trip Space-Parasite, Trygve
Henriksen, Valentine Lewis, Veleda Kniese, Vicki Greer,
Wilbur Yokan, Yannick G. Allard
You're welcome! –Andy Funk–